Christmas Girl

Brooke Baxter

Published by Brooke Baxter, 2021.

This is a work of fiction. Similarities to real people, places, or events are entirely coincidental.

CHRISTMAS GIRL

First edition. November 1, 2021.

Copyright © 2021 Brooke Baxter.

ISBN: 978-0991002214

Written by Brooke Baxter.

Table of Contents

To my family

Chapter 1

"**C**offee?"

Surprised, Clara whirled around and almost knocked the red paper cup out of Clay's hand onto the freshly polished mall floor.

"What are you doing here? I thought you were going to be with your family?"

"Well, I was working late, and figured you might be too. In fact, I thought coffee might be necessary for you to get this scene done before opening day."

Clara accepted the cup, took a long sip, and closed her eyes, enjoying the smell, texture, and warmth of the drink. Besides Christmas, coffee was her favorite thing in the world.

"Thank you. It's perfect. Exactly what I needed."

Clay stepped back to survey the scene Clara created for the mall Santa, the most important person in the world to children everywhere. Clara took such care making sure any child, or adult, believed they were in Santa's workshop. There were benches for elves to make final adjustments to a simple wooden toy for each child as they left Santa's lap. She included a giant hot chocolate bar, because everyone knew Santa survived on hot chocolate. And, somehow, she even had the aroma of chocolate chip cookies wafting throughout the display. Santa's chair was a deep red velvet with gold detail, and there was a small ottoman for him to put his feet on when on a break, while he sipped his cocoa and nibbled on cookies, all while in full view of any shoppers who passed by.

Clay walked all around the display. "Wow, it's even more impressive this year."

The mall changed the location for pictures with Santa this year. Because it was centrally located, and not up against a wall, she had to make sure there was no obvious front and back to the display. So, as the children left Santa's lap, they would walk through a stable. She labeled each stall with a reindeer name: Dasher, Dancer, Prancer, Vixen, Comet, Cupid, Donner, Blitzen, and of course the last stall belonged to Rudolph, the most famous reindeer of all.

The city health codes wouldn't allow living animals in the mall, so Clara conveniently placed signs explaining the reindeer were out training, but would be back soon. Signs encouraged children to leave a message for their favorite reindeer in chalk on the door or wall of their stall.

She watched for Clay's reaction as he walked around her design.

Clara explained, "I hoped that really bringing them into the scene would help children and their families feel the magic of Christmas. I wanted them to feel like they were an important part of the season."

"Well, I think you've succeeded. I feel like I am a part of the magic, and I know Santa isn't real!"

"Clay, you better take that back, or you will have a sad Christmas morning with no presents!"

They laughed comfortably.

"Are you sure you don't want to come with me, or meet me at my parents' later? There'll be tons of food, games, and embarrassing stories. It'll be fun!"

Clara turned away from the display and smiled. He was always doing sweet things for her. Since they met in that coffee shop years ago, he was always trying to include her in his life. Clay was the reason she landed her biggest account that first year. As a partner in a prominent accounting firm, he was the one who suggested Clara for their Christmas decorating one year. She wowed the rest of the partners and had the account for the large downtown building that housed the firm since that year. From there her business grew, and she now consulted all over the country, and had a staff to help. But she did all the work herself for her favorite accounts.

"Thank you for inviting me. You know I love being around your family, but I'm exhausted! This is the end of my decorating season, and I really want to rest before the parties begin. You know how hectic that is for me. Besides, my parents are expecting me for Thanksgiving dinner. I still need to decorate their house and tree."

"Okay. But you'll be missed."

"Please! Everyone will be so busy stuffing their faces and playing games that no one will even notice I am not there."

"I'll notice you aren't there."

Clara smiled and gave him a quick hug. "Look, you better get on the road. You have a long drive even without crazy holiday traffic."

Clay nodded and said he would let her know he got to his parents' home safely and then turned to walk toward the parking lot. When he got a few steps from the door, he turned and called out over the Christmas music, "Hey, Clara! Happy Thanksgiving!"

Chapter 2

A fter making sure every detail of the Santa's Workshop scene was perfect, Clara walked through the mall, inspecting the other window displays she created.

The Winter Wonderland in the windows of Macy's was complete with snow-covered trees, red and green sleds, and a cottage with a happy family inside.

Down the concourse, she saw the gingerbread house display created for a sweets shop. During the holidays, they specialized in all things gingerbread. Families could preorder the parts of a gingerbread house to put together at home. The shop offered selections of gingerbread, ginger cookies and pastries; even specialty gingerbread coffee and hot cocoa were available options on the menu this time of year.

She continued on, smiling as she stood in front of the Elf Workshop she built for the toy store. Clara loved this one. The elves invited children to watch as they checked lists and made toys. She arranged for the toys to be delivered to the local children's hospital, children's homes, and homeless shelters on Christmas Eve. The names the elves checked off the list were the names of actual children who would receive the toys. She even secured a grant to pay for the expensive and elaborate project. Clara smiled, thinking about the imagination and work that went into this display.

And that is why they pay you the big bucks.

She was right. This attention to the smallest detail grew her business from volunteering to decorate classrooms in middle school, to decorating the children's hospital in high school for community service points, and even set designs for Christmas productions in college. She was in high demand and had several multi-year contracts and no last-minute cancellations. Businesses knew they might never make the list again. In fact, her waiting list was six pages long. Even if she hired an expansive staff, she would never get to all of them.

That was part of the magic. If the business was too big, she would lose the creativity and detail everyone wanted at Christmas. No, Clara would not expand her business and bring on other designers. She only needed additional assistants who could help assemble the displays she created.

Next, she stopped to admire the nativity scene in the bookstore window. She took a few liberties with this one and made the stable and manger out of books. The shop owners loved her clever idea. She wasn't sure they would agree to her plan because it would tie up so much of their inventory. But they were so excited, they pulled books they had multiples of right away and had crates of copies for her to use when she came with her team. She used shredded paper for the straw on the ground and placed stuffed animal characters from well-known children's books around the stable. She knew it was irreverent and made a mental note to check back after Thanksgiving for the crowd's reaction.

Finally, she walked to the mall entrances, making sure everything was ready for the big day. She hung holly over the archway leading into the mall, and oversized trees and candy canes littered the concourse intersections. She checked the doors and straightened the wreaths. Everything was in its place.

Satisfied there was nothing left to do, she walked back to gather her things at Santa's Workshop. Passing a candy-striped trash can, she took one last swallow of the coffee, now room temperature, and tossed it in the bin.

As she walked, she ran into Sam. He was her favorite security guard. Old enough to be her dad, he always offered encouragement and compliments on her designs. He was also the only one who actually knew her name and used it. The others just complained about having to always let that "Christmas Girl" in the mall at all hours. Sam was different. Even when she was at the mall over the summer, looking for a new swimsuit, and he ran into her, he asked about her summer and how her designs were coming. She would often confide in him about upcoming themes and ask for his opinion. He was always willing to help and give advice on how the logistics would work in a mall setting. Often, his input shifted her plans, making them even better in the end. Sam wanted her to succeed. He always told her she was the daughter he and his wife wished they had. Instead, they had two boys who rarely came home for a visit.

"Hey, Sam! What do you think?" Clara asked.

"As usual, you made the magic happen. I don't know how you do it, come up with original designs each year," Sam answered.

"Thank you. What are you doing here so late the night before Thanksgiving? I thought you'd be home helping Maria get dinner ready for tomorrow."

"No, not this year. Everyone will be with their in-laws. It will be just us. I worked tonight so I could be the first one to see all of your finished displays." Sam gave her a playful wink. "Plus, I had to make sure nothing was hazardous and would collapse on a kid. Nothing like a lawsuit at Christmas."

They both laughed.

"Hey, why don't you come by tomorrow night for dessert? Maria would love to see you, and since the boys aren't coming, there are plenty of pies to share. She has been baking for two weeks. Dessert was always their favorite part of Thanksgiving."

Clara thought for a minute, wondering how her parents would feel if she spent a holiday away from them. She felt sad that Sam and Maria must feel invisible and discarded. No, she would never do that to her parents.

"I'd love to come by for dessert."

"Call when you're on your way. I know you have dinner with your parents, but save plenty of room for Maria's cranberry cobbler. It's delicious."

"It's a date! Seven o'clock work for you?" Clara asked.

"Seven is perfect."

Clara had been to their home once before when Maria hosted a small Christmas party for her church group. She asked Clara to help with a table setting and some decorating. Clara was happy to do it. It wasn't often that someone asked her to do something so small and intimate, and she jumped at the chance. Of course, she wouldn't take any pay for the job. She loved Sam and Maria and wanted to do something nice for them. Ever since, the three had been close friends. That made it even more difficult to think about their boys abandoning them on Thanksgiving. Hopefully, they wouldn't do the same at Christmas.

Gathering her things and taking one last look at Santa's Workshop, Clara walked to her car and drove toward home. It was late, and she was ready for a shower and bed. Tomorrow was going to be a busy day.

Chapter 3

Clara woke up ready for the day. Rolling over, she hit the off button on the top of the clock. Clara never embraced using her cell phone as an alarm clock. Phones were for business, and clocks and watches were for telling time.

Awake and out of bed, she made her way to the kitchen for coffee. There was something wonderful about a first cup of coffee. The entire process was something that Clara enjoyed. No automatic coffeemaker for her. She put the kettle of water on the stove and as she waited for it to boil, she put six scoops of freshly ground beans in the bottom of her French press. At the whistle, Clara returned to the kettle and waited until the bubbles ceased. Then she carefully saturated every coffee ground, filling the canister. After the allotted time, she carefully pushed the press down, gently, gently, watching the thick crema push through the press's filter, rising to the top. Finally, it was ready to pour. No cream or sugar necessary. This was perfection.

She surveyed her tidy home and felt something was missing. Of course, it was time to bring out the tree and Christmas village, but she couldn't help feeling something else was missing as she curled up on the sofa with a fluffy blanket and her cat, Mistletoe, settling in beside her.

On the outside, things seemed great. Clara had purchased a condo all by herself. She built a thriving business, and she maintained a few close friendships, but still something nagged at her. She was great at creating these scenes for people to lose themselves in magic, but she wasn't feeling any of it herself this year. It seemed to elude her, no matter how much she tried to capture it. Truthfully, it had been awhile since she felt it. Yet somehow, she still helped others enjoy the magic of Christmas.

Clara didn't have time to dwell on this now. As she enjoyed her coffee, she consulted her planner for the day. There was the Turkey Trot at the community center, then a late lunch with her family, and finally pie with Sam and Maria. It was a full day.

She returned to the kitchen and put her empty cup in the dishwasher and cleaned the French press so it would be ready for the same ritual the next morning. After brushing her teeth and pulling on running tights, she fought with the sports bra before tying the laces on her running shoes. On her way out the door, she fed her trusty companion Mistletoe, a stray she adopted as a kitten.

Parking at the Turkey Trot entrance, she looked for Sophie. Sophie was Clara's best friend. They met in middle school and were opposites. Unlike Clara's red hair and green eyes, average height and build, Sophie was a brunette with icy-blue eyes and porcelain skin. She was tall and thin and the life of the party. While Clara was quiet and introverted, Sophie would walk into a room and command everyone's attention. And she didn't notice the effect she had on everyone. It was amazing to watch. When they met in homeroom, that first day of eighth grade, they became fast friends, to the surprise of their classmates. Clara moved to that school at the end of seventh grade from out of state and hadn't connected with a group of friends until Sophie.

They bonded over their crazy love of Christmas. Sophie was the first to call Clara "Christmas Girl" because of her red hair and green eyes. One Halloween, Sophie convinced Clara to dress as an elf, because, as she explained, "You look like a walking Christmas card." They both thought this was a terrific idea, until they arrived at the Halloween dance. Everyone's teasing drove Clara to tears and she hid in the bathroom. Sophie, angry people were hateful to her friend, defended her and announced they were going to a "real party," not some dumb school dance. She called her brother to pick them up, and they went back to Sophie's house for scary movies and junk food. That was Sophie's way. She never tolerated people being rude or taking advantage of others. Even now, as a court-appointed attorney, her job was to defend those who had no one else in their corner.

And she was good at her job.

As she passed through the crowd of runners and walkers, Clara heard her name and saw Sophie waving her over to the sign-in table. Sophie already collected their numbers and pins and was struggling to get her own number attached to the front of her shirt. They helped each other with the numbers and found their place in the crowd at the starting line.

This was a tradition since high school. Neither of them actually raced. It was a Turkey Trot, not a Turkey Race, they rationalized. Mostly it was a time to hang out while pre-burning the monstrous number of calories they would consume at dinner.

At the sound of the gun, they were off, dodging slower runners and walkers with baby joggers, commenting about people walking with baby "joggers." Why weren't they jogging? It wasn't a baby "walker." As they weaved through the thinning crowd, they talked about their plans for the day.

"I am going to my parents for Thanksgiving dinner and later to Sam and Maria's for dessert," Clara explained.

"The boys didn't show up, I guess?" asked Sophie.

"No. And they didn't even let them know until a few days ago. Maria had already started cooking and preparing all the pies."

Clara and Sophie had gone to school with Sam and Maria's sons. They were self-absorbed jerks back then, and apparently never grew out of it.

"And, what about Clay? Will you see him today?"

"You know he went to see his family for the long weekend."

"Yes, and I also know that he invited you to come along," Sophie teased her friend.

"He's always inviting me to things. It was fun going with him and his family to the lake over the summer, but I needed to finish designs and be here for the day after Thanksgiving to make sure they hold up to the crowds and make any necessary adjustments," Clara said.

"You could have gone. Never in all of your years of creating displays have you ever had to make any adjustments!"

"Well, you never know. This might be the year I need to make a last-minute change so you don't have to defend me in a lawsuit! Plus, if I went with him, I wouldn't be here for our annual run."

"Whatever. Clay is perfect for you. It is actually pathetic the way he waits for you, but he might not wait forever," Sophie warned.

"Look, Clay is a friend. Besides, he dates and tells me all about it. If he was interested in me, I am sure he would tell me."

"Okay, if you say so—"

"Watch out for the baby jogger," Clara said, cutting her friend off mid-sentence.

Finishing the race and pumpkin pancake breakfast, they hugged goodbye and promised to get in touch to make Black Friday shopping plans, another yearly tradition.

Back at her condo, Clara showered, drank two bottles of water, and dressed. Her parents expected her at three o'clock. There was plenty of time to get ready and maybe even have another cup of coffee.

Pulling out her phone, she noticed several messages. There were various Happy Thanksgiving messages from professional contacts.

Scrolling, she noticed a message from Clay, with a video attached. Hitting Play, she sat at the table to watch.

"Hey, Clara! Just wanted to show you what you are missing!"

He went from room to room, describing all the activity: the cooking, eating, game watching, kids outside playing, and finally the Christmas decorating.

"My mom really wishes you were here to help with the decorating!"

From somewhere off-camera, Clara heard Clay's mom yell, "Don't tell her that! I really wish she was here because we miss spending time with her, you idiot!"

Laughing, Clay continued, "Well, anyway, my mom is sending a care package of great food. I'll deliver it when I get back tomorrow. I hope you have a great Thanksgiving Day with your family and will talk to you soon."

Clara smiled. Clay was right. She was missing out. That was the Thanksgiving she always wanted. Lots of food, lots of family, and lots of excitement about the coming holiday, the most important, fabulous, wonderful holiday of them all: Christmas!

Still thinking about Clay and his family, she swiped on lip gloss, glanced at her reflection, and headed to her parents for what was sure to be the usual Thanksgiving dinner.

Chapter 4

C lara left a few minutes early for the drive across town. Traffic was unpredictable on Thanksgiving Day. She was excited to hear the announcement that her favorite radio station was playing only Christmas music until Christmas Day. Clara listened to the commercials for sales the next day. She didn't need anything but would be out with the other shoppers just the same.

Clara invited the music to fill her spirit with Christmas cheer. Some people thought that Thanksgiving Day was too early to begin the Christmas season. But she didn't. In her estimation, Thanksgiving was just the dress rehearsal for Christmas.

"I mean really, that is why Santa shows up at the end of every Thanksgiving Day parade!" she rationalized when people questioned her holiday theory.

The familiar jingle for her favorite coffee shop, Cool Beans, pulled her attention from her thoughts.

"On Black Friday, we are giving away a year of free coffee to the first ten customers, and the ten customers throughout the day who have a Santa Claus sticker on the bottom of their cup. So, visit us first, or throughout your shopping day for your caffeine fix."

Now that alone is worth getting out of bed early.

Her phone rang. She pressed the green button and didn't say hello before she heard, "Did you just hear the ad for Cool Beans?"

It was Sophie, who was as excited as Clara about the possibility of a year of free coffee.

"Yes! Obviously, our first stop. What time do you want to get there?" Clara asked.

They decided Sophie would pick Clara up at four o'clock the next morning and they would take their chances at being one of the first ten. If they weren't, they would still take frequent coffee breaks throughout the day, increasing their odds. They weren't big shoppers. The day would be all about people watching, checking on Clara's displays, and spending time together as they ushered in the Christmas season.

"Are you almost there?" Sophie asked.

"About ten minutes away. I'm supposed to be there at three, but I'll be a little early. My sister is already home. She flew in last night," Clara said.

"Okay. Well, tell everyone I said hello. I'll see you tomorrow, bright and early!"

They hung up and Clara smiled to herself, thinking about the upcoming meal and spending the afternoon with her family and then dessert at Sam and Marie's.

The aroma of the various dishes smelled like heaven as she walked through the front door. Immediately, her stomach growled and mouth watered. Thankfully, she wore stretchy pants today. She'd need the extra room.

Clara's parents greeted her warmly. They were always excited to see her. Even though they lived in the same town, she didn't see them as often as she, or they, would like.

As the girls grew up, her mom was always home. Before having children, she worked in advertising. Once she was a mother, she was like the mom on the television shows Clara watched as she was growing up. The mom who always had breakfast on the table when the girls came downstairs, the mom who packed healthy and delicious lunches and wrote notes on the napkin tucked inside. Clara's mom never missed an activity at school, scouts, or church, and drove the girls hundreds of miles a week to different activities.

She cheered them on as they tried new things and sat with them in comforting silence when they failed at some of those new endeavors.

Her mom was crazy about their dad. She supported her husband in his various interests like she supported her girls in theirs. His chief passion was history, and on long vacations, they stopped along freeways and country roads to read and take pictures with the signs marking historical events. An avid reader herself, Clara's mom instilled a love for books and imagination in her. She often credited her ability to create such unique window displays to this love that her mother fostered.

Clara's dad was rarely home when she was younger. He loved his family and worked hard to provide a pleasant home, experiences, and education for his girls. Although he spent time away for work, he enjoyed watching them grow and learn as they became toddlers, young children, teenagers, and now adults. He reveled in their accomplishments and continued to encourage them to work hard.

For as long as she could remember, her dad loved his job. It was long hours and hard work, but as a civil engineer, he traveled the state, designing and overseeing the road and bridge projects.

Clara's dad would always return from his trips with funny stories about crazy drivers and interesting employees he met. Sometimes he told the girls about the little towns he stayed in. One town was tiny. He spent about six months there overseeing a project, and he told the girls the town loved parades. They had a parade for everything: homecoming, winning a state championship (in any sport), Thanksgiving, Christmas, Martin Luther King Jr. Day, Valentine's Day, St. Patrick's Day, and on and on it went. The funny thing was, almost everyone was in the parade, so there were very few people to watch.

Clara loved hearing these stories and wondered what new adventure her dad would tell them about at dinner today.

She heard her sister before she saw her. Squealing from the top of the stairs, Kayla ran down to greet her. Kayla had all the energy that Clara did not have. Even as young children, Kayla was into everything, while Clara was selective. They had different interests and groups of friends, but they loved each other. Clara was five years old and had been so excited to have a little sister when Kayla was born. Their mother tried to dress them in matching little outfits when they were small, but that only lasted until Kayla could talk and demanded to choose what clothes she wanted to wear.

Their mother tried to bend Kayla's will, but that was impossible. Not about clothes, boys, curfews, or anything. Kayla was her own person. Their parents hoped that one day this strength would be a benefit. The latest clash of wills arrived when Kayla announced she was going to graduate school to study viticulture and enology. Otherwise known as winemaking. Kayla's undergraduate degree was in horticulture. She was a naturalist and prided herself in being different. She found this program on a whim, when she couldn't find a job as a horticulturist that would pay her bills, and assumed that a master's degree in winemaking would make all the difference.

Clara's parents hit the roof when they heard about this alternative plan. They suspected that the decision was partly because of the study abroad semesters included in the program. It was longer than the usual two-year program and included semesters in Italy and France and an internship in California.

Eventually, her parents relented. They supported her decision and listened to hours of discussion about wine. Now they at least knew what to buy and how to pair it, although Clara's dad was sure you could find this information from a book and save all that time and expense.

They gathered in the kitchen and each had an assigned task to get the feast on the table. It had always been just the four of them.

They lived far from other family, so they never had big family dinners like Clara would see on television or in movies, or like Clay's family.

She wondered what he was doing right now. *Were they eating, playing a game, napping, watching the parade?* It surprised Clara that she wished she were at his Thanksgiving instead of this one, but she dismissed the thought as she sat down to eat and celebrate with her family.

As they sat, she surveyed the sumptuous spread in front of her. There was turkey, mashed potatoes, sweet potato casserole, green beans wrapped in bacon and drizzled with maple syrup, fresh baked yeast rolls, vegetable casserole with a buttery cracker crust, cranberry sauce, cornbread dressing, gravy, sautéed mushrooms, corn soufflé, green bean casserole, and roasted vegetables.

Kayla brought out her special selection of wines for the occasion, droning on about all the special notes and flavors they should notice. Clara was annoyed at this wine-tasting lesson and wanted to eat while the food was warm. Finally, her dad spoke up more politely, and offered to slice and serve the turkey so they could eat *and* drink the wine that Kayla brought.

Clara admonished herself. This was Thanksgiving, and she should be grateful that her little sister found something to be excited about. After all, she also made some strange career choices.

The food served, they settled into the routine conversations, catching up on each other's lives.

"Clara, tell us about your favorite Christmas displays this year," her dad said.

"It is hard to pick a favorite, much like it must be difficult to pick a favorite child," she answered, shooting a look at her sister and laughing.

"The most challenging was the Santa's Workshop for the mall. It is centrally located, so I made sure there wasn't a well-developed front and a flat back. In previous years, the scene was up against a wall, so it was smaller and I didn't need to worry about the back."

Her mother asked, "So, what was your solution?"

"It's an immersive experience. Children go through the line to see Santa and tell him what they want for Christmas. Then they walk through the workshop and they choose from an assortment of wooden toys on the workbench. From the workshop, they wander through the stable. I labeled each stall with a reindeer name, and they can leave a note on the wall for their favorite reindeer. I made it so that a child just passing by could access the stable part without going through the line to see Santa. Elves working in the stable guide the children and keep them from going through the stable to the workshop and then Santa. I think it will be a real hit this year."

"That sounds amazing!" Kayla interjected.

"Mom, I think the one you might like the best is at the bookstore. They let me use books to build the manger and stable for the nativity scene. I used stuffed animal characters from beloved children's books for the animals and mixed those in with the nativity figures. It's a fun display."

Her mom nodded, saying she looked forward to seeing all the displays her daughter created this year. Her parents took pride in making the circuit to see all the imaginative windows Clara created. They told other passersby that their daughter was the genius behind the scene and they loved seeing the faces of random strangers light up.

The conversation settled into a comfortable rhythm, everyone telling stories of the last few months since they had been together. They ate and drank and enjoyed the meal.

During dessert and coffee, Clara made her usual request to know the plan for December. She brought out her calendar to mark dates she needed to clear for special events with her family. This year, she made a list of the things they could do together. Things like

Christmas movies, getting the family tree and decorating it, shopping and wrapping gifts, baking cookies and other treats, a night of hot cocoa and driving around looking at light displays, a Christmas concert, and finally Christmas Eve and Christmas Day.

She settled her list and pen in its place. Her father cleared his throat and looked at her mother. The girls exchanged a worried look, squirming in their seats.

"Clara, before you plan our Christmas, your mother and I want to tell you girls something," Clara's dad said.

"As you know, I've talked about retiring for a few years. During the last few days, several things transpired. Due to budget cuts from the state, my position is considered 'redundant.' Yesterday was my last day. Anyway, we've thought for years this house is too big for just the two of us. Both of you are off on your own doing amazing things, so we don't need this house."

Clara looked at her mother. She didn't return Clara's gaze, carefully stirring her coffee as if she were afraid it might spill over the edge of the cup onto the white tablecloth.

"Last week, the same day I found out I was going to be retiring, a real estate agent called, asking if we were interested in selling the house. A couple wanted to move into this neighborhood and as you know, homes rarely come up for sale here. They have family at the end of the street, so the Realtor made calls to all the homeowners to see if anyone was interested in selling. We took a few days to discuss it and ultimately tossed out an amount we didn't think anyone would actually pay, and within thirty minutes had a contract. The buyers were so eager to get the house, they paid our asking price and offered to pay for the closing costs and any inspections. The catch is we have to be out by December 5. So, this afternoon, you need to go through your rooms and the attic to see what you want to keep. Then you have to take it with you or put it in storage."

Clara thought she might be having a heart attack. Her vision narrowed. She could feel her blood pumping throughout her body and there was a weird buzzing sound in her ears. Her chest tightened, and she wasn't sure she could breathe. "Why did you wait until today, Thanksgiving, to tell us? This is our home! We grew up here. Didn't you think we would care about this even though we are on our own?"

Her mother tried to console her. "Clara, we would never live in this house forever. We have things we want to do too."

"Like what?" Clara shot back. "And, what about Christmas? You only have a few more days to find a new house, get packed, and move. How will we do all the Christmas things?"

"Oh, here we go! Clara and her Christmas list," Kayla interjected, exasperated.

"Kayla, shut up! You wouldn't even have Christmas if it wasn't for me. You plan nothing, you hardly take part, and frankly, you make everything miserable every Christmas, anyway!"

The conversation continued at a fever pitch until they heard a booming voice. "Girls! I will not tell you again to lower your voices and speak civilly to each other. The house is our decision, not yours. Clara, we know you have this ridiculous obsession with Christmas and every year we humor you, but this year we have to keep things simple. Kayla, your sister is right. You do exactly what you want, with no consideration of how that affects the rest of us. So, this should not make a difference to you in the slightest."

He continued, "About the move. We've decided to take some time to think about our next permanent step. In the meantime, we bought an RV and a Jeep to tow behind it. We are hitting the open road after the closing on December 5. Our first trip will be to drive Route 66. I have worked very hard, put both of you through school, and now you are on your own. We are going to take some time for ourselves and travel. We never had time to do that before, and now we have both the time and the money. So, Clara, those are our plans. I know this is difficult for you, but it is what it is."

Clara could hardly believe what she was hearing. "But, what about a Christmas tree? Where will you put the tree in an RV?"

"Clara, we won't have a tree." Her mother interrupted. "An RV is much too small for a Christmas tree."

"But, how will you celebrate Christmas? What about presents and dinner and movies?"

"We'll let you know where we'll be that week and you can join us. The RV might be tight, so we can make a reservation at a nearby hotel for you. Don't worry, we can still be together at Christmas," her mother explained.

This was more than Clara could take, and she slammed her hands on the table. Coffee spilled from her mother's cup onto the tablecloth. "Have you lost your minds? You make this snap decision to sell our home, then you are moving in two weeks, into an RV for God's sake, and now you think the solution for Christmas is to put me and Kayla in a hotel? On Christmas Eve?"

Clara shook; she was losing control of herself and her Christmas. She was afraid of the next thing that would come out of her mouth.

Kayla said, "Well, it won't be me and you at the hotel for Christmas Eve, Clara. I am going to Italy early and have a flight booked for the day after I finish finals. So, I guess you can just get rid of the stuff in my room or the attic. I won't have much time to go through it, anyway. My study abroad starts in January. The flight was cheaper, and this way I can experience Christmas in Rome. Can you believe it? I will be in Italy for Christmas."

Clara thought maybe she was the one losing her mind! How could all of this be okay with the rest of her family? *Surely her parents would not let Kayla just jet off to Italy to spend Christmas, the most important time of the year, in a strange country, with strangers! Kayla doesn't even speak Italian. How is she going to even enjoy her holiday*

when she can't ask where the bathrooms are, or know how to order a
glass of wine? This was ridiculous.

"That's wonderful news! We'll miss you, but it sounds like an adventure. We can't wait to hear all about it! Be sure to send us plenty of pictures. Will anyone else from your program go at the same time?" Clara's mother asked.

"Well, one of my professors is from Italy, and he offered to let me stay with him and will show me around and take me to all the local places so it won't just be the tourist experience."

"Oh, now I get it. Typical Kayla. Get involved with a hot professor, run off to God knows where, with no thought to how that affects anyone else. Great, that's just great. Don't bother sending me pictures. Just send a text of your itinerary so when it all goes to crap, I know what to tell the American Embassy."

With that parting shot, Clara packed up her belongings. As she reached the door, she turned around. "I guess I'll come back later this week and pick up my things. I'm sorry you all ruined Thanksgiving and Christmas. And, no, I won't be joining you in your RV."

Barely holding back her tears, she made it to her car, turned the key, and threw it into reverse as "I'll Be Home for Christmas" played on the radio.

"Nope, I won't be home for Christmas," she said out loud to the radio. "I don't have a home to come home to."

And with that, she made her way to Sam and Maria's, hoping to salvage the rest of her holiday.

Chapter 5

It was quiet, and the traffic was light as Clara made her way to Sam and Maria's. She hoped her afternoon wouldn't ruin her time with her friends.

The radio played Christmas music. It grated on her nerves. Listening to Christmas music had always brought happiness, transporting her to a wonderful Christmas memory or place in her imagination. Not the case today. Instead, she was sad about the prospect of spending the holiday alone.

She parked in front of Sam and Maria's small home and noticed the drapes in the front window were open. Everything looked perfect. There was plenty of fall decor, and a centerpiece of giant sunflowers was in the center of the table. It looked like a scene from a movie.

Clara felt a glimmer of happiness return and wondered how Sam and Maria's boys could blow off coming home for the holidays. Shaking her head about the ungrateful nature of Sam and Maria's sons, she opened her car door and stepped out into the dark.

Maria came to the door before Clara even had time to knock. She reached out and pulled Clara into the house with a tight hug.

"It's so good to see you! I've missed you and was excited to hear Sam invited you over tonight. We have so many desserts. I hope you saved room for pie," Maria said.

"I'm sorry I didn't call. It's been a weird day."

"Don't worry about that. We are glad you are here," Maria said.

Clara's spirits lifted as she followed Maria. Her stomach growled, and she realized she left her parents' home so quickly, she'd eaten little. The smells were pure heaven. It was as if she walked through a fog of nutmeg, cinnamon, cloves, butter, maple, cranberry, and chocolate.

Sam was in the dining room and turned to greet her when she entered.

"There you are! I'm so glad you came. As you can see, we have plenty of food that we can't eat by ourselves. Come sit down and tell us all about your visit with your parents."

Clara sat down in the chair Sam offered and placed her napkin in her lap. Maria appeared with a tray that held a carafe of hot coffee and cream and sugar cubes.

Wow, thought Clara, *she really went all out.*

She accepted the coffee that Maria poured for her and, for fun, put in two cubes of sugar. Watching the tiny bubbles rise from the cubes made her smile.

"Thank you." She began stirring, careful not to slosh coffee on the table. "Everything looks and smells delicious. I am glad I wore stretchy pants. I will have to try everything!"

Sam and Maria found their places and chatted about their day. They caught her up on all the activities of this holiday that was just the two of them.

"We slept in later than usual, and Maria made the most delicious pumpkin-cranberry pancakes with fresh whipped cream. Then we enjoyed our coffee on the back porch overlooking the lake. The leaves were just beautiful, and it was cool enough to bundle up. After that, we went for a walk around the park. Kids were playing and giggling in the neighborhood playground. I guess their parents shooed them out so they wouldn't be in the way. We watched the parade on television while we finished cooking for the day. The boys always enjoyed watching the giant balloons, waiting to see their favorite floats and characters. The Santa this year at the end looked very authentic. He was a much better Santa than last year; don't you think, Maria?"

Maria nodded her head in agreement. She had just taken a bite of cranberry cobbler.

Clara giggled at the sight of these two. They worked well together to prepare this feast and clearly enjoyed each other's company.

As she dipped her fork into her first nibble of pumpkin pie, she asked, "Did you hear from the boys today? How was their holiday?"

Maria nodded. "They called and of course apologized for not being able to make it. I think they were both planning to eat and watch football. They both work so hard and have their own families now, so we can't expect them to come here for every holiday anymore."

"Although it would have been nice to have had a little more warning they weren't coming," Sam added.

"Yes, but now we have plenty of dessert to share with Clara!" Maria exclaimed.

Clara found it amazing that Maria had such a positive attitude about her family missing a holiday. She wasn't sure she could muster the same level of positivity in a month when she would be alone at Christmas.

"So, tell us about your visit with your family," Maria continued.

"It was a disaster," Clara said, as the story tumbled out of her. "I found out my dad was laid off and given a severance and an early retirement package. Then, someone contacted them about buying their house and they sold it! The home I grew up in will have new people living in it in ten days."

Clara took another bite of pie and a swallow of her coffee.

Maria and Sam sat quietly, eating their dessert and drinking coffee.

"They decided to buy an RV—or maybe they already bought it. I don't remember the details. Anyway, they are going to travel the historic drives throughout the United States. Can you imagine that?

I asked about a Christmas tree, and my mom said that the RV was too small so they wouldn't have one. Then they had the audacity to tell me I could travel to wherever they would be for Christmas Eve and Christmas Day, and they would put me in a hotel, at Christmas. Can you believe that?"

Clara's voice and heartbeat rose as she retold her awful experience from earlier. "I can't believe they are doing this, especially at Christmas. They know how much I love Christmas. What is wrong with them? They are ruining Christmas."

Fighting back tears, she could see the shock on their faces as they listened to her outburst. They hesitated, waiting for her to continue.

"And Kayla! She started some ridiculous graduate program that has something to do with making wine. I can't remember the name. Anyway, she was no help to convince our parents this is a ridiculous plan. In fact, she is leaving right after finals for Italy with one of her professors. That is so like her! I try to make everything nice for everyone, and she just goes and does whatever she wants, with no consideration. And Mom and Dad just sat there, excited about her new adventure."

"A trip to Italy sounds like an amazing opportunity," said Sam.

Clara stopped and looked at Sam. "But she won't be here at Christmas. They ruined Christmas!"

"Maybe you could look at this from a fresh perspective. Now you are free to do all the things you want to do at Christmas, things you enjoy that they always complained about. You can do what you want, when you want, without worrying about anyone else's schedule or conflicts."

Clara paused, considering Maria's suggestion.

"I understand what you're saying, but it isn't as fun by myself. The whole point is to be together. I don't understand why they don't get excited about Christmas. It's Christmas, for heaven's sake! Everyone should be excited about it. It is the 'Most Wonderful Time of the Year' for a reason. It isn't fair that I create wonderful scenes of happy Christmas memories for families and my family won't take part in my Christmas plans."

"It sounds like they are asking you to take part in their plans this year instead," Sam said.

Clara couldn't believe what she was hearing. Sam and Maria were on her parents' side!

"You're right," Sam continued. "You create magic at Christmas for so many people, but not everyone has the same Christmas experience. I'm afraid that you're letting others determine the value of your experience. It will never work out for you if you continue to do that."

Maria interjected, "I'm sorry that you feel bad about this. Surely, it was a shock. Everyone knows how much you look forward to the festivities this time of year. I wonder if maybe you should take some time to think about why this season is so important to you."

Clara thought about what Maria and Sam suggested and quietly nodded her head.

They continued eating, each bite of dessert better than the one before. The conversation moved to happier things. Maria shared funny stories from her visits to the local retirement community, where she led bingo once a week. Sam caught her up on all the mall gossip and news. Even in a down-turned economy, the shops were busy and walkers filled the mall every day.

So full they thought they might pop, Clara helped Sam and Maria clear the table and put away the food. Maria prepared several take-home containers for Clara to enjoy over the next few days.

The three of them worked side by side in the kitchen, Sam washing, Clara drying, and Maria putting the dishes away. It felt comfortable to Clara. Again, she wondered whether the boys even thought about what they were missing right now.

After they washed the dishes and cleaned the kitchen, Clara announced she had an early morning. She and Sophie wanted to win the free coffee for a year at Cool Beans, which meant they had to be in line early the next morning.

At the door, she hugged Sam and Maria, and thanked them for their company and delicious food. She was grateful to end Thanksgiving feeling better.

Driving home, she turned up the Christmas music. "Rocking Around the Christmas Tree" played, and she sang along, feeling lighter than she had since leaving her house that morning.

Later, she set her alarm and snuggled under the covers. Clara thought about Sam and Maria's suggestion as she drifted off to sleep. Tomorrow would be a big day and she needed lots of energy and coffee.

Chapter 6

"Jingle Bells" played, waking Clara up at three o'clock the next morning. Excited, she jumped out of bed, washed and dried her face, dressed, and was in the kitchen for that first glorious cup of coffee within ten minutes. She sent Sophie a message, making sure she was awake. She fed Mistletoe and changed the litter box. Then she quickly scanned the paper for must-have deals.

"Let's see," she said to Mistletoe. "Microwaves and TVs are fifty percent off. Looks like there is a pretty good deal on laptops and printers. Oh, now here is something interesting! A new vacuum to follow you around and pick up any fur on the floor."

She reached over and fluffed Mistletoe's fur between her eyes. That might be something worth checking out, but today was mostly for people watching, coffee drinking, and making sure her displays were holding up.

Half an hour later, her phone buzzed. Sophie was outside, waiting. Clara grabbed her bag and dropped her keys and phone inside. She carefully balanced the two to-go coffee cups while locking the door behind her.

Sophie noticed Clara's hands were full, so she reached over, opened the passenger door, and took one cup.

"Clara, really? You know that we're going to stand in line at a coffee shop, right?"

"And, you will be happy to have coffee to drink while we wait! Besides, this will keep your hands warm."

Sophie took a quick sip from the cup and thanked her for the coffee.

As they drove, Sophie chatted away. She had a great Thanksgiving with her extended family. Her family gathered at her grandparents'. They had a place in the country, and because Sophie was from a large family, there were tons of people and food. She went on and on about the funny things that happened throughout the day. The turkey was raw in the center, a new parent had to deal with a blowout diaper that cleared the room, and one younger cousin decided it would be funny to put antlers on the dog to make a reindeer. It was funny until the dog knocked over the kids' table, trying to remove the antlers.

Fortunately, Sophie had plenty of stories, so Clara didn't have to talk about her miserable Thanksgiving. She would tell her later, but for now she enjoyed listening to Sophie and imagining the chaos of a big family holiday dinner.

They were still laughing and listening to Christmas music on the radio when they pulled into the parking lot. Cool Beans was one of the businesses that was on the outside of the mall with an entrance into the mall. They couldn't believe their good luck! There were only a few people in line, so they rushed out of the car to ensure their opportunity to get free coffee for a year. The coffee here was better than any coffee from a chain coffee shop. They often came here to visit; they had studied here when they were in school, and now it was the first stop they made when going to the mall for anything.

The line moved quickly for early in the morning. There was a special energy as people dreamed of the treasures they might find in the day ahead. As Sophie continued to talk, Clara made a mental note of the route they would need to take, making sure that everything was still in order for her displays in the mall.

Clara and Sophie began people watching. The aim was to find the tackiest Christmas sweater. Although both women dressed in a festive red and green, they thought they were a little more fashionable than some of the other shoppers. In previous years, they had seen adults wearing Christmas pajamas, as if they rolled out of bed and got in line for whatever it was they hoped to buy at seventy-five percent off.

Surveying the crowd, they saw the usual sweaters with red and green and maybe some gold trim, oversized faces of jolly old Saint Nick, even some sweaters with bells on the sleeves that jingled as the wearer walked and jostled packages and bags.

They saw this year's winners at the same time and knocked into each other, trying to get the other's attention.

"I see, oh jeez! I wonder how much time that took?"

Walking into the mall entrance was a family, wearing ridiculous sweaters and linked together with strings of brightly colored and twinkling Christmas lights!

"I guess that is one way to keep track of everyone." Clara giggled.

The day was exciting for Clara. Sophie wasn't interested in shopping either, so there was no pressure to make it to a particular store before the crowds snapped up the deals. They had everything they needed and had short Christmas gift lists to purchase. In fact, Clara had almost everything purchased and wrapped for the people on her list. But, now that her family had changed their plans and residences, she would need to go back through the gifts she planned to give and make sure they were still appropriate. Too many things were changing this Christmas season, and she wished things would just go back to normal.

As they went along with the current of the crowd, Sophie asked, "So, which is your favorite window this year?"

"You know that is like asking a parent which child they love the best, don't you?" Clara answered.

"Yes, and I also know that you secretly have a favorite."

"My favorite is the one that makes the people who see it light up."

"That's a very diplomatic answer. I'll know it by your expression. It'll be the one that also makes you light up the most as we stop to look at it."

"Then why did you ask?" Clara said.

They came to the bakery and stopped, noticing the line coiled in the shop and spilling out into the mall.

"Wow! It's really beautiful!" Sophie said.

They moved around, surveying it from different angles, to see whether the display was accessible to any customers who might damage the props. Clara listened for shoppers' opinions. Once she was sufficiently pleased, they continued walking, repeating this at every scene.

At the bookstore, the crowds commented how clever the nativity was with the shredded pages for straw and the books as building materials for the manger and stable. Clara was excited to see people smile as they walked through the mall entrance she designed. They knew they were walking into a special place.

A major crowd pleaser was the toy store display. There weren't many children shopping the day after Thanksgiving, but every adult in front of the store felt like a child again as they watched the elves check lists, assemble simple wooden toys, and wrap and label the toy, putting it into one of three large red, green, or gold velvet bags to be delivered. From young adults to the elderly, every waiting shopper stood transfixed by what they saw. This was exactly the Santa Workshop of their imaginations.

Clara and Sophie stood in silence, admiring the scene and watching and listening to the crowd. There were oohs and aahs, and people in the lines outside the toy store began telling stories of their favorite toys when they were children.

Joy swept over Clara because of the emotion her creation elicited in these strangers. It was exactly what she hoped for as she drew the design and then gathered everything and put it in place.

She was smiling, proud of herself, when Sophie turned and said, "This one. This one has to be your favorite! I can see why. This is the best one I've seen since you started all of this. Well done!"

"Thank you. This might be my favorite, but you haven't seen Santa yet!"

They continued walking through the mall, sipping on coffee and wondering about the line at Cool Beans. They were coming to the end of their coffee and wanted to use their coffee-for-a-year card.

They made their way past the large department store displays and watched the shoppers' reactions It was always special to watch as people took pictures of and with the scenes she created. She wondered what they did with the pictures. She was happy that people thought they were photo worthy.

Finally, they came to the center of the mall, the intersection of the five concourses. There was Santa in all his glory, sitting on the plush red velvet and gold-trimmed throne, waiting to greet the children already in line as they whispered their greatest Christmas wish in his ear.

Stopping, they stared.

"Wow! He looks real," Sophie said under her breath in case any child was within earshot.

"I know," Clara said.

"Well, be sure to ask him for something you really want. He looks like he might make any Christmas wish come true," Sophie said.

They giggled and Clara said, "Follow me. I want to show you something."

They walked around the side of the display, and she pointed out the details to Sophie. At the back, she walked into the stable when Sophie stopped her.

"Wait! Can we go in through the back?"

"Yes, come with me. This is open to anyone." Clara giggled.

Hearing Clara say this, others standing nearby followed the two inside. They stood in the reindeer stables and exclaimed how much this looked like the real thing. Clara beamed. This place existed only in imaginations and she had brought it to life.

The stable elf explained, "Unfortunately, all the reindeer are in a special training session, getting ready for the big day, but they are always excited to come back at night and read the messages left in their stalls."

Each visitor took a piece of chalk and wandered into the stalls to leave a special message on the wall for their favorite reindeer. As an extra detail, there was a small bio of each reindeer on their stall door. Clara hoped this would help people connect with more reindeer than just Rudolph, the most famous reindeer of all. It worked! She noticed people milling about, reading the bios and writing messages. She and Sophie even took a minute to survey the stable and write a few quick messages in red and green on the chalkboard in each stable.

By now it was lunchtime, and they were starving. They ate in the food court and counted the number of tired and frustrated shoppers, and children having absolute meltdowns. They couldn't understand why anyone would bring a child to shop so early on such a busy day and vowed they would never do that when they had children.

They saw the movie theater marquee. *The Polar Express* was showing throughout the day. Checking the times, they decided it would be a great way to spend the afternoon. They hurried, gathering their trash and dumping everything into the nearest trash bin, as they crossed the food court and headed to the theater.

"Two for *The Polar Express*, please," Sophie said to the cashier behind the window.

Sliding her money into the slot, she took the tickets. Clara was in line for popcorn and drinks.

They found each other in the line waiting to get into the theater. The ticket taker explained that since this was the first showing, it was a smaller crowd, but by the end of the afternoon, they would sell out.

"By the four o'clock showing, people are tired of walking and shopping and want to sit down and rest. That's our busiest Christmas movie showing," the teenager explained.

Entering the theater, they found seats in the middle. A few others streamed in and found seats behind them. There was plenty of room for shoppers and their bags full of the treasures they found that morning.

People were talking softly about what they saw, what they bought, and what they missed out on when the lights went down and the movie began.

Clara's heart fluttered at the opening scene. This was what she wished life was like: Waiting on Christmas Eve, in a warm bed, on a snowy night. Straining to hear the bells on Santa's sleigh. Hoping Santa was real.

Clara settled into her seat, munching on popcorn and sipping her drink. It was the perfect movie to start the Christmas season.

Afterward, the two decided it was time to call it a day. Sophie needed to nap and then prepare for a case that was going to trial on Monday. Clara also needed a nap and was going to begin her Christmas season planning ritual, marking every important date on a special December calendar that hung in her entryway and putting dates in her professional planner. December was a busy time for her as most of her accounts invited her to attend the Christmas parties for the businesses that she decorated.

Home, Clara fed and watered Mistletoe, took off her shoes, turned off her phone, and settled under fluffy blankets on her couch for a nice long nap. She had no plans to be anywhere else for the rest of the day. She deserved a rest and maybe another Christmas movie later.

Drifting off to sleep, she thought of the events of the last couple of days. Her parents and sister still frustrated and confused her, but she thought things might still work out. She found she was happy that her scenes at the mall were so well received and hoped they would continue to help people experience the magic of Christmas.

Chapter 7

Two hours later, a contented Clara opened her eyes. It was getting dark outside, so she turned on the lamp next to the sofa. Mistletoe stretched, annoyed, and sauntered off to find a more suitable place to continue her nap.

Clara checked her messages. Her parents called to check on her after their disastrous family dinner the day before and to invite her to a packing party the following Sunday. There was also a message from Clay explaining that he would drive home Saturday and would stop by with the leftovers his mom packed for Clara.

Clara went into the kitchen and pulled out the containers full of the assorted desserts that Maria sent her home with the night before. She knew she should probably eat something a little healthier, but dessert and coffee sounded good after a long nap. She chose the pumpkin pie and made a fresh mug of coffee. While she ate, Clara flipped through a stack of party invitations, marking the dates in both her professional planner and Christmas calendar. Five parties this year. The same as last year. She already had her party outfit ready to go, shoes and all. She found a few years ago that there were rarely the same people at these events, so there was no need to go to the expense and stress to have something new to wear to each party. This made the season even more enjoyable. She usually looked forward to the parties, until she got there. There was always lots of excellent food and decorations, mostly because she had done the decor, but it wasn't much fun to be at a party with so many people she didn't have a daily connection with. But it was part of the job, and she needed these contacts year after year to get paid for doing what she loved.

Her Christmas calendar had a list of the things that she wanted to do. The list included getting a tree and decorating the inside and outside of her condo, finish shopping and wrapping gifts, driving around to see light displays, Christmas concert, spend a day as a Salvation Army bell ringer, and watch Christmas movies: *A Christmas Story, Christmas Vacation, The Grinch, Christmas With The Kranks, It's a Wonderful Life, Miracle on 34th Street, Elf, Home Alone,* and *White Christmas.* There were enough favorites that she could watch a Christmas movie every night of December, but these were her absolute loves. She also needed to check her Christmas playlist to make sure her favorite carols would be available whenever she wanted them.

Wow. She looked at her list. *I have a lot going on.*

She frowned, remembering that she would most likely be doing these things alone because her parents were moving and Kayla would be out of the country soon. Clara was frustrated again about her family and their total disregard for her and the season.

"How can they all just think this is okay?" she wondered out loud.

Her phone rang.

Oh, I need to change the ringtone on my phone, too! She usually changed it to a Christmas carol during the holidays.

She noticed it was her mom's number and hesitated before answering it. Clara didn't want to deal with whatever her parents had to say now, imagining that perhaps the move was going to be sooner than they expected. It never occurred to her that perhaps their plans changed altogether and they would be available for all the Christmas plans she usually made.

She tapped the green button and answered the call.

"Clara, we wanted to call to tell you we are really sorry about what happened yesterday. You are right. We should have told you as soon as we knew and were in the consideration phase of this decision. It is unfortunate that Kayla has also made other plans, but she didn't tell us until yesterday either."

Clara listened politely to the explanation. She knew her mother was trying to smooth things over, but it didn't change the outcome. Clara would not have the Christmas she always imagined and tried to have every year.

"I know. It is just you know how much I look forward to December and how I love all the fun things that Christmas brings. Things have been so busy the last few months for me with work and now I have to sort and move things from my childhood room and home and figure out what to do with it and try to fit in all that I want to do this Christmas. And, I have to do all these things by myself. It just won't be the same. And to be honest, I am not excited about spending Christmas Eve and Christmas Day in a hotel or RV. We are supposed to be home, doing all the things we usually do."

Clara knew it sounded like she was whining and that was inappropriate for a grown woman, but she couldn't help herself.

"I know you are disappointed and upset, but you are being dramatic. Christmas isn't about doing all the activities. It's about being together and we can do that anywhere."

Clara rolled her eyes, thankful that her mother couldn't see through the phone.

"Why don't you come over on Sunday. We are going to pack and will have plenty of boxes, bubble wrap, tape, and markers. You can work in your room. We'll order pizza and test your sister's wine skills. It'll be fun to spend time together."

Grudgingly, Clara agreed to come Sunday morning and bring coffee and breakfast for everyone before hanging up.

She had planned to decorate her condo but suddenly wasn't in the mood. Instead, she ran a hot bath, made some hot chocolate, grabbed her tattered and well-loved copy of *A Christmas Carol*, and set about to read and relax.

After her bath, she wrapped herself in a fluffy towel and dried off before putting on her green pajamas with the Santas all over them. It was going to be a chilly night, so she dug around in her drawer for her Christmas socks. She was ready for bed but not really sleepy, so she brought her book to bed and continued reading until her eyes drooped and she was losing her place. Mistletoe curled up next to her and after Clara turned off her lamp, they both fell fast asleep.

Saturday, Clara woke bright and early. She felt well rested and ready for the day. This was decorating day! After decorating for everyone else, it was time to get her things in place so she could enjoy them while spending a little more time at home than usual. December was oddly her downtime. After spending months designing, buying, and collecting items, and then putting everything together, she had one month to enjoy Christmas for herself before taking everything down in January and beginning the process for the next Christmas.

After getting some coffee for herself and feeding Mistletoe, she went to the closet in her office and started pulling out the green and red storage boxes. Each year, she carefully labeled them so she knew their contents. There was a specific system. She would start decorating the condo's interior, beginning with her entryway, and work her way through. She had themes for each room, and they would cover her condo in Christmas before the day was over.

Her favorite piece was the leg lamp she placed on a table in the living room window. It faced the street, and she wondered whether anyone ever saw it and laughed.

The kitchen was full of gingerbread houses and men, and she had a gingerbread-scented candle going by her coffeemaker.

Bathrooms were both decorated with snowmen. Even though Clara had never had a white Christmas, snowmen were a cute and easy theme to bring into a bathroom, so it worked.

Clara decorated her bedroom like a Christmas tree farm. She had three trees, of varying sizes, to put up in her room, and she strung white lights over the trio like a Christmas tree lot. Each tree had lights on them and she loved to snuggle in her bed at night and look at the lights as she drifted off to sleep.

Her living room was her favorite. Besides the massive tree with multicolored lights, she had vintage toys of all kinds scattered about the room. There were cinnamon- and pine-scented candles everywhere. Each ornament was special to her. She had collected them since she was a teenager and was very particular about adding one or two a year. Some were from vacations; she picked others up during her shopping trips for design jobs. There were expensive ornaments and ornaments that were less than a dollar. Each ornament represented a snapshot of her life. Decorating the tree each year was like going from memory to memory. The additions for this year were antique blown-glass ornaments that looked like candy. They were bright colors, and caught the light from the tree and glistened against the flocked branches.

Her tree was always a beautiful mix of vintage and modern Christmas ornaments. This year, she also added a Santa climbing up a ladder. The ladder attached to the inside of the tree and when turned on, Santa would climb up the ladder, carrying a string of lit lights over his shoulder that went all the way down into a red velvet bag placed next to the bottom of the ladder. When he reached the top of the ladder, Santa would step back down the rungs to the bottom and start again.

Clara finished decorating the tree and room, and put all the boxes back in the office closet where they belonged. She came back in and sat on the sofa to survey her work. It was exactly as she imagined a home should look at Christmas. Not cluttered, but definitely full of Christmas cheer.

Her stomach growled. Looking at her watch, she noticed it was almost four o'clock. She was so busy getting her home ready for Christmas she didn't even stop to eat. As she was heading into the kitchen to find something to warm up, there was a knock at the door. She opened it to find Clay with a basket full of Tupperware.

"I thought you might be hungry. Today is your decorating day and once you get started, I know you don't stop until everything looks perfect. Can I come in?"

Clara was excited to see him and opened the door wider, inviting him into her Christmas dreamland.

"Wow! You did all of this today?"

Clay stopped and just took it all in. Christmas was everywhere. When he would pick her up for his company's Christmas party, she was always ready to go and so he would only really see the entryway. He had been to her home several times over the years for movie and game nights and barbecues in the summer, but this was his first time to see it at Christmas.

"Yes. Do you want the grand tour?" she asked as she took the food from him and led him into the kitchen.

"As you can see, this is the kitchen and dining area. Because I actually have to cook and eat in here, I can't decorate as much as I would like," she explained.

Walking back out of the kitchen, he followed her to the living room.

"This is my favorite room during Christmas and where I spend most of my time. These are all my favorite toys from when I was a little girl, or that I picked up along the way."

She pointed out her special things and watched as he took it all in. It was like watching people see her Christmas displays, and she could tell it impressed him.

"Come this way." She walked into the hallway and stopped at the bathroom to flip on the light.

"You even decorated your bathroom?"

"Yes, both of them. Don't you?" she asked.

"Um, no. I barely have a tree. Some years I don't even do that," Clay explained.

"Are you serious? Where do you put all of your presents?" she asked.

"I don't know. I guess I send them to the person I am buying it for or they sit on my table."

Clara frowned and he quickly added, "But this year, I will have a tree. Maybe you can come and help me decorate it."

"I would love to!" It surprised Clara that she felt excited to help Clay with a tree and figured it must be because she wouldn't be helping her parents with their family tree.

"Come on in here. Speaking of trees." She opened the door to her bedroom and showed him her Christmas tree farm decorations. It was really beautiful from this angle, and she knew it was impressive. This year, she added some framed artwork that looked like vintage Christmas tree farm signs with pricing all around the room. She also added an old red truck with a Christmas tree in the back, tiny twinkling lights wrapped around it so that it really showed up.

Her attention to detail dazzled Clay, and she knew it. She laughed, watching him take it all in.

"I can't believe you did all of this in one day! How long does it take to put it all away in a month?" he asked.

"This is what I do for a living. If it took me forever to decorate, then I would never get paid and would starve to death," she said. "And, it only takes a day to put it all up. But this isn't everything. I haven't even started on the outside yet. Come back in a couple of days and see the fully decorated product, inside and out!"

"Okay, it's a date!" he said.

Walking back to the kitchen, Clara asked, "Are you hungry? I'm starving and can't wait to eat what your mom sent."

"Yes! I hoped you'd share. She sent nothing home for me. She said I had already eaten everything, and this was for you."

From the kitchen, Clara started her Christmas playlist, and they unpacked the food Clay's mom sent while listening to Christmas classics. They ate at the table, and Clara felt Clay watching for her reaction.

As if on cue, Clara said, "This is delicious! Did you eat like this growing up?"

"Only at the holidays. My mom is a wonderful cook. Actually, she owns a small café and does all the cooking. Before she married and had children, she had been a chef at a fancy restaurant. She traveled to different countries, learning about different dishes, and brought them back to the restaurant. Then she stayed home with us. As we got older, she had an idea for a café in our hometown and that was that. My mom loves her café and everyone in town loves it too. She is busy and thrilled with what she has built. She doesn't cook at home much these days, but she really wows at the holidays. Thanksgiving and Christmas dinners are her specialty."

As they ate, Clay told her all about his visit with his family. She thought he was lucky. He and Sophie had the Thanksgiving and family that she wanted, and she wondered whether they appreciated it.

Finally, there was a break in the conversation, and he asked about her visit with her family. He knew they lived in the area and she saw them frequently, but the holidays were always special times for her and her family.

"Well, it wasn't as wonderful as your visit with your family," she said, filling him in on the details.

"So, tomorrow I will go to a 'packing party' to help my parents pack things up. My sister and I have to focus on our rooms, things we saved in the attic and garage, and then anything else we want before Mom and Dad sell the rest."

"I know it's disappointing, but try to make it as happy an occasion as you can."

Hearing that sentiment from everyone was frustrating. She was an adult, and she knew that her parents and sister could make their own decisions, but it just seemed that they were always resisting her perfect Christmas. All she wanted to do was have the Christmas that she saw in all the Christmas movies.

She didn't want to argue with Clay, so she agreed and said that she would try to make the best of it.

After they cleaned up, Clay announced he better go home. He came straight from his parents' and still needed to pick up his dog from the boarder before they closed. Clara walked him to the door and as he went to leave, he turned and reminded her to have fun the next day. She closed the door behind him and tried to imagine a world in which packing a house in a day would be fun.

Chapter 8

C lara arrived bright and early with coffee and muffins in tow. Her parents were already up and sorting, but Kayla wasn't out of bed yet. She sat at the table with her parents and visited about their plans over breakfast.

"Everything is still on track for the fifth. Today we'll choose what to take and what goes into storage. The rest will go to you or your sister. We'll sell anything that doesn't fit those categories. We need to move fast today. There's a lot to do. I can't believe how much we accumulated over the years."

Her dad was still talking as Clara surveyed the situation. From the kitchen table, she could see the living room, dining room, and kitchen. *Just that would take a week.*

"Okay. Have you given any thought to coming back for Christmas? You could stay with me."

"Clara, honestly. Where would we park the RV? Plus, we'll be half a country away by Christmas. It's much easier if you come to us," her mother explained.

"You know I have work. The party season lasts until Christmas Eve. It isn't possible for me to travel at Christmas. Besides, even if I did, it wouldn't be the same. Won't you miss our usual holiday?"

Clara couldn't understand why her parents were insisting on this ridiculous plan.

"We already checked and the RV park has a community room and hosts a holiday dinner for everyone staying during Christmas. We read the reviews and everyone enjoys it. It's potluck and they have a Santa. It sounds fun," her dad said.

"Are you kidding me? You're planning on celebrating Christmas with strangers, eating strange food? Don't you think this is weird? This is the worst Christmas ever. I can't believe this is your plan." Clara got up from the table, put her paper cup and plate in the trash, and went to her room.

She spent the day sorting items from her childhood, making a keep pile and a donate pile. As crazy as she was for Christmas, she wasn't very sentimental about most of the things in her room and had kept little over the years. Almost everything went into the donate or trash pile. She only kept a few toys and books. She wrapped each item and labeled the box. After she took it to her car, she went into the attic to claim the Christmas decorations.

No one objected to her taking all the decorations. She knew what was in each box because she was the one who unpacked and repacked each box, replacing what may have broken anyway. For now, she planned to keep them in storage to use for her displays.

It was early afternoon when they sat at the table again. Her parents and sister discussed their plans and when her sister was flying back to school. Clara barely listened. She was still angry and disappointed about the way their Christmas was turning out. If they noticed, no one said anything.

Finally, everyone went back to work. By evening, they had packed most of the house. The donate boxes filled one room. They had labeled all the furniture with price stickers. And all the other "for sale" items were stacked in another room.

After an exhausting day, they said goodnight and Clara hugged her sister.

"I hope you have a pleasant flight tomorrow. Keep in touch and let me know your plans," Clara said.

Clara walked to her car, lonely and tired, and couldn't wait to get home to her little slice of Christmas after dropping the carload of decorations off in storage.

Pushing open her front door, she balanced her box of toys on her hip. She unpacked the box and set the old toys around the base of the Christmas tree. Pleased with this new arrangement, she checked on Mistletoe and went straight to bed.

She couldn't sleep, so she put on a Christmas movie in the hope it would relax her and lull her to sleep with images of how Christmas should be. She looked through her collection and settled on *Miracle on 34th Street*.

This had been a favorite since she was a little girl. Beginning with Thanksgiving and the parade, then Santa saving Susan and her mother, and Christmas, for everyone, this movie had it all.

Clara nestled herself in bed, cozy under the covers, and watched the movie. All the while wishing she had a magical Santa who would make everything perfect for her.

Chapter 9

Clara had one more packing party with her parents before they moved into their RV. At their last dinner, there was plenty of uncomfortable silence and lots of small talk. No one wanted to argue on their last night together. She wondered whether they had second thoughts at all. By now everyone accepted she would not join them for Christmas.

They hugged and promised to keep in touch. Her dad gave her an itinerary with the names and contact numbers of the RV and state parks where they planned to stay along Route 66. Glancing at it, she noticed plenty of tourist traps. They planned to stop at the Blue Whale of Catoosa and at Pops in Oklahoma; Leaning Tower of Texas, Tower Station, and the Cadillac Ranch in Texas; the Blue Hole in New Mexico; the Meteor Crater and the Petrified Forest National Park and the Painted Desert in Arizona; and the Calico Ghost Town, Elmer's Bottle Tree Ranch, the Original McDonald's Museum, and the Santa Monica Pier in California. It looked like a fun trip, if it wasn't in December.

She watched them pull away and waved one last time as they turned the corner and drove out of sight. Clara, needing to feel some family connection, sent a message to her sister that her parents were officially homeless now and on their trip. She included their travel plans and asked Kayla to respond so that she knew for sure her sister was getting her messages.

Thankfully, Sophie had an open lunch break, and they agreed to meet close to her office.

"How was it seeing them off?" Sophie asked as the server delivered their food.

"Weird. I could tell they were excited about the trip, but I think it's becoming real to them they don't have a home and this isn't a vacation. I think it's a little scary. They've always been so settled. Plus, you know, Christmas. I couldn't help myself and got them a tiny potted rosemary plant, you know, one shaped like a tree. Just so they have something Christmas tree-like. They can always use it for cooking. And it smells wonderful, especially in a small space."

Sophie rolled her eyes as she took a bite of her salad. "You and Christmas."

Clara was shocked by Sophie's comment. "What do you mean? It is Christmas, and it's nice to have some kind of decoration. It's festive."

"For some people, it's a pain. Water it, keep it from tipping and dumping everywhere when you are driving," Sophie explained.

Clara thought about this for a moment as she swallowed her food. "I didn't think about that. I can't stand the thought of no tree or decorations or presents at Christmas. I was trying to be nice."

"I know you were, Christmas Girl," Sophie said. "This must be very hard for you. Let's make some plans together to help fill in the rest of your month."

Clara agreed and as they finished their meal, Sophie caught Clara up on the cases she was working. There always seemed to be an abundance of them, and they were interesting.

Later that afternoon, Clay called to ask whether she would meet him at the Christmas tree lot at the mall. He wanted her to help him find the perfect tree and then decorate it. She agreed, and they scheduled a time to meet.

Clara ducked into Cool Beans to once again use her free coffee for a year card. She ordered two Americanos to go. Even the seasonal baristas knew her name and commented about her displays in the mall. They especially like Santa's Workshop. Taking her coffee, she thanked them and, wishing them a Merry Christmas, left to meet Clay.

He was right where they agreed to meet. Clay was like that. If he made plans, he carried them through. He was reliable, easygoing, and a loyal friend. That was what she liked about him. It was comfortable to spend time with him because there were no surprises.

He smiled as he accepted his coffee. "I hoped you might put that card to good use and bring coffee."

"How did you know I had a free coffee card?" Clara didn't remember telling him.

"I ran into Sophie here before work one morning and she told me."

"Well, this must be why you chose this lot when there must be one in every big parking lot in the city," Clara said.

They walked into the huge white tent to see the trees. The pine smell was powerful and invigorating. Clara inhaled deeply, filling her lungs with the smell of Christmas.

They developed a system. Clay found a potential tree and held it up while Clara inspected it. First, she took a needle and snapped it, checking for freshness. Then she had Clay tap the tree on the ground to see whether needles fell. No one wanted a floor full of pine needles in a week. If it passed those initial tests, she would walk around it, looking for symmetry and any gaps in the boughs.

An hour later, she still hadn't found the perfect tree.

"Does it usually take this long to find a Christmas tree?"

"No, but it takes this long to find the perfect tree," Clara answered.

"I don't mean to offend you, I know Christmas is your thing, but this place is closing in another forty-five minutes and I think we need to move the process along. I am getting hungry. Aren't you?"

She sighed. *Clay's right,* she thought. *It doesn't have to be perfect; it just has to be good enough.* Unlike her tree, it would probably stand in a corner and he wouldn't decorate it all the way around anyway.

Taking one last look around the lot, they found one. It was taller than Clay, and fresh, with minimal needle drop, and was mostly symmetrical. There was only one gap and before she could say anything about that, Clay quickly interjected, "I'll just put that side in the corner so I don't have to put any ornaments on it."

He paid for it, and in a few minutes the man wrapped and strapped it to his car. As they were getting ready to leave, she asked him about ornaments.

Clay smiled sheepishly, explaining that he had red and green plastic ball ornaments.

"That sounds nice," she said, "but would you consider adding some different ornaments to your tree this year?"

"Sure. What do you have in mind?"

"Well, a couple of options, really. We could go to just about any store in town and buy something, or I have all of my parents' old ornaments in storage. I packed each theme in different boxes. You can help yourself to any of them."

Clay agreed to follow her to the storage unit and shop her stash.

"Wow," he said when she rolled up the door. It was Christmas, everywhere, top to bottom, side to side, and front to back. Everything was neatly in its place, but there was so much of it.

Clara watched him take it all in and laughed. "Remember, this is what I do for work. It would be like if you had a storage unit filled with bankers' boxes full of profit-and-loss ledgers."

Clay nodded his head in agreement.

"Well, go in and start shopping!" Clara directed.

Clay explored his options. There were boxes labeled Snowman, Santa, Gingerbread, Christmas Movie Decor, Christmas Around the World, Farmhouse Christmas, Trains,

Snow Globes, Nativity, Mistletoe and Holly, Fancy, Presents and Stockings, and Simple Glass Multicolor.

Clara watched Clay as he took it all in and paused at each section of the unit. She could tell he was trying to imagine where he would put his tree and how this theme might work in his home.

She had never watched someone else consider this process, and it was fascinating. Her family usually complained and then just went with whatever theme she wanted to use that year. In fact, as she looked at the boxes and labels, it occurred to her that even though these were her parents' ornaments, she had purchased most of them.

Clay finally turned to her. "I think I'll take the bin marked 'Trains.' Is that okay?"

"Sure. How about we also take the 'Simple Glass Multicolor' box to fill in any gaps?" she offered.

He agreed, and she grabbed several strings of lights. Clara also picked up a bit of greenery and ribbon to make a tree topper.

Clara and Clay loaded the boxes into her car and headed toward Clay's house.

After untying the tree and unloading the boxes, Clara realized she didn't confirm he had a base for the tree, so she asked.

"Of course I have a base. This isn't my first Christmas tree. It's my first perfect Christmas tree."

They laughed as he retrieved it from a shelf in the garage. She noticed his garage was perfectly organized, with everything in its proper place.

They took a moment to survey the living room, imagining the tree in different places.

"In the corner next to the fireplace," they both said at the same time.

"Why there?" Clara asked.

"There is an outlet for the lights next to the hearth, and I can see it while I cook in the kitchen or watch television on the sofa," Clay explained. "Why do you think it belongs there?"

"Because it'll be the first thing to welcome you when you walk in the door. Also, anyone passing by will see a Christmas display and not just an obnoxious tree."

"You certainly have an eye for details," he said.

She offered her Christmas playlist, and they began moving furniture, making room for the tree.

By now they were starving and took a quick break to order takeout. While they waited, Clay strung the lights on the tree. Clara supervised, making sure there was an appropriate amount of space between each strand. She was working at the kitchen table, making a tree topper out of ribbon and holly, mistletoe, and lamb's ear. She chose a red and black plaid ribbon with gold running through it to match the color scheme of the trains.

The food arrived, and they sat on the floor, surrounded by boxes, while they ate.

After a few minutes of silent chewing, Clay asked, "What's your favorite Christmas movie?"

She thought for a minute. "*A Christmas Story*. It has everything. The disappointment and challenges of regular life made better by the magic of Christmas and the one present only Santa can bring. Definitely, *A Christmas Story*. What about you?"

"*Christmas Vacation*. The chaos of it all reminds me of the Christmases I had as a child. You know, all the family coming in from out of town who we only saw once a year, the crazy things that would go wrong, and right, and my dad trying so hard for everyone to have the perfect Christmas."

"What's your favorite Christmas food?" Clara stuffed the crust from her pizza into her mouth.

"This might be gross, but I love cranberry sauce. Specifically, the one that takes the shape of the can and jiggles on the plate when it slides onto it."

"Not gross at all. Now, if you said the whole berry kind, that would be bad. That stuff is disgusting." Clara shuddered.

They worked together for a few more hours, placing ornaments perfectly. Clara resisted the urge to ask Clay to put ornaments on all around the tree. After putting the tree topper on and cleaning up the boxes, Clay turned off the overhead light and they stood back, taking it all in.

It was perfect! The lights were just right; the ornaments were properly balanced, and the topper brought the entire design together. They smiled, watching the train chug its way around the base of the tree.

It looked like something out of a Christmas movie. Clara was pleased with their efforts. She could tell that Clay liked it, even if he really didn't care whether he had a tree.

By now it was close to midnight, and she still needed to put the boxes back in the storage unit before going home. She didn't enjoy having things left out or undone before she went to sleep. Clay was adamant that she wasn't going to the storage unit that late at night by herself. He assured her there was plenty of room in his garage for them. Besides, the bins would need to be repacked when it was time to take the tree down. Reluctantly, she agreed. She didn't want her boxes to take up space in his orderly and organized garage, but when they went to stack the boxes, she saw that there was a perfect place for them.

Looking at her watch, Clara quickly calculated how much sleep she would get if she was in bed in an hour. "I really need to get going, and you have work tomorrow."

He walked her to the car and thanked her for her help. "I can't wait to send pictures to my parents. My mom can never understand why I don't take the time to put up a tree unless they are coming for a visit."

"I hope she's pleased, but I really hope you enjoy it."

Clay reminded her to let him know she got home safely as he shut her door. It was in his nature to make sure of things like that. She promised she would, and within ten minutes he had a text thanking him for letting her help him decorate his tree. He responded with a thank-you of his own, and she went to sleep, content for the first time since her parents' big announcement.

Tomorrow was a big day for her. It would be the kickoff of the Christmas party season, and she needed to be ready for a night of small talk and Christmas cheer.

Chapter 10

Clara loved Christmas. She didn't enjoy the parties the companies invited her to. But she felt compelled to attend. All her accounts had parties and she was invited to most of them. Clara also worried it might be unprofessional. The night was usually hours of small talk with people she only saw once a year, and they had nothing in common. The food was excellent and sometimes there was entertainment. Over the years, there had been comedians, magicians, concerts, and casino games. Some parties were more fun than others. Occasionally she found being invisible to the other partygoers helped her have an enjoyable evening.

She wondered what this Christmas party season might be like as she showered and dressed for the first party of the month. Clara bought a black dress for the season and planned to change her accessories for each party. The knee-length dress had a deep v in both front and back. It was simple, elegant, and flattering.

Clara stepped into it, pleased with her reflection. Her red hair was in soft waves, framing her face, and she wore minimal makeup. Clara reached in her closet for her most comfortable black heels and black clutch and was ready to go. Giving herself one more glance to check everything was in place, she said goodbye to Mistletoe and drove to the party.

A large law firm hosted tonight's party downtown. They owned the building that housed several other businesses and had a first-floor lobby that was all glass on the side facing the street. Every year, they gave her a theme for the window display. They expected her to carry that theme into other areas of the lobby for continuity. This year the theme was "Naughty or Nice."

Fitting for a law firm, Clara thought when she met with the office manager at the design meeting. There was a fireplace with a glowing fire, and Santa sat in a red velvet, gold-trimmed overstuffed chair with the list in one hand and his trusty red pen in another. To make the list, she found dot matrix printing paper and carefully removed the perforated edges. She had several boxes of the paper with different lengths pulled out for effect. She put the names of the law firm partners on the list, which they all thought was hilarious. The animated Santa moved and looked like he was really moving down the list.

Next to the chair was a table with a large cup of hot chocolate. Behind him was a Christmas tree decorated with red and green glass ornaments and small wooden toys. In the center of the lobby, between the reception desk and the escalator, was a massive tree. Fifteen feet high, it required her assistants to use a scaffold to place the ornaments around the tree all the way to the top. It was impressive and took an eight-hour day to assemble and decorate.

Clara handed her keys to the valet and put the ticket in her purse. Entering the building, she noticed the reactions of the spouses and dates of the employees as they entered the decorated lobby. There were plenty of oohs and aahs. It felt good knowing she helped them feel the magic of Christmas.

Things looked beautiful at night. She had only seen the lobby during the day and although that was festive and fun, walking through it now, it was elegant and the perfect setting for a party.

It wasn't a formal dinner, but there were several tables with an assortment of foods available throughout the evening. She made herself a small plate, collected her drink, and walked to a table to sit, for the allotted time. At some point, she would gracefully find a partner, thank them for a lovely evening, and make the drive home to her cozy condo and watch a Christmas movie as she drifted off to sleep.

She watched the other partygoers. This was her favorite game. She tried to see what they were talking about. If she couldn't make it out clearly, she created dialog in her head. She also tried to identify married couples, those on an awkward first date, and who were like her, just wishing this night would be over soon.

Someone announced from the entrance that Santa had arrived. A moment later, the lobby doors opened and there he was!

Dressed from head to toe in red and white, with the iconic black belt and enormous gold buckle, he walked through the crowd. Waving with one hand and holding an enormous red bag with the other, he made his way through the crowd. He walked to the tree, where there was now a red overstuffed chair, like the one in the scene in the window, took a bow, and sat down. Now there were gifts under the tree that hadn't been there before. Clara wondered who arranged this because the firm hadn't asked her to secure a Santa or wrap gifts.

The Santa was familiar, but she couldn't place him. He looked real, but all Santas look real. Otherwise, the illusion wouldn't work. Throughout the evening, Santa would call out a partygoer's name and announce whether they were on the naughty or nice list. The guests were, of course, on the nice list, but some employees found themselves on the naughty list.

Prior to the party, they nominated each other for one list or the other, with evidence why they should be in that column. It reminded her of high school superlatives. Jim: naughty list for always leaving your paper in the copier. Erica: nice list for calling in the office coffee order. Kate: naughty list for taking too much time in the conference room creating and organizing files. Rob: nice list for always being ten minutes early for every meeting. It went on. It was all in good fun and no one seemed to take any personal shots.

But these were all inside jokes. It was tedious for those who didn't work there. As Santa called the names, he would give the person a gift depending on which list they found themselves. The gifts ranged from cash and gift cards, to memberships and trips. *It must be nice to work for such a successful law firm*, she thought.

During a lull in the festivities, Clara felt someone watching her. She looked up to see Santa wink at her. Surprised, she looked around, confirming he was making eye contact with her.

She didn't see anyone else looking in his direction. When she looked back at him, he gave her a slight wave and a smile. She waved and smiled back and decided on that note that it was time to call it a night. The drinks were flowing and probably no one would notice her exit. On the way to the valet, she found a partner, thanked her for the invitation and lovely evening. Wishing her a Merry Christmas, she retrieved her car and went home.

A week later, it was time to repeat the process. The second party on her calendar was for a large bank. Out came the black dress, fresh from the cleaners. On went the black stockings and heels. This time she put her hair up. Again, makeup was just mascara and lipstick. She accessorized with gold jewelry and a gold clutch. She looked in the mirror and was pleased. *Simple but elegant*, she thought as she retrieved her keys from the hook by the door, said goodnight to Mistletoe, and drove into the night.

At the design meeting for the bank, they requested an *It's a Wonderful Life* theme. The economy had taken a hit in recent times and they thought this was a fitting theme since the movie was about a building and loan business. They weren't exactly the same thing, but it worked for the theme. After watching the movie again for ideas, Clara used vintage trees and ornaments. She decorated everything in angels and bells, and angels that were bells, and placed cardboard suitcases around, plastered with stickers of the places George Bailey intended to go. She found a prop that looked like the cab that Ernie drove, and had a sign that read, "Welcome to Bedford Falls." It was simple and looked as if she took scenes from the movie and incorporated them throughout the lobby. She knew it was impressive.

Music from classic Christmas movies played throughout the venue. There was the usual food, bar, and small talk. She overheard many conversations about the movie and what it meant to people over the years. People were shocked when someone in their group admitted they had never seen the movie. Clara thought it was hard to believe considering it played nonstop in the days leading up to Christmas and was always on the top Christmas movies lists.

About an hour into the party, once all the guests had arrived, in walked Santa Claus. Everyone cheered as he passed through the crowd. Clara noticed as he passed her table, he looked directly at her, nodded, and winked in her direction. She was sure this was the same Santa from the last party. She watched him move through the crowd, careful not to whack anyone with the large bag of gifts, and settle into the same throne from the previous party.

Like the previous party, guests came forward when they heard their name and received a gift. It was fun to see adults get so excited about accepting a gift from Santa, even though they knew it was really a gift from the bank. Santa was simply handing them out. Later, someone brought Santa a plate of food and a drink. He settled in as part of the decorations for the rest of the party. Clara wondered how he got this job, the Santa on the expensive party circuit. She was curious about who he was and what he did the rest of the year. He turned and, looking directly at her, smiled and gave a slight wave.

She smiled and waved back and stood to clear her place, find the bank manager, thank him for the invitation and a lovely evening and return home to her cozy Christmas condo and watch yet another Christmas movie, drink hot cocoa, and drift off to sleep.

The third party was several days later. The hotel manager asked her to create a Winter Wonderland in the lobby. The hotel also wanted her to bring some of the design elements into other areas in the hotel such as the café, registration desk, and outside the elevator on each floor.

This had been a fun and messy project for Clara. She brought in flocked trees and commissioned a glass painter to paint frost on the windows for an icy illusion. There were snowmen throughout wearing gloves, scarves, and stocking caps. She decorated with trees with greenery and red birds. There, next to the café, there was a giant snow globe that had displayed a winter scene, with snow swirling around. On the registration desk was a Christmas village of snow-covered homes and other buildings and an ice-skating rink with skaters who glided across the ice.

Clara curated a playlist that had the words snow, winter, wonder, snowman, and tree in them for the hotel to play. She also added coatracks full of winter gear at entryways, just for display. Finally, there were snowmen and smaller flocked trees at each elevator on all floors to carry the theme throughout the hotel. It was simple but spectacular.

Tonight, the hotel was having their Christmas party in one ballroom usually reserved for conferences and receptions.

Getting ready, she fixed her hair—this time half up, half down and curled—swiped on lipstick, and coated her lashes with mascara. She pulled out the black cocktail dress and unwrapped it from the plastic covering and put it on. She finished her look with sheer black stockings, black heels, and silver accessories. Once again, she gave Mistletoe a pat, grabbed her keys from the hook, and off she went.

The hotel was across town and at least a half hour drive from her condo. As she drove, Clara sang along to the Christmas music the local radio station played.

She handed her keys to the valet and put the claim ticket into her purse. It was lonely and boring to go to these parties and not know anyone. As she walked across the lobby toward the ballroom, she wondered whether Santa would be at this party too.

Clara could hear the partygoers before she found the ballroom. This was a more festive group. It comprised a more diverse crowd than the last two parties, and like the mall Christmas party, that always made things a little more interesting.

She walked through the crowd, getting the lay of the land. There were tables of food, an open bar, and tables for seating covered in white linen with red and green decor. The DJ sat in one corner, and there was a small dance floor toward the front of the lobby. She wondered whether anyone would really dance. Next to the DJ, she noticed a gigantic Christmas tree decorated in snowflakes and icicles, with what seemed like thousands of tiny twinkling white lights. In front of the tree, she noticed the red velvet overstuffed chair.

I guess Santa will be here tonight.

Walking through the crowd to the food table, she accepted a small plate of the usual party food. None of it looked very interesting until she noticed the dessert table. It was full of pastries and cookies. Across from the dessert table was a hot cocoa station.

She took her plate and sat down. As usual, she found an empty table away from the crowd. She hoped this would keep the small talk to a minimum. It usually worked. She didn't plan to be there very long.

Nibbling her food, she waited for the crowd to dissipate near the hot cocoa bar. Clara heard a familiar voice and turned her attention in the direction it was coming from. She looked into the crowd and saw Clay. *Finally, this might be fun after all.*

As she wondered what he was doing here, she noticed the woman walking beside him. It hadn't occurred to her that Clay would be here. But he didn't work for the hotel, so he must be her date. She suddenly felt embarrassed that she was excited to see him, thinking they would have fun together, and realized that it would be awkward to spend time with him and his date.

Clara was looking for an escape, a way to leave before he noticed her, when she heard her name called out.

"Clara, hey! I wasn't sure if you'd be here too," Clay said.

She thought he sounded excited, and his reaction confused her because he was obviously on a date with this woman.

Clara looked up from her seat. "Well, you know I go to all the parties this time of year."

He smiled and explained to the woman next to him, "Clara designs Christmas window displays. Probably all the ones you see around town, the memorable ones, those are most likely her designs."

"Oh, that must be so much fun!" the woman exclaimed, her voice a little too high pitched and annoying, like a cartoon character. "But, what do you do the rest of the year if you only work in November and December?" she asked, looking confused.

Really, she thought, *what can he possibly see in this woman? Does she really think that I only work two months a year?*

She calmly answered, "I actually work all year. Christmas is a pretty big deal, so most companies plan in January or February. I meet with them and we talk about their vision. Then I begin the design process and collect the things I need for the job, and hire helpers to put everything together. Then there is all the paperwork to do, contracts to write, and accounts and billing to maintain. Clay helps me with all of that, so at tax time things are ready to go."

Clay smiled when she mentioned his name. Clara thought she noticed the woman stiffen a bit at his reaction.

He asked whether they could sit with her, and before she could answer, they set their plates and drinks down as he pulled the seat out for his date. He was always polite like that. Once they sat down, Clara introduced herself to this person.

She reached out her hand. "Since Clay didn't properly introduce us, I'm Clara. I designed all of this."

The woman responded, "I am Alexis. It is nice to meet you. Clay talks about you a lot. By the way, his Christmas tree is stunning. He said you helped with that."

Clara was pleased to hear that he talked about her. She never considered that possibility. It irritated Clara to know Alexis had been in his living room. *How long has he known this woman?* She realized in the over ten years they had known each other, she had only been to his house a handful of times.

Clay, oblivious to how awkward this situation was quickly becoming for the two women, announced he was going to the hot cocoa bar and asked whether anyone needed or wanted anything.

Alexis said no and excused herself to use the restroom.

Clara took this opportunity to follow Clay to the hot cocoa bar.

"I wasn't expecting you to be here. Since when do you work at this hotel?" Clara asked.

"Our firm is trying to get this account, and they appointed me to make a meeting happen between the partners and management. Alexis is their executive account manager. After our meeting, she invited me to the party. I think it is a trial run to see how I get along with the other managerial staff. Anyway, I thought you might be here and it would be fun."

Clara smiled when she heard this.

"As I was getting ready to leave, I had a flat tire. There wasn't time to change my clothes, and my tire, and then get ready again. I knew that if you were going, you were most likely already here because you get everywhere early. I was about to call a cab when my phone rang. It was Alexis asking if I was planning to come so she could add my name to the list at the door. I explained the situation, and she said that she could come by and give me a ride since I was on the way. She was at my house a few minutes later. I didn't even have time to go back inside before she was in my driveway."

So that explained how she knew what the tree looked like. Clara remembered the reason she wanted to put the tree in that corner was so people could see it from the street.

"By the way, as she pulled out of my driveway, she commented on how the tree and fireplace looked so beautiful in my window, 'almost like a Christmas window display,' she said. I kid you not, she said it just like that," Clay said, mimicking her high-pitched squeal.

They laughed, checking to make sure no one heard them. The line at the hot cocoa bar was thinning, and when it was finally their turn, they couldn't believe all of their options. There was dark chocolate, milk chocolate, salted caramel chocolate, peppermint chocolate, white chocolate, coconut hot chocolate, and spicy chocolate. They made their selection and moved to the add-ins. There they found marshmallows of all sizes and flavors, whipped cream, cinnamon sticks, candy canes, chocolate shavings, toasted coconut, shots of Bailey's liqueur, mini chocolate chips, and crushed peppermint. After choosing their add-ins, they were each handed a mug and made their way back to the table.

Alexis rejoined them and noticed they both went to the hot cocoa bar in her absence. It looked like she wasn't happy about it.

"Clara, you won't mind if I take Clay around to introduce him, do you? I am sure you know how important it is to make business connections at these kinds of events."

Even Alexis's voice was irritating. Clara couldn't stand when women behaved like that, especially to each other.

"Of course. This is a business event for me as well," Clara answered.

Alexis led Clay away. Clara had the urge to message Sophie to tell her what happened. But as she pointed out, this was a business function and it would be rude and unprofessional to be seen on her phone, so she resisted.

She began people watching, but Clay and Alexis constantly drew her gaze. He seemed completely unaware Alexis was flirting with him. It was embarrassing to watch but Clara couldn't seem to look away.

They finally returned to the table and as Clara turned to talk to Clay, Santa arrived.

The doors opened with a great flourish and the DJ played a rendition of "Here Comes Santa Claus" as he walked through the crowd with his giant red bag and made his way to the red chair.

Once settled and the music faded, Santa surveyed the crowd. He held up a white gloved hand to shield his eyes from the bright spotlight and made eye contact with Clara. He winked and waved. She looked around and noticed that no one was waving back, so she sheepishly made eye contact with him again and nodded and gave a slight wave, wondering why Santa sought her out at all three parties.

Clara was just about to excuse herself. She already knew the way the rest of this was going to go.

Clay leaned over. "That Santa looks like the real thing! I wonder where they found him."

Clara was surprised that Clay didn't mention Santa waving at someone. *Maybe he didn't notice.* Then she wondered whether anyone saw him look at her and wave. Come to think of it, no one noticed at any of the parties.

She was considering this when, out of the corner of her eye, she noticed Alexis say something to Clay, and he nodded. The next thing Clara knew, they were both headed to the dance floor to join the other revelers dance to what the DJ was playing.

The line at the bar had dwindled, but the line at the hot cocoa bar had grown. More people moved to the dance floor. The crowd had left the tables littered with plates, cups, and belongings. People were in large and small groups, talking and laughing. She suddenly felt more out of place than usual and gathered her things to leave.

She could feel someone watching her and looked up. Alexis was leaning in to talk to Clay, and he looked over at Clara. He noticed that Clara was gathering her things to leave, so he turned and walked toward her, with Alexis trailing behind.

"Leaving already?" he asked.

"Yeah, I have an early morning tomorrow and it's getting late." She continued to clear her place at the table and reached in her purse to find her claim ticket for the valet.

"I'll call it a night too. Would you give me a ride home?" Clay asked.

Before Clara could answer, Alexis interjected, "Clay, the party's really just getting started. Santa hasn't even given out the presents yet. I can drive you home later. That way you can meet more of the management team."

Clay turned to Clara as if he were waiting for her to say something and when she hesitated, he answered, "Okay, if it isn't too much trouble."

Alexis smiled and looked at Clara. "It is no trouble at all."

Clara told them both goodnight. As Clay followed Alexis toward a group of people at one table, he turned to look at Clara. She thought he looked a little confused and gave him a reassuring smile. He smiled back and then turned his attention to the group of people Alexis was dragging him toward.

As Clara passed through the crowd, she stopped by the table with the executives and thanked them for the invitation and the lovely evening. They gushed over her designs in the lobby and asked her to call them after the first of the year to secure another contract for next Christmas. She agreed, wished them all a Merry Christmas, and as she headed out, she turned once more and saw Santa watching her. She smiled, and he smiled back. Then she collected her car and drove home for her after-party ritual of hot chocolate, warm covers, and a Christmas movie.

Chapter 11

C lara woke up irritated. She tossed and turned all night, and her dreams were all over the place. Sitting up, she noticed her neck was sore and her back tight.

When she excused herself from the party, she said she had an early morning. That wasn't true. She had nothing to do today except a few errands and some Christmas shopping.

Drinking her first cup of coffee, Clara checked her messages and read from a stack of mail. There were postcards from her parents in the pile.

"Looks like they are having fun," she muttered.

Her mother wrote about the Christmas lights and displays in a little town they passed through. "You would love it! It seemed deserted, but the town square was full of decorated trees and there were lit decorations and displays throughout the park."

Clara felt a pang of sadness. She missed her parents. Clara didn't want to spend Christmas alone, but she didn't want to go to a hotel either.

Clara put a few Christmas cards from professional contacts and old acquaintances on her mantel after tossing the envelopes.

She stretched and made a second cup of coffee, while checking her messages. Kayla called from Italy, telling her what a wonderful time she was having and described all the Christmas festivities there. Clara made a face and mimicked her sister's voice, going on and on about how wonderful things were.

Her parents left a message to let her know the itinerary changed. They had had a few delays and weren't as far in their trip as they planned. They were having fun and hoped she was enjoying all the

Christmas parties and they hoped to hear from her soon and would check back in in the next few days.

The last message was from Clay. He was checking to make sure that she made it home safely because she didn't let him know.

He is so considerate. Irritation washed over her again and she couldn't understand why. Her feelings were all over the place.

She sent a quick message to thank him for checking up on her, letting him know she arrived home safe, and asked him about the rest of the party.

The phone rang in her hand. She looked at the number; it was Sophie.

"Hello."

"Hello, yourself! What are you doing today?" Sophie asked.

"Today I was planning to run some errands and finish a bit of shopping. Why?"

"I have the rare day off. Want some company so we can catch up?"

"Yes! What time will you be ready?" Clara asked.

She was excited to spend the day with her best friend. Maybe this would give her some perspective about what she was feeling about Clay, her family, and Christmas.

"I just woke up. Pick me up in an hour?"

"Sounds great. See you then," Clara answered and headed to the shower to get ready for her day.

An hour later, Sophie was getting in the front seat of Clara's car. "Mmm, it smells so good in here!"

"It's a cinnamon coffee cake air freshener. I thought it was appropriate for the season," Clara answered.

"Excellent choice, but we may have to hit a bakery. It's making me hungry."

They planned their day. First stop was Cool Beans. Next, the mall. Then the dry cleaner because Clara needed her dress again in a couple of days. After lunch, they would catch a movie if they still had any energy.

Cool Beans was busy, but the line moved fast. Most customers ordered their coffee to go. Clara and Sophie liked to guess what people ordered. A mom wearing jeans and sneakers with young children would often order a vanilla or pumpkin spice latte, unless they dressed in yoga pants or other workout gear. Then it would most likely be a chai latte. Black coffee for older men, but a junior business executive in a suit would have an Americano. The college students were unpredictable. Engrossed in the laptop on the table, they wouldn't notice what they were drinking. Some ordered a pour over or regular brew coffee, others tea. Really, who comes to a coffee shop and orders tea? The two always snickered when they saw that.

They ordered their usual and visited with their favorite barista. Picking up their coffee, they thanked him and wished him a Merry Christmas. They each dropped a few dollars in the tip jar as they made their way to their favorite table.

"Tell me about the parties this year," Sophie demanded as they sat down.

"The usual. Lots of food, music, beautiful decorations, and strangers who don't know me or why I am there." Clara debated telling Sophie about the Santa. "Clay was at the party last night." Clara then paused and took a long sip.

"Really?"

"He was with a woman who works for the hotel. She is an executive of some sort."

"Where you surprised to see him there, in your domain?" Sophie asked.

"Well, yeah, kind of. I mean, I see him every year at his firm's Christmas party, so it isn't like I never see him at a party. It was weird that he walked in with a date. At least, I thought it was a date at first, and I think she thought it was a date, or maybe she was trying to make it a date, I don't know," Clara explained.

"Why do you think it wasn't a date?" Sophie asked.

"The woman's name is Alexis, and she definitely stayed pretty close to him most of the time I was there. She kept wanting to introduce him to other people who work for the hotel, so she kept whisking him away every time he and I would talk. It was irritating," Clara said.

"How did he meet her?"

"His accounting firm is trying to get their business. He was the partner assigned to meet with them to assess what they need and develop a plan. They met at that meeting and she invited him. He said as he was leaving for the party, he had a flat tire. Before he could call a cab, she called to confirm he was coming. He told her he would, but he would be late, because of the tire. She offered to pick him up. Evidently, she was already on her way to the party and was pretty close to his house."

"He knew you would be at the party. Why didn't he call and see if you could give him a ride?"

"He said he knew I was probably already at the party and he didn't want me to have to leave, drive back across town, and then go back."

Clara continued, "It was weird. I have known him for a very long time, and I know he dates. I just never thought I'd see him on a date. And, she seemed to think it was a date, or at least she wanted it to be a date. Maybe the first of many dates."

"Sounds like someone is a little jealous," Sophie teased.

"I'm not jealous. He made it a point to tell me about the situation. I would have given him a ride home when I was leaving, but she insisted he stay and make more professional contacts. He left me a message asking if I arrived home safely since I didn't call him to let him know," Clara said.

"Sounds like it was less of a date and more of a coincidence," Sophie offered. "Besides, that guy is really into you. And I think you might feel the same way. Don't wait too long. It sounds like there may be other women who are more than happy to claim him."

Clara tired of talking about this. It made her uncomfortable, and she didn't want to sort out her feelings right then. She needed time to think. She hoped Alexis wasn't really going to be in the picture. It would mess up everything. She was counting on Sophie and Clay to make up for her parents and sister not taking part in Christmas this year. If Clay started dating this woman, it would ruin her plans. Clara would be a third wheel, and she wasn't excited about that thought.

They set their mugs on the bar and, gathering their purses, made their way into the mall.

The mall was its finest at Christmas. Even the chain stores with tacky cardboard cut-out decorations made the place festive. There was a distinct energy in the mall at Christmas, and Clara loved it.

Merging into the crowd, they walked toward the bookstore. Clara needed gifts for her parents and sister. She wanted an atlas for her parents, and leatherbound journals and pens for all three to document their travels.

In the bookstore, she carefully chose the journals. She decided on the lined version for her parents and the grid pattern for her sister. She thought her sister might want to make hers into more of a scrapbook, and the grid paper would make that option easier. Of course, one never knew what Kayla would do, so she could also just write in the journal as it was. After scribbling with all the samples on the provided paper, Clara chose three pens that would be perfect for the journals. She wasn't sure how to send the gifts, especially as it was getting closer to Christmas. She would need to work out the shipping details later that day to get them in the mail tomorrow. It would probably be more to ship the gifts than purchase them, but Clara was happy she found something that was practical and personal.

The first errand complete, they walked back into the mall. A cloud of perfume enveloped them as they entered a large department store. The middle-aged woman hired for the holiday handed them each a sample, and sneezing and coughing, they thanked her and continued on their way.

Clara needed a gift for Sam and Maria. She wasn't sure whether their boys would be home for Christmas, and she wanted to make sure they had something to open.

"What are you looking for?" Sophie asked.

"I'm not sure. They have everything they need."

They walked through the clothing sections, circled the purse and accessories, and finding nothing suitable, rode up the escalator to the home section. Wandering through the displays, she saw something that might be perfect. On one of the most recent visits to their home, she saw a stack of records. The vinyls dated back to their teen years. Clara had asked whether they still listened to them, and Maria explained they had long ago given away the record player when listening to vinyl fell out of fashion. She couldn't part with all the records because they held too many precious memories.

In the housewares section, Clara saw a display of record players. They were a newer design, and they had updated technology, but she was sure this was the perfect gift. She paid for the player and took it to customer service to be wrapped. She didn't want Sam to see it if they ran into him that day.

Retrieving the wrapped and labeled record player, Clara asked Sophie if they could take the packages she had to the car before continuing their shopping. Sophie helped her manage the bags and bulky record player box, and they loaded everything into Clara's trunk.

Re-entering the mall, they took a left toward the center. Clara had one more gift to buy. She needed something for Clay. She already had her gift for Sophie wrapped and under her tree, waiting for Christmas. Sophie had loved *To Kill A Mockingbird* since high school. That book played a large role in why she became a lawyer. She loved the opportunity to step in and help someone in a desperate situation. Sophie made a little money, but she didn't need it. She had received a large inheritance as a teenager. Her parents put the money in a trust for her education. She reinvested the rest and had a sizeable amount to supplement her meager wages as a court-appointed attorney.

Clara was so excited when she came across a signed edition at a local bookstore. It was an extravagant gift, but she knew it would be something that Sophie would cherish forever.

"So, who do we have left?" Sophie asked.

"Clay," Clara said.

"You still haven't bought his gift? I can't believe it is two weeks before Christmas and you are still shopping and wrapping gifts." Sophie looked at her friend with concern.

"Well, things this year have been a little different. September, October, and November were especially busy this year. The new designs took extra time, and then you know what happened at Thanksgiving. I don't know. I just haven't been feeling it this Christmas."

"Are you sick? Should I get you to a hospital?" Sophie teased.

"No, just a little burnout. Things aren't like usual this year, and it's making it difficult to get into the spirit this year," Clara answered.

Clara looked past Sophie and saw him. Looking at the large Santa's Workshop display, full of children and their families, she noticed the mall Santa for the first time. He was helping a child off his lap when their eyes met, and he smiled and winked at her. She just stood there and gave him a slight wave to make sure he was looking at her. Before the next child climbed in his lap, he gave a quick wave and then directed his attention to the squirmy little one eager to tell Santa all of his Christmas wishes.

Sophie looked at Clara and asked what she was looking at.

"It is him!" Clara said, excitedly.

"Yeah, it's Santa. Do you want to get in line and take a picture with him? That won't look weird at all. A grown woman sitting on Santa's lap, making a list of demands," Sophie said. "Seems a little extreme, even for you."

"No, I don't want a picture with him. I think he must know me," Clara explained.

"Yeah, I'm sure he does." Sophie rolled her eyes. "He sees you when you are sleeping, he knows when you're awake, he sees you when you're bad or—"

Clara interrupted, "I know the song and I know what you are thinking. I am not crazy. I've seen him at every Christmas party this year."

"Yeah, well, he looks like the real thing. I am sure he makes appearances at parties. He can't be making much as a mall Santa, and he only works like two months a year. Makes sense he would supplement his income by working the party circuit."

"He must know me from here," Clara said, disappointed.

Sophie, still a bit confused, asked, "Why do you think he knows you?"

Clara told Sophie everything as they walked through the mall. She explained that at every party she had been to, Santa made an appearance with his big red bag full of presents. Then Clara told her the best part. At each party, he singled her out with a smile, wink, and even a wave. And he didn't do that to anyone else. She was pretty sure that no one else noticed the attention he paid to her.

"I thought maybe he was magical, but he must know me from the mall. We must have been here at the same time. I spent a lot of time here in November getting things set up. That must be it."

Clara's face fell. It was fun to imagine Santa, the real Santa, noticed her. Knowing he was just a mall Santa shattered the illusion. She wondered whether he would be at the next party and if so, what would happen. In the meantime, she had a mission. She needed to find the perfect gift for Clay.

They continued on, talking about different people they saw, Sophie's work and Christmas plans, and just enjoyed being with each other in this cheerful place.

"What did you plan on getting for Clay?" Sophie asked.

"I am not sure. It has to be something that he will like. I hate giving gifts just because."

"What do you give an accountant who can buy whatever he wants?" Sophie asked. "I know—maybe you can give him a tire patch kit or a AAA membership. It would keep him from ending up on dates that may or may not be actual dates in the future." She laughed.

"Are you serious? I can't give him that. Besides, I'm sure he called someone first thing this morning to get the tire fixed. He doesn't wait on things like that. It messes up his orderly life. That guy is an accountant to the bones."

"What guy?"

Clara heard a voice she recognized right behind them and turned around to face Clay.

"What guy are you talking about, Clara?" Clay smiled.

"Oh, um..." Clara hesitated before Sophie jumped in.

"As if it is any of your business, she was just telling me about this really successful man she met at a party last night."

"Was she now? It sounded like the two of you are planning to get me a membership to AAA so I would never be on a pretend date again, or something like that. I couldn't quite make out exact details of your conversation over the children whining in the line to see Santa and the Christmas music blaring. By the way, I already have a membership to AAA, which is why I am here. But I really appreciate the thought," Clay said.

Clara thought she might die of embarrassment right there in the middle of the mall. "Well, I am glad to hear that you got that tire taken care of and that you are here. What a surprise."

She regained her composure and would not give him the satisfaction of seeing her uncomfortable, knowing he had been listening to their conversation.

Sophie tried desperately to save her friend and offered, "We were just going to get some lunch. Would you like to join us? How much longer do you have to wait on your tires?"

Clara glanced at Sophie, and Sophie nodded.

"Yeah, come with us. We are going to eat and then maybe watch a movie. It'll be fun," Clara agreed.

"I don't know. A few minutes ago, it sounded like you still had some very important Christmas shopping to do. Do you think you really have time for a leisurely lunch and movie? That gift will not buy and wrap itself, you know," Clay teased and then fell into step with them.

They walked to the food court with Clara in the middle of Sophie and Clay. The conversation turned from shopping to lunch. Specifically, which establishment had the best options.

The three decided they would each get what they wanted and find one another at the table to eat. Sophie went to get in the line at the pizza place. Clara hesitated, trying to decide between Chinese and a sub sandwich, and Clay walked off to find a hamburger.

Clara settled on Chinese, and she thought about Clay while she was standing in line. She wondered what he really thought about her and overhearing her talk about him. He didn't seem irritated. In fact, it kind of seemed like he was happy. Probably to have something to tease her about. Ever since she went to his family's Fourth of July weekend at the lake last summer, there was a shift in their relationship.

Her order was up and, taking it to the table, she decided she wouldn't spend any more time overthinking. This was a rare treat to spend time with her friends. Walking through the maze of tables, she noticed Clay was already at a table. Clay moved and pulled out the chair next to him for Clara.

"Why haven't you touched your burger?" she asked.

"Because I was waiting until you got here. I didn't want to be rude." He picked up his loaded hamburger and took a large bite. Swallowing, he said, "Now I can finally eat. Took you long enough."

They were laughing when Sophie arrived with a single piece of pizza that draped over the sides of her plate.

"What's so funny?" she asked.

"Nothing," they answered in unison.

Sophie pulled out her chair, sat down, and rolled her eyes.

They visited about what their Christmas plans were. Sophie was going to visit her grandparents again for Christmas Eve and Christmas Day. Clay wasn't sure whether his plans were to go to his parents' cabin again or whether he wanted to have his family come celebrate at his house.

"Besides, it would be a shame to waste the perfect tree." He looked at Clara.

She laughed. "It is a beautiful tree."

Clay noticed her reaction and explained, "Clara helped me pick out the perfect tree, then let me shop her Christmas decoration stash, and directed me as I decorated it. It looks like something she would put in one of her window displays. My favorite part of the day is coming home to my beautiful tree."

"Wait, you helped Clay get and decorate a tree? Why haven't you ever helped me? I want a perfect tree too!"

"You never asked," said Clara, matter-of-fact.

"I think it is too late this year, but put me down for next year for sure. My family is coming to my house next year for Christmas, and I want it to be beautiful," Sophie said.

The conversation continued. It was mostly Clay and Clara, with Sophie occasionally adding something.

Looking at her watch, Clara told Clay that they were going to watch a movie that afternoon. "If your car isn't ready, would you like to go with us?"

"It depends. What movie are you going to see?" he asked.

Clara glanced at the movie theater marquee. "It looks like today they are showing *A Christmas Story*," she said excitedly.

Clay said, "It's a date!"

Sophie glanced down at her phone and furrowed her brow reading an important message. "I am sorry, guys. I have to go. Something came up at the office," she lied.

Clara looked confused. "I thought you took the day off."

"I am very sorry. We can catch a movie this weekend, maybe. Go on, have fun. Call me tonight." She smiled at Clara.

"Wait, how will you get home?" Clara asked. "I drove."

"Oh, shoot. I didn't think about that. I guess I will call a cab," Sophie said, typing the name of the cab company in her phone for the number.

"Wait. Clara, why don't you let her take your car? I can drive you to get it after the movie."

Clara thought about this for a minute, while Sophie could barely contain her grin, and agreed.

"Sophie, will you still be at the office, or should we drive to your house in a couple of hours?" Clay asked.

"I should be home. If I'm still tied up at the office, I'll let you know."

Sophie gathered her trash and took it to a nearby bin. She returned to gather her purse and the few purchases she made. Clara handed over her keys and reminded her to drive carefully. The holiday traffic would be heavy this time of day. Sophie thanked her for letting her borrow her car and as she walked away, looked back and said, "Have fun and enjoy the movie. I'll see you later."

They had some time before the movie started, so they cleaned the table and walked around the mall. She asked Clay about the party the night before and how it went after she went home for the night.

"It was okay. I don't know how you go to so many parties during the season. It is exhausting. Get all dressed up, then have the same small talk a hundred times."

"I love the idea of going to a Christmas party. It always seems like it will be fun to get dressed up and see the decorations and watch the crowd as they celebrate the season. I am always a little disappointed in the end for the same reason. But it allows me to people watch," Clara said.

"What do you mean?" Clay asked.

"Come sit down," Clara instructed and pulled him over to one of the open benches in the middle of the concourse.

"Now pretend we are tired and just resting for a minute while we wait for someone. Casually look around and find someone interesting to watch. Then try to figure out what they are doing, or just make it up as you go."

"Okay," answered Clay. "What about that family there?"

They saw a family of four approaching them. There was a man, woman, and two small children. One child was crying and on the verge of an all-out tantrum. The family stopped, and the parents tried to console the little boy, explaining that they were on their way to see Santa.

As Clara watched, she said, "They had a terrible morning. The mom wants everything perfect, and the dad really doesn't see the point. He doesn't want to argue, so he took a day off work to get the kids' picture with Santa. See the matching clothes? I bet she's a pumpkin spice latte mom. Now she is promising him a toy if he'll settle down and behave. The sister is rolling her eyes because no one is promising her a toy and she is already behaving." As she finished talking, the little boy across the way rubbed his eyes, took his dad's hand, and the family began walking toward Santa.

"That was good," Clay said, "Let me try."

He looked around, trying to find someone to watch. Finally, he settled on a group of college students walking down the mall with cookies and coffee cups in their hands and packages hanging from the crook of their arms. They were a mixed group with both guys and girls, but two stood out.

"You see that group there, the college kids coming from the cookie place? They're finally on break, took their last finals today. I bet they're not all the same major, but they are all glad to have a little freedom and less responsibility for a few days. See how the guy in the red sweater keeps glancing over at the girl on the left, the one who is absolutely not paying him any attention? He is desperate to ask her out, but time is running short. She will leave for Christmas and he's afraid he's losing his chance. He even has a present but can't figure out when or if he should give it to her. What if she likes someone else? What if she doesn't like him at all?"

Just then, as the poor guy glanced again at the girl, he tripped, drawing attention to himself from the rest of the group. He played it off and somehow didn't fall.

"This is painful. He's so distracted by this girl, who doesn't even notice him, that he tripped over his own feet!"

They tried not to giggle. As they passed, Clay made eye contact with the young man and smiled and gave him a thumbs-up. The college student just looked at him, confused, and said, "I'm sorry, do I know you?"

Clara couldn't contain her laughter any more. "You can't invite the people you are watching into the people watching!"

In a second, they were both holding their sides, laughing so hard.

Getting himself together, Clay glanced down at his watch. "Come on. We better head to the theater if we are going to make the movie on time."

As they walked, Clara's phone vibrated. She pulled it out and saw a message from Sophie. It read, "Have fun at the movie. I want to hear all about it later."

Clara realized Sophie didn't have a work emergency at all. She was scheming to force Clara and Clay to be alone. Clara was a little irritated that her friend cut the day short, but it was fun to hang out with Clay.

"Everything okay?"

"Yes. Sophie was just letting me know she would be home so you can take me there later to get my car."

"Oh, okay."

Arriving at the movie theater, they walked up to the ticket counter and Clay purchased two for *A Christmas Story*. Clara thanked him and offered to get the popcorn and drinks. Clay refused, saying, "I crashed your fun day, so the least I can do is get the tickets, popcorn, and Cokes."

They stood in line together and ordered one popcorn to share, two large drinks, and one box of Junior Mints.

Settled into their seats, they snacked on the popcorn and mints while they sipped Cokes.

Clara thought about how comfortable it was to spend time with Clay. There were never awkward silences. They always had things to talk about and had known each other for a while so there were plenty of inside jokes.

A few minutes later, the lights dimmed in the theater and the screen glowed with ads offering refreshments and reminding patrons to silence their phones and crying babies. Clara thought she felt someone watching her and as she looked to the side, caught Clay looking in her direction. He quickly redirected his attention to the screen and took a long drink from his Coke.

They sat in silence, watching the story of a little boy named Ralphie who wanted a Red Ryder BB gun for Christmas He laughed at the trouble Ralphie got in and the scenes that Ralphie imagined, always seeing himself as the hero of the vignette.

Christmas movies were predictable that way: everything always worked out in the end.

When the movie was over and the lights came on, they picked up the half-eaten popcorn, candy box, and cups, making sure they didn't leave a mess behind. Clara noticed Clay was as concerned as she was with making sure no one had any extra cleaning to do around their seats. She couldn't stand to leave a theater and see all the trash and spilled drinks others left behind.

Once outside the theater, Clara asked Clay what time his car would be ready.

"Why, are you ready to get rid of me so soon?" Clay teased.

"No, I just didn't know if the tire place had contacted you yet."

Clay checked his messages and there wasn't one from the tire company, but there was one from Alexis. "No message from the tire store."

"Then come with me. I want to show you something." She grabbed his hand and pulled him through the crowd.

There was little time to think about where they were going when suddenly they came across an enormous group of people in a winding line. Parents and children were all waiting to see Santa and tell them everything they wanted for Christmas.

They found a place to stand on the edge of the crowd, and she said, "Have you ever seen a more real-looking Santa in your life?"

He looked over the crowd and his eyes finally settled on the large, white-bearded man in the red chair. "He looks pretty good. Whoever found him did a fantastic job." He looked at her. "The best part isn't the Santa, though. This is an amazing display you created for him." Clay squeezed her hand and led her out of the crowd.

She wondered whether she should tell Clay her story of the Santa to get his opinion. As they passed by, Santa turned his head toward her, smiled, winked, and gave her a slight nod before picking up the next child in line and setting him on his lap.

Clara stopped. "Did you see that?"

"See what?"

"That Santa just smiled and winked at me," Clara said.

"That's nice. I bet he does that to all the pretty girls," Clay teased.

"No, you don't understand." Clara told him her crazy secret. "This Santa has been at every Christmas party I have been to this season. I guess he is popular, and he should be. He really looks like the real thing.

"Anyway," she continued, "at every party, he singles me out and makes eye contact with me. Me, and no one else. At first, I thought maybe he was magical, but now Sophie and I wonder if maybe he recognizes me from the mall. He must have seen me here putting finishing touches on designs. I don't know."

Clay looked at her, "Maybe he is the real thing," Clay said.

"Come on, you know you don't really believe that. You just think I might be crazy."

"There is only one way to find out. Ask him for something that you wouldn't ask from anyone else and see what happens."

"Are you serious? You expect a grown woman to go stand in that line, with no children, and sit on his lap and ask for something for Christmas?"

"Well, when you put it that way, it does sound strange, but who knows? You both put in a lot of time around here and at parties...maybe you could ask him in an unofficial setting. I bet he doesn't have to sit in a special red chair to hear a request."

Clara smiled. She could tell that Clay was being serious and not making fun of her. She thought for a minute. "You are right. I think I will do that."

They continued to walk around the scene, and she pointed out all the special things she created for the children and their families to enjoy as part of their visit to Santa. Clay complimented her creativity and attention to detail and left a note for a reindeer. She beamed at his praise, thankful that someone she cared about took the time to immerse themselves in the scene she created.

Clay's phone vibrated and saw the message: his car was ready to be picked up. The tire shop didn't close for another hour, so he slipped the phone back into his pocket.

"Okay, so what now?" Clay asked.

"How about coffee? I have that year of free coffee card to burn."

"Then what are we waiting for?" Clay asked, and they headed to the mall entrance to walk across the way to Cool Beans.

They talked over a leisurely cup of coffee. Clara caught him up on her parents and sister. It was upsetting, but she was getting used to the idea that she may just be alone for Christmas. Clay told her about his holiday plans. He wanted his family to come to his home this year. It would be easier for him instead of having to travel. He had plenty of room for guests, since he lived alone, and his married siblings would be with their in-laws this Christmas. He assumed his parents might consider coming, if for no other reason than to see this perfect tree he kept bragging about.

As they drained the last swallows from their coffee cups, Clay said, "Looks like I can pick up my car. Are you ready to go?"

"Yes." Clara gathered her purse and coat from the chair next to her.

They walked across the parking lot and across a street to get to the tire shop. Clay went inside to retrieve the keys.

"Hey, do you have to get home right away?"

Thinking he must have an errand to run, Clara said, "No, why?"

"I was thinking we could go to dinner," he said. "Unless you have other plans."

"No, I don't have any other plans." She thought for a minute and then answered, "Dinner sounds great."

"How about Mamma Mia's?"

"Sure," Clara said.

They drove across town, listening to Christmas music. It surprised Clara that he had the radio set to this station. It came on as soon as he started the ignition. So, it wasn't for her benefit.

"I didn't know you listened to this station," she said.

"Only during Christmas. It is fun this time of year to listen to it. The music makes me feel happy as I drive around."

They continued to sit in a comfortable silence, just being together, as they drove. Clay was a very cautious driver, observed Clara. He never sped or rolled through stop signs. And he wasn't prone to road rage when someone made a mistake or cut him off. He was steady and even-tempered, and Clara was comfortable being with him.

They parked near the restaurant entrance and, grabbing their coats, locked the car and walked toward the door. Clay opened the door and held it for her, and told the hostess they would need a table for two.

"Table or booth?" she asked.

"Booth," they answered, then laughed.

Grabbing two menus, she led them across the dimly lit restaurant. Christmas jazz was playing, and it was festive and elegant as they made their way to a booth toward the back of the dining room.

Once settled, the hostess served breadsticks and water. A few minutes later, they ordered. The server took their orders and then left them to visit again.

They started people watching while they waited. This time they were trying to decide who was on a first date, blind date, married, about to be engaged, or about to break up.

It was fun. They miscalled one couple, that they were both on the edge of a break, until they brought the couple dessert. Then suddenly, the guy got out of his chair, went down on one knee, and proposed. The entire restaurant celebrated when she said, "Yes!"

Clay looked at Clara. "I guess we called that one wrong."

"Yep. He was just nervous and acting weird, and she got irritated because she didn't know what was going on with him. Maybe he should have been clear about his intentions before coming to the restaurant."

"I don't like public proposals. They seem so contrived, like they benefit the crowd. I think it should be a private moment. You are asking someone to decide to spend the rest of their lives with you. They should be able to answer yes or no without the pressure of a group of strangers looking on. It always makes me nervous to see them. What if she had said no? It would humiliate him," Clara said.

"I see your point, but I wonder if you would consider an alternative. Perhaps, taking that risk is what it is all about. That guy is putting his ego on the line and loves her so much that he will risk public humiliation to let her know how much he loves her and can't stand the thought of a life without her," Clay answered.

"Maybe you have a point," she said.

Changing the subject, Clara asked, "So how did it go with Alexis last night? She seemed very interested in getting to know you better."

"Did she? I didn't notice."

"Well, I did. It was kind of annoying, to be honest."

"And why was that?" Clay asked.

"She kept looking at me and reminding me, in not-so-subtle ways, that she asked you to come to the party and basically you came together. It was obnoxious."

Just then, the server brought their meals and set them on the table.

They both ate in silence for a while before Clay asked between bites, "What was so obnoxious about Alexis?"

"You know. It was kind of desperate. She is an intelligent, accomplished, and beautiful woman. Men probably give her all the attention she can handle. She doesn't need to act like that. She was obviously the most attractive woman in the room. It would have been more acceptable for her to have treated your presence as a business associate rather than a forced date."

"Why do you think it was a forced date? Maybe I took it as a date," Clay said.

Clara didn't think Alexis was the type of woman Clay would be interested in. "Did you?" she asked, surprised.

"Well, no, but she is pretty and since you pointed out her intelligence and accomplishments, she might be perfect for me," Clay said.

Clara hoped he was joking. She couldn't see Clay with anyone else. Clara was suddenly acutely aware that maybe she wanted to be more than just good friends with Clay. *Maybe Sophie is right.* She suddenly could not look at him for fear he would know what she was thinking. They had been good friends for quite some time, and he was pretty good at reading her expressions.

"Are you serious? Would you really consider dating Alexis, like in a relationship?" She took another bite of her dinner.

"No, I am not interested in her in the least. I just accepted the invitation because I really thought it was a business opportunity. Don't worry, I am not getting married soon, at least not to her," he teased.

They continued eating and even ordered a dessert to share.

"So now that you have commented on my dating relationships and saved me from being trapped by the obnoxious Alexis, what about you? Have you been secretly dating anyone I should know about?"

"Don't you think if I was, they would be on the party circuit with me?" she asked. "It's hard for me to meet anyone who'd put up with my Christmas obsession. My job is Christmas all year round, and that is too much for most people."

"Well, it's their loss. I, for one, love your exuberance about the holiday. It makes my dreary world brighter."

They finished dessert and coffee, and Clay asked for the check and paid for dinner. She noticed he left a generous tip. He was very generous all year, not just Christmastime.

As they drove to Sophie's, Clay asked about the rest of the parties that she had on her schedule. She still had the party at the university, and of course the party at Clay's accounting firm. There were only a few more until the season would be over and she could retire the black cocktail dress.

She told him the theme of the parties and wondered whether Santa would be there again like he had the other parties. Clay agreed that it was likely he would make an appearance. It seemed to be something new that everyone was including in their parties this year.

They pulled up to Sophie's house and noticed there weren't many lights on, but Clara's car was in the driveway.

"Are you sure she is home?" Clay asked.

"She said she was when I called her from the restaurant to let her know we were on our way."

"Before you go, I have a proposition for you," Clay said.

"Okay," Clara said suspiciously.

"You know I overheard you talking about what you were looking for me for Christmas. First, you should know that you don't have to get me a gift. Second, if you really feel compelled, there is something I would like."

Clara giggled. "Okay, but you know I am not Santa."

Clay said, "Well, you obviously have some kind of connection with him. You've been telling me about it all day." Clay continued, "Seriously, all I want is to be your date for the next party."

Clara hesitated for a second and then said, "Really, that's it? I had a much bigger budget for your gift this year."

"Well, add it to the budget for next year's gift then," he joked, and then said, "I am serious. I want to go with you to the next party. It will be fun, and I really want to see Santa try to flirt with you while you have a date."

"Okay, then it is a date. I'll send you the details when I get home."

Clay smiled at Clara and then walked around the car to open her door. "Don't forget to let me know you got home okay and be sure to send me all the details for the party."

Clara laughed as she agreed and turned to go up the walkway to Sophie's front door to retrieve her keys. She had a lot to tell her friend.

Chapter 12

C lara was excited about the next party. It was at the university, in one of the open study lounges of the Student Center. The theme was Christmas Around the World. The administration wanted international students to experience something familiar, like other students.

Clara spent a great deal of time researching customs in other countries. Wherever people celebrated, it seemed family, joy, and magic were part of the experience. She made sure this was clear in her design.

Because this was a date and a work obligation, she took extra care getting ready.

Sophie had about lost her mind when Clara gave her a report of the day with Clay after she left the food court. "See, I told you! I knew it. He's waiting for you."

"We'll see. What if it's terrible? How will we stay friends?" Clara was concerned about that possibility.

"Don't worry. You spend every minute you can together throughout the year. Why would it be any different tonight? You spent almost the entire day together just a few days ago. You've eaten with Clay, gone to family events with him, helped him decorate and pick out a tree, and he has even seen you when you were sick. Remember when you had the flu, and we alternated days bringing you soup and juice? He's not worried about one terrible date. Just have fun. Who knows, maybe Santa will have a surprise for you at this party." Sophie laughed, and continued, "I think you are worrying way too much."

Clara thought about her conversation with Sophie while getting dressed. Christmas music playing in the background, she took the time to spritz herself with perfume and painted her nails a cheery Christmas red. She fussed over her hair more than usual and took a little longer getting her makeup just right. She was usually a mascara and lip gloss girl, but tonight she added more color to her lips and cheeks.

Dressed in her black dress, this time with pearl earrings, necklace, and bracelet, she heard a knock at the door as she slipped her feet into black heels.

Her stomach fluttered as she walked across the living room to the front door. *Get it together.* She took a deep breath before opening the door.

Clay stood a few feet from the door. He wore a dark suit with a blue tie that made his icy-blue eyes stand out. He smiled at her and stepped inside. "Wow! You look amazing."

She grabbed her purse, said goodbye to Mistletoe, and turned off the lights as they walked out the door. Clay found a parking spot close to her front door, so they didn't have far to walk. It was a frosty night and settling into the seat, she noticed he had warmed it on the drive to pick her up. Clara thought it was nice of him to think of that detail.

He got in the driver's seat and they were off. It was quiet at first, as if both of them were unsure of what to say.

This is ridiculous, she thought. *We've never had a hard time talking to each other.*

He must have thought the same thing. They decided to just go for it and started talking at exactly the same time.

Laughing, each hesitated to let the other go first. Finally, Clay said, "So tell me about this party. What are we walking into tonight?"

"Let's see. This was one of my favorites. I researched Christmas traditions from other places. The university gave me a list of countries their international students represent, and I started there. I wanted to make sure that every student would feel right at home. You'll see Yule logs, Christmas trees decorated with seashells, a giant advent calendar, poinsettias all over the place, and lights that look like candles in the windows. I brought in oil palms and mango trees and decorated those. There'll be plenty of greenery, you know, like garlands and wreaths made of holly. And because this is a place for college students, I hung mistletoe in various places. Of course, there are a variety of nativities, and Christmas trees of all sizes with decorations commonly found in other countries.

"Oh, and a variety of Santa figures. Of course, there's Father Christmas, Kris Kringle, Père Noel, Papa Noel, Saint Nicholas, Grandfather Frost, Christmas Man, and Santa Claus. Every country does something slightly different with their version of Santa."

"I can't wait to see it."

"Thank you. I hope I haven't oversold it."

They continued to visit like any other time they were together. When they arrived at the university parking lot, Clay opened her door and helped her out of the car.

Clara had created beautiful sections of decor that flowed one into the next. Many had elements from lots of different places that were blended together. She even put Christmas pillows on the couches and hung stockings from the staircase that led to the upper floor.

"This is really something," he said as they walked toward the crowd of guests. The dean of student affairs saw them and rushed over to welcome Clara and gush over the decorations.

"We had so much positive feedback about the Student Center this year. In fact, the director noticed students were using it more during this time than any other for studying and study breaks. Even our international students came here instead of staying in the international dorms. We'll call in January to sign a contract for next year," the dean explained.

Clara smiled and thanked him for the compliment and the opportunity to create something so special. She remembered her own college years and wished she had had a place like this to come to.

She introduced Clay to the dean, before the dean excused himself to welcome faculty as they arrived.

Clara and Clay walked through the gathering of guests and found a place to sit. Clay's hand was on the small of her back as they walked through the crowd and she noticed that he stood a little closer to her than usual.

This party was different from the previous weeks'. There was live Christmas music tonight. It was a benefit of having an accomplished music department. A sit-down dinner instead of a buffet of finger foods and desserts. Another perk of a university. They had a hospitality department ready to show off their skills. They arranged each table with eight place settings, complete with the forks and spoons necessary for a formal dinner.

Clara and Clay chose a table on the edge of the crowd. This would be optimal for people watching and wouldn't be as loud as sitting next to the musicians.

At the appointed time, dinner was served. There were several courses, and each was as delicious as the one before. Over dessert and coffee, which was delicious, Clay leaned over and asked Clara, "I never had food like this in college, did you?"

She shook her head and laughed. "No, and it was probably a good thing. If the food had been like this, I would've never left the dining hall."

Eventually, the student waitstaff cleared the tables and offered more coffee, which Clara accepted. As part of the entertainment, the choral department gave a short concert with samplings of Christmas music from all over the world.

"They are really keeping true to the theme, aren't they," Clay said.

"Yes, it's nice to have a party like this. So many other parties I have been to are more like mixers. This one is more structured. You have something to do if you don't know the other guests."

At the end of the concert, there was an announcement. A very special guest was arriving soon. The musicians began playing "Here Comes Santa Claus," and in walked Santa, his big red bag filled with gifts.

Clay leaned in close. "I wonder if that bag is full of books. This looks like a crowd that reads a lot."

Clara shushed him and watched, waiting to see whether Santa would acknowledge her.

Santa made his way to the front and sat in his overstuffed red chair. The crowd was excited to see him, and the energy in the room shifted. She wondered whether everyone else felt it too.

Clara was about to turn and ask Clay, when she noticed Santa survey the crowd as if he were looking for someone. She watched him scan from left to right. When he found her, he broke into a wide smile. She smiled back, and he winked at her and gave a subtle wave. She waved back.

"Who are you waving to?" Clay asked.

"Santa Claus. Didn't you see him wave at me?"

"No, I must have missed it. Wait, is that the same Santa that was at the hotel party?"

"I think so. He looks like the one from the mall too. When I saw him there, the other day, I wondered if that's how he knows me. But, to be honest, they all have to look similar or the whole thing won't work."

"Have you talked to him?" Clay asked.

"No. I mean, not that I am aware of. At least not in all of his Santa clothes, that is for sure. And, I think I would remember talking to a person who looked like Santa."

They stayed awhile longer. The music was pleasant and the crowd more subdued than usual.

Clara felt comfortable with Clay. He asked about her family and whether she had decided on her plans for Christmas without them.

"They seem great. Kayla is off in Italy, drinking lots of wine and experiencing traditions there. She never has trouble meeting people and making friends and has quite the group now. She plans to stay there. I sent her Christmas gift. Shipping was a fortune! I hope she enjoys it. She occasionally sends me messages and pictures of the places she is going and the people she is meeting."

Clara continued, "My parents send me postcards from all the tourist traps along the way. They've met a lot of interesting characters and report they're having the time of their lives. They definitely aren't coming back for a visit at Christmas."

"So, have you decided what you are doing?" Clay asked.

"They don't seem to mind going off and doing something different this year, and maybe I should do the same. Just have a quiet Christmas at home and watch movies, play with Mistletoe, bake lots of desserts and eat them all. It's only one day."

"What would you normally do together?"

"It isn't so much about Christmas Day. In the days leading to Christmas, we would get hot cocoa and drive around, looking at lights. Most years, we attend a Christmas concert and spend a day baking a variety of Christmas cookies. There is a day set aside for shopping and wrapping gifts. And, we watch at least one Christmas movie. We try to keep change to drop in the bell ringer's red bucket. I always insist on a family picture wearing ugly Christmas sweaters when we get and decorate the tree. And we take gifts to the nursing home for people who don't have regular visitors."

"That is a lot. Do you plan it all?"

"I do. They go along, but they aren't really into it. I know they like to be together at Christmas, but they consider me obsessed about the whole thing. They always say I should live in a Christmas movie. But it is only one month. I feel like I have to be intentional or I'll miss out."

"I find your obsession charming. You couldn't have done all this without being crazy about Christmas."

Clay held her hand as he encouraged her and for the first time in a long time, she felt like someone didn't think she was weird about Christmas. She felt appreciated.

"Thank you for saying that. This year has been so different. I haven't quite known what to do with myself in between parties. I enjoy being home, surrounded by my cozy decorations, but things aren't as fun as usual. I really haven't had the experience I wish I could have."

Sitting in silence, Clara could tell that Clay was deep in thought. She hoped she hadn't said too much as they listened to the jazz band continue playing.

Finally, he turned to her. "What if you created new traditions this Christmas? It might be the perfect time to make a change, since others decided for you."

Clara considered this possibility.

"What would your perfect Christmas be like?" Clay asked.

"It would be cold and exciting. There would be family around, and everyone gets along, even if things aren't perfect. There would be mounds of presents wrapped beautifully. Lots of hot chocolate and Christmas cookies. Matching pajamas, full stockings, Christmas movies playing, the fireplace lit, everyone laughing and telling stories about previous Christmases, maybe snow, and lots of relaxing after all the festivities. You know, like a Christmas movie," she said, and they both laughed.

"Things in Christmas movies are perfect. That's what I imagine the perfect Christmas would be like," Clara said.

"Wow," Clay said, looking very serious. "You are right, that's pretty intense."

Then he laughed. "I'm kidding. It sounds wonderful and I hope you have a movie-perfect Christmas. In fact, I hope you get everything you want for Christmas."

She looked at him and smiled, believing that he really hoped she would get everything she wished for.

When it was time to leave, they found the dean and thanked him for the invitation and a wonderful time. He thanked them for coming and again complimented Clara on all the beautiful decor.

They walked across the cold parking lot together and once again Clay opened the door for Clara and then walked around to the driver's side. Clara was content. This was a fun and relaxing evening, and she felt differently about the events of the last month.

They drove back to her condo, and Clay walked her to the front door. Once there, she turned to face him. This was usually an awkward part of the date, but she didn't feel awkward at all. In fact, she wasn't really ready for the date to be over, but it was getting late and Clay had to work the next day.

Clara reached out and took one of Clay's hands. "Merry Christmas. I hoped you liked your gift."

"Thank you, I did. It might be one of the best Christmas gifts ever."

Clara blushed. "I am glad you liked it."

"I was thinking," Clay said. "I know this was my Christmas gift, but what do you think about going out again, on a non-Christmas gift date?"

Clara thought about this for a second. "Are you asking me out?"

"Yes. So..."

"I have to check my calendar, but I think I can arrange it," she teased.

"Okay. I'll call you tomorrow." Clay smiled and leaned in for a quick kiss on her cheek. "Good night, Clara. Thank you for my Christmas gift." He turned and walked back to his car.

She opened her door and let herself in, thinking that Sophie may have been right all along.

Chapter 13

C lara got up and had her usual first cup of coffee as she fed Mistletoe. Taking her mug to the sofa, she checked her messages and found notifications from her family. Kayla thanked her for the gift and was excited to fill it with pictures and journal entries. Her parents also received their package and had filled it with stories from their trip. They let Clara know they were farther along on their trip and planned to stay there a few more days. They were still hoping that Clara would change her mind and join them for Christmas, but understood if she couldn't.

Clara replied to her parents that she had obligations until the day before Christmas. She explained she missed them and was glad to hear they were having a wonderful trip, but she planned to stay home and watch movies and relax Christmas Day.

She was excited to meet Sophie for coffee. Her feelings about Clay were a surprise after the date and she was excited to talk it out with Sophie. She hoped Sophie would keep the teasing to a minimum.

Sophie was at their favorite table at Cool Beans arrived. She had already begun her Christmas vacation and wanted to make the most of every moment. Sophie had a lot of travel planned for the next two weeks and she needed to pack, but she was desperate for details from Clara's date with Clay the night before.

Clara placed her order and sat down.

"I knew it! I knew you would have a good time," Sophie said. "It must have gone very well for you to be smiling this much."

"If you must know, I had a wonderful evening!"

"Details. And leave nothing out."

As the barista set her coffee on the table in front of her, Clara began recounting the details from the night before. Clara told about how comfortable it was to be with him and how they talked and people watched for the entire party.

"Now the good stuff. Did he kiss you goodnight?"

"Not exactly. He asked me to go on another date, a proper date, not like last night, and then he leaned in and kissed my cheek and said good night."

"That's it?" Sophie asked.

"Yep, that's it," Clara answered.

"So, what do you think?"

"I'm surprised, but I think I like him. It's kind of weird, though. We've been friends for a long time, and I've not considered anything romantic with him. This is uncharted territory for me. I'm not really sure how to proceed."

"I'll tell you how to proceed. You go on this date, and the next date, and so on. Don't worry about planning things out so much. Just have fun and see what happens," Sophie encouraged. "When are you going out again?"

"He called this morning and said he had something planned for tomorrow. He said to be ready early, and dress comfortably. Other than that, he wouldn't say where we're going or what we're doing," Clara said.

"Since he didn't tell you to pack a bag, I assume he's not whisking you away on a romantic trip."

Sophie was listing all the possibilities when Clara interrupted, "Wait a minute! Your imagination is moving way too fast. One date does not lead to a romantic weekend away."

"I'm just trying to cover all possibilities. Did he give time frames—like, is it just the morning?"

"No, he said what I told you."

"I can't wait for you to call me tomorrow with all the details. You will call me, right?" Sophie asked.

"Yes, of course."

Sophie looked at her watch. "I really wish I could stay and visit all morning, but I have a thousand things to do before I leave. I better get going. I'm excited for you. Clay is great."

They stood and hugged before Sophie rushed out to run her errands before the trip. Clara took Sophie's empty cup to the counter and ordered another coffee.

"I see Cool Beans is going to lose a fortune on you two," joked their favorite barista.

"Hey, they offered and we stood in the freezing line for it." Clara laughed, thinking that it was true. They might never offer this again. Cool Beans was definitely going to lose money if Clara and Sophie were getting free coffee for the next year.

Clara ordered a cup to go and walked around the mall before heading home. After all these years, she still loved the mall at Christmastime. As she walked by the Santa display, sipping her coffee, she watched all the children as they waited for their turn. She remembered all the times she stood in line with her family, waiting to tell him what she wanted for Christmas. Every year, she got exactly what she asked for. Now she wondered how her parents pulled that off, especially the year she purposely didn't tell anyone except Santa what she wanted. At school, some kids were spreading this terrible rumor that Santa wasn't real. That it was parents who put the presents under the tree. She tested the theory and only told Santa what she wanted. No matter how much her parents or sister asked her, she held firm. Only Santa would know what she really wanted. That way she would know for sure whether he was real or not.

It must have driven her parents crazy because they knew the stakes were high. Somehow, they figured it out and when she came downstairs Christmas morning, there it was. From that point on,

Christmas, and Santa especially, would be magical and there was no disputing it.

Clara's heart was heavy, reminiscing. She missed her parents and sister. But she thought of Clay's suggestion that maybe she should create Christmas traditions for herself. She was considering what that might be like when Sam called her name.

"Well, my day just got a hundred times better! It's so good to see you." Sam enveloped her in a friendly embrace. "How have you been? I haven't seen you since Thanksgiving."

Clara walked with him as he made his rounds and gave him a brief update on her parents and sister, telling him about her date with Clay.

"It sounds like your parents and sister are having fun on their adventures. It also sounds like Christmas hasn't been too bad for you either." He smiled.

"No, I guess it hasn't. I'm going to stay here for Christmas. It is too hard to plan to meet my parents and really, it would be too weird to celebrate in a hotel or RV. I think it might be time to try something different myself. I'm just not sure what."

Sam nodded. "We'll be in town and would love for you to come over and spend Christmas with us. As far as we know, the boys will be home, so the more the merrier."

"I appreciate that and you know I can never pass up Maria's cooking. I may pop over."

"The invitation is always open. You don't have to decide now. Call if you decide to come and we'll be happy to set another place at the table."

They hugged goodbye, saying they'd see each other at the mall Christmas party. The mall party was the day before Christmas Eve and it was usually her favorite party of the year. It was much more casual. The party would go late into the night, but she was around people who weren't as formal and stuffy and didn't judge if she wanted to leave early.

She walked back through the mall, wondering about Clay's surprise for the next day. She took Sophie's advice and went with the flow. Besides, Clay knew her pretty well, and she felt she could trust him to plan something she would enjoy.

Just then she saw Santa. One child was climbing off his lap while another was walking toward him, eager to tell him what was on their Christmas wish list. Before the child got to Santa, he turned and smiled and winked at her. She smiled back, thinking things were looking up.

The next morning, there was a knock on the door at seven fifteen. She was still nursing her first cup of coffee and dressed in her red footed pajamas that had a Christmas sweater pattern on them. She picked up her coffee and walked to the door, opening it to find Clay there, fully dressed in jeans, a sweater, and hiking boots. He handed her the coffee cup he was holding, and they stood looking at each other for a second before bursting into laughter.

"Um, I know I said to dress comfortably, but you should know we'll be in public. If this is what you want to wear, that's fine with me, but other people may look at you funny."

"Obviously, this is not what I'd wear in public! I wasn't expecting you this early, and I thought you'd call when you were on your way. Give me a few minutes and I'll be ready."

He settled on the sofa and Mistletoe walked by, brushing up against his leg. He reached down and gave her a quick scratch behind her ears, and she purred before walking off and leaving him alone in the living room.

"You never told me what we're doing today," Clara called from her bedroom.

"I told you it was a fun surprise," Clay replied, "but you better hurry or we won't have time to do everything."

Clara walked out, dressed similarly to Clay. She wore jeans, a Christmas sweater, and boots, and had thrown her hair into an easy ponytail that cascaded over her right shoulder.

"Okay, let's go." She pulled him up off the couch.

Once in the car, he said, "I know this is not the Christmas season you had in mind, so I thought we would take that list of yours, the things you usually do at Christmastime, and pack the season into one day."

"Are you serious?"

"Yes. That is why I had to pick you up so early! I'm glad to see you clean up so nicely, so fast. Daylight is burning!"

He asked her to reach into the glove box and pull out the paper trimmed in red and green.

"This is our list. We have to accomplish all of this in one day. If you'll notice, there are nine things on this list. It bothers me that there isn't an even number, but I guess nine will have to do since that's all that you mentioned at the party."

"You planned all this since the other night?" Clara knew what it took to plan activities for a month and had tremendous respect for anyone who could do this so efficiently in less than forty-eight hours.

"Yes, well, I am an accountant. We are efficient. Now, what's first?"

"Let's see. Number one: find a tree and decorate it. We already did that a few weeks ago."

"Well, that was before you mentioned all the things. So, we are going to the mall where you can sponsor a tree for charity. I checked and there are a few left. Let's go find whatever decorations are left on the shelves and claim a tree," Clay said as they pulled into the parking lot of a local discount store.

They decided on a green and red theme and bought all the green and red decorations they could find. Because the mall would auction off the tree, the ornaments would go with it. Satisfied they had enough for any sized tree, they put their purchases in the trunk of Clay's car and were off.

The mall was busy. This close to Christmas, the last-minute shoppers were crowding the place. They stopped at Cool Beans for coffee to go and then walked through the mall to the "tree lot." It was a roped-off area with lights strung over the top, just like the tree lots all over town. Clay found the person in charge and paid the fee for them to claim a tree. They chose the most perfect of the trees that were left. All the trees were beautiful and represented some really wonderful local charities.

"Thankfully, you're a pro at this," Clay said as they unwound lights and checked to make sure they were all lit. "Otherwise, we might not get to the rest of the list."

Clara sorted the ornaments. She carefully put them on tiny green hooks that would blend in with the greenery on the tree. Finished, she looked up and saw Clay was ready to put the lights on the tree. They worked together to make sure there were no gaps, and began putting on the rest of the ornaments. She had decorated lots of trees before but never like this, and she was enjoying every minute.

Finishing, they both stepped back to see what they had accomplished.

"It's beautiful," Clay said.

"It's my favorite tree of the season," Clara added. "Thank you for bringing me here. I guess I walk by this every year and admire all the beautiful trees, but I never thought to take part."

They collected their trash and put it in the bin at the edge of the lot. The tree lot organizer thanked them for participating.

Stopping right outside the tree lot area, Clay asked for the list.

"Find and decorate a Christmas tree, check," he said as he put a red check in the box next to the item on the list.

"Wait, a candy cane pen?" asked Clara, laughing. "You really went all out."

"As we go by the entrance to the mall, you'll need this." He handed her a small bag full of coins.

She took the coins and as they got closer to the glass doors, she could hear the faint sound of the bell ringers. This was one of her favorite parts of Christmas. She loved everything about the bell ringers and always kept change on hand, so she had something to drop in every bucket.

Clara ran ahead and found the bell ringer just outside the glass door. Clay caught up with her when she was dropping the last of the coins in the red bucket.

"Merry Christmas," the bell ringer said.

"Merry Christmas," Clara replied and smiled at Clay and the bell ringer.

"Number two: drop money in a bell ringer's bucket, check." Clay marked it off the list. "Hey, smell this." Clay handed Clara the pen. "It smells like peppermint."

Clara smelled it and laughed, anticipating how much fun today was going to be. "What's next on the list?" she asked eagerly.

"Number three: shopping and wrapping," Clay read. "Do you have any last-minute shopping to do?"

"No, I'm done. And, if you remember, I already gave you your gift. It was the last thing I needed to shop for," Clara said.

"Ah yes, the date. That was my favorite Christmas gift so far." He took her hand and walked through the mall. "In that case, let's pick up a few gifts for the nursing home visit that is planned for later in the day," Clay suggested.

"Sounds good. I assume you might have a list of possible appropriate gifts," Clara said.

"Yes, I do." Clay pulled out the list, and they found suggestions such as socks and slippers, word search books, lotion and other toiletries, light blankets, and small pillows.

"Then let's get to work."

They spent the next hour collecting things from the list and standing in line at the gift-wrapping station. For one dollar per gift, they supplied all the paper, tape, ribbon, and gift tags a shopper would need to take everything home wrapped and ready for the tree. They wrapped the gifts, labeling them for a man or woman and, if appropriate, the size of the item. It surprised Clara that Clay was good at wrapping gifts.

She complimented his wrapping, and he explained, "As a kid, I went through an origami phase."

With the gifts wrapped and placed back in their bags for easier toting, they headed to the car. Clay popped the trunk and placed the gifts flat so they wouldn't topple and mess up the bows. In the car, sitting on warmed seats, and listening to the Christmas radio station, Clay pulled out the list once again.

"Number three: shopping and wrapping Christmas gifts. Check," he said, and marked it off the list with a flourish.

"Now what?"

"Christmas baking," Clay read.

"Where are we going for that?" Clara asked.

"You'll see," Clay said mysteriously as he pulled out of the parking lot.

On the way, Clara asked Clay what his favorite Christmas song was.

"Let's see...probably 'Winter Wonderland,'" Clay said thoughtfully. "What about you?"

"'Last Christmas,'" Clara said.

"Seriously? You are the first person I have ever heard say, out loud, that's their favorite Christmas song," Clay said as he laughed.

"Don't make fun of me. It might not be everyone's favorite, but when anyone hears it, they immediately get in the Christmas mood," Clara said, defending her choice.

"I guess, but you only ever hear that song playing in stores or on the radio. It is never on anyone's playlist."

Clara retrieved her phone from her purse and showed him her holiday playlist. At the top of the list, he saw, "Last Christmas."

"Okay, to each their own. I won't hold it against you."

She put her phone away and Clay reached over to hold her hand again. This was comfortable. She enjoyed spending time with Clay, and he was obviously interested in spending more time with her and not just as friends. She heard Sophie's words rolling around in her mind about enjoying the moment.

She leaned her head back onto the headrest.

Clay looked over. "Tired already?"

"No, just happy and relaxed."

"Well, rest up. We still have a lot on the list. Christmas season in a day is going to be busy."

They pulled into his driveway, and he came around and opened her door. As she stepped out, she asked, "Why are we here?"

"Let's go in and see."

Clay unlocked the door and when they walked in the kitchen, she could see that he had been really busy. There were recipe cards next to bundled ingredients. It was all very organized, and she took a minute to take it all in.

"How much baking are we doing?"

"I told my mom I needed a few recipes, and she went a little crazy. We have gingerbread men here. Over there is the sugar cookie recipe and ingredients. On the table, we have everything we need to make snowman mints. And, finally, on the bar is everything for chocolate chip cookies. She wanted to send me a recipe for fruitcake, but I said that wouldn't be necessary."

Amazed at the preparation and organization this took, Clara surveyed the kitchen. "Have you slept since the party the other night?"

"Not a lot. I wanted to make sure you got the perfect Christmas," Clay said.

"Thank you, Clay. This is amazing. Where do we start?"

"I think we should make the gingerbread and sugar cookie dough first. That way, we can let it chill before we use the cookie cutters. Then, while the oven is preheating, we can make the chocolate chip cookie dough and get them in the oven. As they bake, we can roll out the other dough and use the cookie cutters to make the different shapes. They can go in the oven while we make the snowmen mints and then once the cookies have cooled, we can decorate them."

"You *are* efficient," Clara said.

"In most cases, yes, but this was overwhelming even for me. These instructions came from my mom," Clay answered sheepishly.

"All right, let's get started." Clara walked toward the gingerbread area when Clay stopped her.

"Wait, first put this on." He handed her the most festive Christmas apron she had ever seen. She put it over her head and tied it in the back.

"Where did you find these?" she asked as Clay put his over his clothes.

"At the store, when I bought all the ingredients. They were on clearance this close to Christmas, and even though you said nothing about a special apron, I thought we had to have them. Look, they even light up." He pressed Rudolph's nose.

Blinking lights trimmed the aprons as they worked.

It was fun and messy work. Finally, sitting for a few minutes in between baking and decorating, Clay made them hot chocolate, and they sat on the sofa to rest.

"This is so much fun, but who is going to eat these cookies?" Clara asked.

"I figured you would take some home and my family has agreed to come for Christmas. They will go fast with that crew."

"It's so nice that they agreed to come. I'm sure your decorations will impress them." Clara grinned.

"Yes, they are used to a lopsided tree with ornaments haphazardly placed in the front. You know, why don't you come over for Christmas? I know you can't meet your parents, and my family would love to see you. They always ask about you and really enjoyed spending time with you at the lake this summer."

"Thank you. I might. Sam and Maria also invited me to eat with them. Maybe I'll make the rounds and celebrate with everyone! It'll be like having several Christmases in one day," Clara exclaimed.

As they drank the last of the cocoa, the kitchen timer alerted them it was time to take the cookies out of the oven. Clara and Clay cleaned the kitchen as everything cooled. They brought out the sugar cookies and gingerbread men and decorated them. By the end of the decorating, they were both covered in flour and icing.

Clara noticed her reflection. "Can we swing back by my place? I need to change."

"No time for that, and not to worry, I have everything covered. Wait here," Clay instructed as he went down the hall into his bedroom. He came back a few minutes later with two sweaters folded over his arm. Laughing, he held one out to her. "Here you go. These are the ugliest Christmas sweaters I could find. Will they do?" he asked, barely able to keep from laughing.

"I don't know." Clara frowned. "Are you sure these are the ugliest sweaters you could find?" Then, bursting into laughter, she held it out. "Are we really going to wear these? I mean, I'm used to ugly Christmas sweaters, but you're usually a much better dresser."

"You said ugly sweaters—we are wearing ugly sweaters. It's on the list and we have to do everything on the list," Clay explained as he pulled the cookie-covered sweater off and put the Christmas sweater on over a T-shirt.

"You go change while I package cookies for you to take home," Clay offered.

When she came out wearing the ugly sweater, Clay said, "That is one ugly sweater, but you still look great! Come on, let's go. We still have a lot on the list." Clay took out his list and said, "Number four: Christmas baking, check," and placed a check next to the item.

They drove to a local theater. Clay was trying to make it to a matinee showing of *Elf.* They arrived in plenty of time and after purchasing tickets, they walked around the arcade. Clay noticed a photo booth and pulled Clara inside. They closed the curtain, and he put money in the slot. The lights blinked, counting down to the flash. They made silly poses for each of the five snapshots. Clay pushed the button for doubles and two strips with the five photos came out of the machine. Laughing, they each took one and shook it to dry the ink.

Clay pulled out the list and his candy cane pen again. "Number five: picture wearing matching ugly Christmas sweaters. Check," and he marked it off the list.

They stood in line for popcorn and Cokes, starving because they hadn't eaten lunch. Neither wanted candy. They'd sampled too many of the Christmas cookies.

Clay handed the attendant their tickets. Once inside, they found seats in the middle of the second to top row. They were the best seats.

As they waited for the movie to start, Clay asked, "So, how's your day been so far?"

"The best day in a long, long time," Clara answered.

"I'm glad." Clay reached over for her hand and squeezed it.

The movie started, and they watched Buddy the Elf navigate new relationships and how to manage the perfect Christmas with the people he loved.

Walking out to the car, Clay pulled the list out again. "Number six: watch a Christmas movie. Check," he said again and marked it off with his special candy cane pen.

The sun was setting as they headed from the parking lot onto the street. "Where to next?" Clara asked.

"The list says to drop off gifts at the nursing home. I found one near here and they said we could come by today."

They drove with the Christmas music playing and laughed about their day so far. When they arrived, Clay opened Clara's door as usual, and they retrieved the gifts from the back of the car.

"I wish we had something different to put them in," Clara said. "We can't carry them all without dropping something, but plastic store bags just don't look festive."

"I'm way ahead of you." Clay pulled out a big red and green cloth bag with a drawstring at the top.

Clay carefully slung it over his shoulder and Clara walked ahead, holding open the door.

"How do I look?" Clay asked.

"Like a younger, fitter Santa." Clara laughed.

The manager met them in the lobby and thanked them for the gifts, explaining many of the residents didn't have visitors and they would be excited to have gifts to open on Christmas morning.

Clay and Clara turned to leave, and the manager called out, "Merry Christmas!"

"Okay, let's see the list," Clay said. "Number seven: deliver gifts to the nursing home. Check." He marked it off and then frowned. "It looks like we are coming to the end of the list. Only a couple things left."

Clara was tired but happy and didn't want the day to end. Pushing that from her mind, she concentrated on thinking about what they were doing next. She took the list from him and read, "Number eight: Christmas concert. Where did you find a Christmas concert for tonight?"

"You'll see."

They drove across town to a park. The parking lot was full, which was unusual at night, especially a cold night. Clay went around to the trunk and collected a couple of blankets and chairs. They each grabbed one, and he closed the trunk. Carrying their supplies, they walked across the park to where the crowd was gathering. The lawn was covered with families and couples bundled up, sitting on blankets or chairs. Park staff managed a large fire off to the side and a platform built in the shape of a Christmas tree faced the crowd.

They found a place close enough to the fire to feel the warmth but not smell like smoke after, and settled in.

"How did you find this?" Clara asked.

"I had to do some pretty serious research. Most of the Christmas concerts had already happened, but I found a notice on the board in our breakroom for this, and I thought it might be fun. An employee in our firm is in this choir and wanted to make sure we were all invited if we were looking for something festive to do, or to impress a girl we like." He smiled. "So, are you impressed?"

"Yes, very! I've never heard of this. I can't wait."

In a few minutes, the choir came in and found their places on the tree-shaped platform. They dressed like carolers, wearing dark jeans and various shades of green sweaters. The brightly colored scarves, hats, and gloves completed the look and it looked like a decorated Christmas tree. Clara and Clay settled in to enjoy an hour of festive Christmas music.

Clara felt Clay watching her throughout the concert. She turned and smiled at him, thankful that he was the one that made the perfect day for her.

When the concert was over, Clay took out the list once again and read, "Number eight: Christmas concert. Check," and marked it off the list.

At the car, they loaded the blankets and chairs in the trunk and Clay pulled something out of the trunk before opening the door for Clara. Settling in the driver's seat, he handed Clara a thermos and two mugs, and a gift bag full of snacks.

"Number nine: drink hot cocoa and drive around, looking at Christmas lights," he said.

She poured the hot chocolate into the mugs and put marshmallows in both. Handing him the mug, she said, "This has been the best day. Thank you."

"You're welcome. I wanted you to have the perfect Christmas season, even if we packed it into one day."

He drove to Candy Cane Lane, where they parked outside the neighborhood and walked through the streets. The neighborhood was famous for their cooperative Christmas light displays. Every year they chose a theme and all the homes decorated accordingly. It was festive and exciting and a great place to see lights.

Mugs in hand, they talked about which light display they liked and which was over the top. Clara and Clay spent time people watching as little kids had meltdowns while their parents were trying to create the perfect Christmas memories. They tried to identify other couples on dates like they were and guessed how long they had been in relationships. They strolled up and down each street. Holding hands, they sipped their hot cocoa as they went and talked about Christmas memories from when they were kids.

"My family always decorated the outside of the house. My mom, no surprise, always had gingerbread-themed decorations for the yard and we trimmed our house in red and white lights. I mean every bit of our house. From the street, it looked like a gingerbread house. She had green and red net lights over the shrubs, and candy cane lights lining the edge of the driveway and sidewalk. We had gingerbread men on the lawn and we covered the mailbox in battery-powered lights," Clay said.

"Do they still decorate like that?" Clara asked.

"Since we've grown up and moved out, they don't go as overboard, but they still do some lights at least. How about you? How did your family decorate at Christmas?"

"Well, I don't remember before I took it over. At some point, probably in middle school, I decided we needed to decorate more and so I learned how to hang lights around the front door and over the years it grew from there. My dad always hung lights on the house, but I don't think he really enjoyed doing it. I think he did it because that's what you do. As I got older and went into this business, they just let me do what I wanted with the house. Every year I would choose a theme and using what we already had, I'd add to the collection. That's why I have so much in storage right now. When they downsized, I took all the decorations, lights, and ornaments. I might not have to buy anything next year for the displays. Everything I need is probably already in a box, waiting to be rediscovered."

They found themselves back at the car. Clay opened her door and put the thermos and mugs back in the trunk so they wouldn't be rolling around at their feet. He thought of the smallest details.

Sitting back in the driver's seat, he took out the list one last time and read, "Number nine: drink hot cocoa and drive around looking at Christmas lights. Check. Well, we didn't really drive around—we walked around. Does that still count?" Clay asked Clara.

"Yes, it counts," she answered.

Clay started the car, and they drove back across town to Clara's condo.

They were quiet as they drove, each exhausted from the day and unsure how to end the date. Traffic was light for a Saturday night during the holidays, so the trip across town didn't take long.

At Clara's condo, Clay came around and opened her door as she gathered her things. Clay had his hand at Clara's waist as he walked her to the door. She had left the light on and as they stood there, she said, "Thank you for a wonderful day. It really was the best Christmas season I have had in a long time."

"You're welcome. I was thinking, we had such a good first date, and today was a success. Would you be my date for the firm's Christmas party this week? I know it is a work thing for you—actually, it is a work thing for me too—but I thought it might be fun to go together. You know, as a date."

Clara pretended to think about it. "I don't know. You shouldn't date the people you work with," Clara said, watching Clay frown a bit.

"I'm kidding." She continued, "Of course I'll go with you."

Clay's face broke into a grin. "Okay, I'll call you later. I guess I better go."

"Wait! I know it bothered you that the list only had nine things on it. I think I can add a tenth to make it complete."

She pointed up to the porch light and as he looked, he laughed. Hanging from the light was a bunch of mistletoe wrapped in red and green sparkly ribbon with a perfect bow.

Clay leaned in to kiss her, making sure that they were directly under the mistletoe. This time it wasn't on her cheek.

"Good night, Clara."

Smiling, Clara said, "Good night, Clay. Thank you for the perfect day."

She watched as Clay turned and walked to his car. She felt him watching her as she went inside and closed the front door behind her.

She couldn't believe what a great day it was. Everything was finally looking up. She only had two Christmas parties left and would have a date for one of them at least. Work had been great this year, but she was ready for a few weeks off in January. Clay surprised her with everything she thought she was going to miss out on this year. Everything was perfect.

She called Sophie, like she promised, and gave her a summary of the date.

"I told you! I have been telling you for years he was perfect for you, and you just kept ignoring me," Sophie said. "Are you going out again?"

"Yes. He's made it a habit to make plans to see me again before he leaves."

"That's because he doesn't want anyone else to sweep you off your feet," Sophie explained.

"I don't know about that. I'm excited. It's exciting to date someone, but I'm a little nervous that if it doesn't work out, we won't be able to be friends anymore and the two of you are my best friends."

"Well," said Sophie, "if it doesn't work out, we'll still be friends. I don't want to date you, so you are safe there."

They laughed as they said goodbye and promised to keep in touch over the holiday. It wasn't until they got off the phone that Clara realized she didn't even ask Sophie about her trip so far. She made a mental note to do that first the next time they talked.

Clara put her phone away and got ready for bed. As she snuggled under her covers with Mistletoe at her feet, she was excited about what was to come.

Chapter 14

C lara awoke to two messages from Clay. The first a picture of him eating a cookie, still wearing a crazy Christmas sweater. The second to let her know when he'd pick her up for the party.

She was excited to go to the party with Clay. Usually, this was a favorite party of the season because Clay made sure they sat together. Clara wondered whether this time would feel different.

Clara went about her day, running a few errands, relaxing, and watching Christmas movies. She munched on cookies baked the day before and marveled at the perfection in Christmas movies: the towns were beautiful, the decorations elegant, there were presents everywhere, people love and help each other, and Santa makes everyone's dreams come true. For the first time in a long time, she felt maybe her Christmas could be perfect too.

Late in the afternoon, there was a knock at the door. She went to open it, and Clay stood with coffee and sandwiches from her favorite deli.

"I spent all day getting things ready for my family's visit and knew I didn't want to cook, so I thought I would grab dinner to go. I thought you might like some too," Clay explained. "I tried to call first, but you didn't answer. I figured I'd take a chance you might be hungry."

Clara invited him in and looked at her phone. She hadn't heard it ring and realized that the ringer was still off from when they went to the movies.

She took plates to the living room, and they ate while they talked and watched the end of *Miracle on 34th Street*.

"I love this movie," Clara said wistfully. She was full from the sandwich and was sipping her coffee now.

"Because they prove Santa is real?" Clay asked.

"It's not just that. By the end, everyone believes again. In Santa, magic, and humanity. And, I love the ending. Everything works out perfectly for little Susan, and of course her mom ends up with the cute guy," Clara said.

"Well, on that note, I better get going. I don't want to wear out my welcome before the party." Clay got up from the sofa, taking away the plates and the paper from the sandwiches. Walking into the kitchen, he threw away the trash and put the dishes in the dishwasher.

She met him as he walked toward the front door and thanked him for dinner and coffee. "You saved me from a dinner of cookies and cocoa."

"You're welcome. It was partly an excuse to come by and hang out," Clay said. "I hope you don't mind."

"Not at all."

Just before opening the door to leave, Clay looked up toward the light in the entryway. "I don't see any mistletoe hanging. Should we move this outside, or is it okay to kiss you? I'm not sure of the rules here." Clay sounded serious.

"I think under the circumstances it's perfectly okay to kiss me without being under the mistletoe. Besides, what will you do in June?"

Clay leaned in and kissed her. Then he pulled back suddenly. "Wait, June? That's six months from now," he said, teasing.

Clara stammered, unsure of how to respond. The comment had come out unfiltered.

"Well, yes. I mean...well, I am not sure what I mean," she stammered.

Clay rescued her. "See you tomorrow," he said, laughing, and walked to his car.

The next few days were full of errands, people watching, and seeing Clay. They met for coffee, lunch, or in the evenings when he got off work. Things were going so well with the shift in their relationship she wondered why she ever worried.

She heard from her parents and was glad to hear them so happy. They were having fun on their trip and told her to expect a package for Christmas. Her sister even sent a letter full of details. She was meeting the most interesting people and learning more of the language. Kayla told stories of orders in restaurants gone wrong when she mixed up or mispronounced words, but her Italian was getting better every day.

Sophie checked in regularly, living vicariously through Clara. She was experiencing her own dating slump, and it was fun to hear all about Clara's new experiences. Sophie was having fun on her trip and they were making plans to see each other when she got home.

The day of the party finally arrived, and Clara was excited. She picked up the black dress from the cleaner's and spent the afternoon getting ready. This time she chose gold accessories: delicate layered gold necklaces, gold chandelier earrings with tiny diamond details, and a multi-strand gold bracelet.

Hair up, she completed her look with mascara, a little blush, and went for a bolder lip. Her green eyes popped against the other colors and she smiled.

Clara slipped into black heels and transferred the necessities to her black clutch with the gold clasp, and gave herself a spritz of perfume. She nodded, taking a quick look in the mirror, and she smiled at her reflection.

Clay knocked at the door and she opened it to see him there with her favorite coffee. She could tell she made quite an impression.

Clay stepped in, holding out the coffee. "It worked last time," he joked as she took it from him and swallowed a generous sip.

"Thank you. You can never go wrong with coffee."

"You look amazing. Ready to go?" he asked.

"Give me just a minute," she answered.

She turned off the lights, leaving the tree on. And as they walked to the front door, she checked Mistletoe's water and gave her a scratch behind her ears. "All set. Let's go," Clara said.

At the car, Clay opened her door. Once again, he had warmed the seat, so Clara wouldn't have to sit on cold leather. In the driver's seat, Clay turned to look at her. "Every year I've asked you to come, and you never seemed to consider it as a date. It was always a work obligation. I am excited that this year it's different."

The party was in full swing in the building's lobby. It was a large firm that was housed in a historic two-story building in the beautiful downtown area. Several years ago, the city attempted to revitalize the area to attract more businesses to the district. It worked, but the area kept its old charm.

The theme the firm chose this year was Christmas at the Movies. She turned the front windows into a display with props from classic Christmas movies and even had a marquee over the lobby entrance with titles and show times. There were vintage popcorn carts, with real popcorn, and old drink machines full of glass bottles of soda. Around the lobby, she decorated with different scenes. There was a Red Ryder BB gun and a leg lamp on an end table from *A Christmas Story*, a tree decorated with little bells and angels from *It's a Wonderful Life*, and a corner with a World's Best Coffee sign and a tremendously overdecorated tree for *Elf*.

They worked their way through the crowd and found a seat. Each table had a specific movie theme. Their table was decorated with a small toy piano that played music, a scrawny and leaning tree with one red ball on it and a blue blanket at the base, larger bulbed Christmas lights strewn about the table, and a red dog house.

"*A Charlie Brown Christmas*," they said in unison, sitting down.

"Look," Clay said. "Christmas movie bingo." At each place setting was a bingo card and a red or green Christmas stamp. The bingo card was full of the titles of classic Christmas movies.

A server took their order and they could hear the murmur of the crowd over Christmas music in the background. A coworker stopped to speak with Clay and as he was introducing Clara, they heard, "Clay, there you are!"

Alexis navigated the crowd with purpose. She was loud and drew attention to herself.

"Why haven't you returned my calls?" she asked, approaching their table.

"I've been busy the last few days and since you didn't say it was important, I thought I'd get back to you after Christmas. I'm sorry, was there something you needed right away?"

Clara's body tensed at this public exchange, but she was more uncomfortable about a private conversation. She didn't want Clay to return Alexis's calls. Alexis was obviously interested in having more than a business relationship with him.

"I apologize. We can set up a time and I will be happy to have a conference call with you and the others on the team next week. Why don't you call my assistant tomorrow and they can help you get that set up as soon as possible?"

Alexis frowned. Clearly, she was used to being in control of situations and didn't enjoy getting a private or public brush-off. "Oh, okay. Well, it wasn't a business call really, except we haven't decided which accounting firm to work with."

Alexis looked over Clay to Clara.

"It was just that we had so much fun together at the last party, I thought we could come to this one together, that way I wouldn't have to spend the evening alone. I don't know anyone except you, and I'm sorry...what's your name?" She looked at Clara, smiling.

"Clara," Clay said. "This is Clara, and Clara, you remember—"

"Alexis, isn't it," Clara interrupted.

"Yes. Since this chair is empty, I am sure you won't mind if I sit here." Alexis practically jerked the chair out from under the table and slinked her way from standing over them to sitting close to Clay.

Clara simmered silently through the meal. She knew Clay was in a difficult position. The firm had invited Alexis to the party, just like all potential and current corporate clients, but she was taking advantage of the situation. This woman would stop at nothing to keep Clay's attention. She redirected the conversation every time Clay and Clara could talk; she complained about the food and made snarky comments about the decorations and displays. It was obvious Alexis was trying to dominate Clay's attention, and that he kept going along with it was irritating. She knew he was polite, but this was too much.

After the meal, the bar opened, and servers filled the dessert tables. Alexis excused herself to the restroom and finally there was peace at the table.

"She's a little much," Clara said when Alexis was out of earshot.

"Yeah, but she's a big account, and that's why she's here. I'm going to see if one of the other partners can entertain her for a while."

Clara felt more secure knowing that he was not falling for Alexis's overtures.

"Why didn't you return her calls? And by the way, how many times did she call you?" Clara asked.

"Because I was busy. And, it didn't sound like a business call. I thought about what you said after the hotel Christmas party, and I didn't want to encourage her. I'm interested in someone else." He took her hand and gave it a squeeze.

Alexis returned with two cups of holiday punch.

"Be careful with that stuff. It sneaks up on you fast," Clay warned.

Clara thought it was nice of him to warn Alexis of the effects of the punch. He was right; it was powerful stuff.

"These aren't both for me." She set one down in front of him. "I am sorry, Clara. I could only carry two," she continued as she sat back down.

"Thank you, but I don't touch the punch. I learned that at my first Christmas party." Clay pushed it away.

Clara smiled, knowing that Clay didn't want Alexis's attention.

Once everyone settled in with their dessert and coffee, Santa entered. He walked through the crowd, winding around the tables and finally found his red throne. The overstuffed red chair with gold trim was at the front of the room where every partygoer could see Santa and he could see them. She watched him scan the room and, again, he noticed her. She was ready this time and gave a slight wave and nod as their eyes locked. Santa chuckled and winked and nodded back to her. Clara almost burst with excitement. She realized this experience had gone from weird to downright fun and something she looked forward to.

"There he is, your not-so-secret admirer," Clay leaned over and whispered into her ear.

Clara noticed Santa looking at them as Clay spoke and she giggled. "I know!"

Alexis was too busy sipping her second glass of holiday punch to notice the exchange. Clara had a fleeting worry about Alexis and the punch, but put it aside. *She is an adult and Clay warned her. The headache tomorrow will be her own fault*, Clara rationalized.

Santa invited the guests to find their seats for a game of Christmas movie trivia. Clara and Clay found their bingo cards and stamps while the waitstaff cleared the plates. Clara noticed Alexis had hers out too and seemed ready to win.

"I love bingo," Alexis slurred loudly.

Clara winced. The effects of that Christmas punch were showing.

"This is Christmas movie bingo, with a twist. On your bingo card, you'll notice the titles of several movies. I'll draw a title from this bag and call it out. The twist is, it's an alternate title. You will need to mark your card with the actual title it represents. To have bingo, you'll need to have the correct titles in a row—up, down, or across. Good luck!"

Clara was excited. She knew all the Christmas movies and was sure this was the time to put that knowledge to good use.

Clay smiled. "I don't know why anyone else is bothering to play."

Santa's gloved hand pulled out the first title, and he called out, "*Gussy Up the Vestibule*." There was a moment of silence, and Clara could almost hear the wheels turning in everyone's brain. In a flash, she recognized *Deck the Halls* and marked it on her card.

"The next title is *To Subsist in an Awe-Inspiring Vivacity*!"

Clara looked around the room and noticed only a few were marking their cards. She thought for a minute and stamped the box marked *It's a Wonderful Life*.

"Two for two," Clay said. "Let me see your card."

"No way! Think about the words. They are synonyms."

Clay sat back and thought a minute, grinned and then marked a box.

"What did you mark?" Clara asked.

"You'll just have to wait and see, won't you?" Clay laughed.

"Everyone ready?" Santa paused and then read, "*Expire Solidly*."

"Finally, an easy one," Clay said as he marked his card.

Looking around, Clara noticed several people nodding and smiling as they recognized it was *Die Hard*.

"I don't know if that's really a Christmas movie," Clara said as she marked her card.

"Wait," Alexis yelled. "*Die Hard* isn't a Christmas movie."

Clara leaned over to Clay. "Finally, something we have in common."

It was clear that Clay tried to ignore Alexis. She was on her third glass of the punch.

"Okay, everyone ready? The next clue is *One Anecdote of Noel.*"

Easy, thought Clara as she marked *A Christmas Story*.

She looked around and saw the guests at the table decorated with a leg lamp, as they figured out the clue. There were a few shouts of "Yes!" This was fun. Clara couldn't wait for the next clue.

"The next title is *Nativity Alongside the Turning Device.*"

Clara hesitated, mentally flipping through the movie titles she knew. Timidly, she marked *Christmas With The Kranks*. She wasn't the only one unsure. There weren't any confident exclamations.

"Next title," Santa boomed from his red throne. "*That One Pessimist Purloining Advent.*"

Clay marked his card first this time and with a great flourish said, "I know this one for sure!" Laughing, he hid his card from Clara as she tried to get a peek. "All of those hours of studying SAT vocabulary tests finally came in handy. This is the first time I've heard the word purloin in twenty years!"

Clara laughed as she thought about the title. *Aha*, she thought, and marked *The Grinch Who Stole Christmas*.

Clay was still relishing his success when Santa read out the next title.

"*Stipulation of Kris Kringle!*"

Clara thought this was a giveaway clue. She was right; it seemed most guests knew it was *The Santa Clause*.

Alexis whined this was too hard and Christmas parties should be fun, not like school. Clara wondered how she got through school. She looked at Clay and rolled her eyes.

Ever the gentleman, Clay leaned in close and said, "Give her a break. She'll be miserable tomorrow."

It troubled her he would defend this woman who was obviously so rude to her. She had little time to dwell on this because Santa was ready with the next title.

"*Supernatural Occurrence Covering Fifty-Six Minus Twenty-Two Pavement-Covered Trail.*"

"Wow, that's a lot of words. What did he say?" Alexis asked Clay.

Santa, like everyone else, heard her question and repeated the clue.

Clara knew right away it was *Miracle on 34th Street* and marked the box. She was one away from bingo and wondered who else was close.

Alexis was overtly trying to get closer to Clay. Clara couldn't tell whether it was because she was having trouble sitting up straight or because she wasn't able to control her inhibitions. Clara couldn't understand why Clay didn't move to the other side of her or do something. This was ridiculous. Clay looked at her and shrugged, as if he were uncertain what to do when an attractive, inebriated woman was practically throwing herself at him.

"Next clue," Santa bellowed. "*Winter Solstice Canticle.*"

Clara thought, still distracted by the scene happening in the two chairs next to her. It surprised her the answer didn't come immediately. She looked at the remaining boxes on her card and inspiration struck. She marked *A Christmas Carol.*

In the meantime, Clay was still trying to get Alexis to quiet down and play the game.

Clara thought about intervening, but was unsure what she could do to help. Clara couldn't believe a professional woman would behave in such a way. It was embarrassing.

Clara had little time to think about helping Clay with a solution as Santa called out the next title: "*Alabaster Yuletide!*"

Clara looked at her card, marked *White Christmas,* and shouted, "BINGO!"

The outburst drew Alexis's attention from Clay to Clara, and she slurred, "Of course you have bingo!"

"Good job," Santa said. "Read your card and we'll see how well you know your Christmas movie titles."

Clara read, *"White Christmas, Miracle on 34th Street, A Christmas Carol, Die Hard,* and *A Christmas Story!"*

"We have a winner," Santa exclaimed and smiled broadly at Clara. "Let me look in my bag to see what you've won. Come on up here, young lady, and claim your prize."

Clara looked down at Clay.

He smiled and laughed and waved her to the front. "Go on, let's see what you won," he said.

She looked down at his card and noticed it was mostly blank and was angry Alexis had diverted his attention.

She smiled back and made her way to the front. Standing next to Santa, she waited for her prize as he rummaged around in his bag. He withdrew a bunch of dried mistletoe wrapped in red and green ribbon at the base and embellished with glitter and tiny Christmas bells. Handing it to her, Santa quietly said, "I think this is quite fitting, don't you," and winked as he nodded toward Clay.

The crowd burst into applause, and Clara made her way back to her seat. She wasn't one for public displays of affection, but she was tired of Alexis's behavior, so she held the mistletoe overhead. Clay looked around quickly and leaned over to give Clara a quick kiss on the cheek. As everyone applauded, Alexis grinned at her. This wasn't what Clara expected. She thought for sure that Clay would kiss her, really kiss her, like a person on a date, not like a person caught on the kiss cam at a ball game. *Maybe she had mistaken the last few weeks.*

Santa announced, "This concludes the bingo game. Enjoy the rest of your evening."

The serving staff were removing some tables for a makeshift dance floor. She knew Clay wasn't much of a dancer, so she excused herself to go to the restroom. Trying to be helpful, she asked Alexis whether she wanted to go as well. Maybe that would give Clay a minute of peace.

Alexis looked at her. "No, you go ahead. I don't need to."

Clara looked at Clay and shrugged. She would bring coffee for Alexis. Maybe it would help sober her up.

Clara laid the mistletoe on the table along with her purse, and set off across the party to the restroom. She glanced back once and noticed that Clay and Alexis were both laughing. It irritated Clara, wondering what they found funny as she rounded the corner in search of the ladies' room.

People stopped and congratulated her on her big win. Those who worked for the firm also complimented her on her designs. She had worked for them for years, so they knew her. She was gracious and thanked them, saying that she looked forward to next year.

Drying her hands and making a quick check of her hair and makeup, she left the mirror in the restroom, satisfied everything was still in place. In the hallway, she could still hear the party in full swing. With the dance floor in place, the music was louder. Clay's reaction to the mistletoe still confused her. Maybe it was too much for him at a party with colleagues. Perhaps she shouldn't have put him in that situation, she considered. Besides, he had enough to deal with, with Alexis's pawing all over him.

She decided Clay didn't intentionally do anything to hurt or confuse her and settled on remembering how he had been acting the last couple of weeks. Clara decided the cheek kiss wasn't a reflection on how he felt about her. He was just being a gentleman. She was filled with warm thoughts of Clay and their new romance.

She walked back into the party and couldn't believe what she saw. Clay was on the dance floor with Alexis, his back to the door.

In her left hand, Alexis held Clara's mistletoe. A second later, Alexis looked directly at her over Clay's shoulder, held the mistletoe over his head, and kissed him full on the mouth. Clara stopped, feeling as if someone knocked the wind from her lungs. Her heart beat so fast that she thought it might explode. The kiss seemed to last a really long time and Clara stood there, unable to move.

Then she was furious. *How can he just stand there and kiss her*, Clara thought as she stormed through the party to her table. Hastily grabbing her things, she fled the party before she cried. It was humiliating. She didn't have her car; she came to the party with Clay. Unsure what to do, she went out the front door, thankful for the local bars and restaurants in the downtown area. There were cabs at the ready for those who'd had too much to drink to drive home safely. Getting into the back of the first cab, she could barely say her address before bursting into tears.

Just blocks from the party, her phone rang, and she declined the call. Then the messages came in. Clay panicked and wanted her to call him back. *Not soon*, she thought as she rode across town with rivers of black mascara running down her cheeks.

Home, she headed straight to her bedroom and pulled out her warmest and fuzziest pajamas. Enveloped in soothing softness, she washed the black streams of mascara from her face. Her red patchy cheeks were evidence tonight hadn't gone the way she imagined.

Walking to her bed, she scooped up Mistletoe. She needed something to snuggle and for once Mistletoe obliged. Her phone buzzed on the nightstand. Clara looked over, and it was another call from Clay. No doubt this upset him, but she wasn't interested in hearing what he had to say. She would deal with it tomorrow. She was too emotionally and physically exhausted. He'd have to wait until she felt like talking. Clay was the one who did something wrong.

Why can't my life be like a Christmas movie, she thought, drifting off to sleep.

The sun had happily shone for several hours before Clara woke up and dragged herself out from under the layers of warm blankets. She never slept this late, but last night had been brutal and her last party of the season was tonight. It was at the mall and was the most-low key of them all. It wouldn't require getting dressed up. Most people were coming from their shifts at different shops, and the ones who were off usually wore jeans and a festive sweater.

Her chest tightened and tears threatened to roll down her cheeks as the events of last night played through her head like a scene from a movie. She still hurt and couldn't believe what happened. Things were so perfect. Now she was out a good friend too. This was exactly why she didn't want to get involved romantically in the first place.

Drinking a few sips of coffee, Clara glanced at her phone.

Twelve messages from Clay. Against her better judgment, she played them, to see what he had to say for himself.

"Clara, where'd you go? Call me."

"Clara, it's not what you think. Please call me back."

"Clara, I ran out to catch you, but you were driving off in a cab and didn't see me. Please call me. I'm worried."

"Clara, please, call me back. I need to tell you what happened."

"Clara, I know it upset you. I really, really need to talk to you. Please, call me back when you get this."

"Clara, this is the last message I am leaving tonight. Please call me when you wake up. I really need to tell you what happened."

"Good morning. It's me, Clay. I didn't sleep at all last night. Please call me. I need to tell you what happened so you will understand. It wasn't what you think."

"Clara, please call me. I can't stand not being able to fix this."

The others were basically the same message over and over. Finally, the last message was, "Clara, since you won't return my calls, it's clear you don't want to talk. Please go outside. I put something on your doorstep and I'm really, really sorry about what happened. I won't keep bothering you because you need some space. But I hope you'll let me explain. Christmas is in two days and I really want to spend it with you and my family. The invitation is still open. Please come. I don't want you to be alone on Christmas. Please call me so we can work this out."

Intrigued, she crossed the room, with Mistletoe following closely behind. Not wanting to find Clay standing outside, she looked through the peephole first. Unless he was lying flat on the ground, she was confident he wasn't there. Slowly, opening the door, she recognized the Cool Beans logo right away. There on the doorstep was a bag from her favorite coffee shop filled with her favorite pastries and an insulated cup of her favorite drink. At the bottom of the bag, she found a letter in Clay's handwriting.

Inside, she grabbed a plate and napkin and settled on the sofa. It was peaceful in her condo, and she was thankful for the coffee. She had just finished her first cup. The coffee Clay left for her was still warm.

"That was thoughtful, at least," Clara said out loud to Mistletoe.

Her plate filled with pastries, Clara licked her fingers and wiped them on the napkin before picking up the letter. She wasn't sure she wanted to read it, but she hated all the tension between them. Even if they wouldn't be a couple, she needed her friend, and he'd never given her a reason to think he would intentionally hurt her.

With a deep, shaky breath, she slid her finger under the seal of the envelope. Clara recognized his handwriting and wondered how many times he had written it to get it the way he wanted before leaving it for her.

Dear Clara,

I am so sorry about what happened last night at the party. I would never hurt you. Please believe me. We have known each other a long time, and I believe I've shown myself to be a loyal friend who wouldn't do anything to put our relationship in jeopardy.

I know what you saw, and what you think it means. Several people told me what it looked like from your perspective. That must have been awful, and I wonder if I would have reacted the same way if the roles were reversed. Let me tell you what actually happened, in its entirety, and then you can decide how you want to proceed. I hope this makes sense.

After you left to use the restroom, I was trying to manage Alexis. That was a mistake. She had had too much of the holiday punch and I was trying to protect her from making an embarrassing scene since she is a professional. I didn't want her reputation damaged because she couldn't hold her punch. I see now that was a terrible mistake.

She kept wanting to dance and was getting louder and more belligerent about it. At one point, she went to the dance floor and started dancing with a man known for being overly friendly with the women. The women at work avoid him because of his reputation. I didn't want Alexis to do something she would regret, so I stepped in. She had taken your prize, and I knew it would irritate you. I thought I could rescue her from Jeff, get your prize back, and have everything under control. Unfortunately, that's not what you saw.

Once I got her unwrapped from him, she basically fell onto me. I wasn't dancing with her—I was supporting her weight so she wouldn't fall on the floor. With my back to you, I can see it looked like we were dancing. Before I knew what was happening, she was kissing me. As quickly and safely as I could, I pushed her off. She may have had too much of the holiday punch, but I hadn't had a drop and didn't want to kiss anyone but you. When I got back to my seat and saw you left, my heart dropped, knowing you must have seen something awful. A few friends explained that you left upset and in a hurry. I ran out, but you were already in a cab, pulling away from the curb, and didn't hear me shouting for you, or if you did, you didn't turn around.

I have a lot of regrets from last night. Now that you know what really happened, I hope you believe I wanted nothing to do with that woman. I wish I had kissed you properly under the mistletoe and left early. Perhaps none of this would have ever happened and we would still be as happy as we were this time yesterday.

Please forgive me and please call me. I want to fix this before Christmas. I'll wait for your call.

Love,

Clay

Smiling, Clara *could* see Clay trying to be a gentleman and keep someone else out of harm's way. That was part of what she loved about him. But it still bothered her, and she wasn't ready to talk about it. It felt like such a betrayal. She needed some time to sort out her feelings and determine what she wanted to do next.

The shrill ring of her phone broke into her thoughts. It was Sophie.

"Hey, what happened last night? I woke up to several messages from 'Perfect Clay' asking me to call him because you won't return his calls? He sounded really frantic."

"I wish you were here. It was a terrible night." The story tumbled out of Clara, and Sophie was quiet on the other end, letting her friend vent and cry about the events of the night before.

"I'm so, so sorry that happened." Sophie's soothing tone was comforting. "But you know Clay, and he wouldn't do anything like that on purpose."

"I know, but it doesn't matter. It was so humiliating. This is also a work function that I left abruptly. I should have never even thought about a relationship like this with him. Now everyone knows what happened. I don't even know if I can take that account next year and it was my first huge one," Clara wailed again, thinking not only was Christmas ruined, but now her business was too.

"I think you need to calm down. Take a deep breath." Sophie hesitated. There was a jagged breath on the other end of the call. "Now, let's look at the evidence. You weren't the one who misbehaved. Alexis is the one who will wake up today embarrassed. She acted inappropriately in front of business colleagues. Alexis is the one who has some explaining and apologizing to do, not you. From the letter, it sounds like Clay's coworkers filled him in and had compassion for you for what you saw. No one is going to think anything bad about you because there isn't anything bad to think."

Clara considered what Sophie said. It made sense and helped calm her down.

"But what about Clay? I tried to tell him before that she was into him, and he blew it off. Then he seemed to worry more about her than me and how I felt about the situation."

"You have been the happiest I have ever known you to be over the last few weeks. It would be a shame to end that over this. You know how Clay tries to take care of everyone. That is what he was trying to do, and it just got out of control. I think he is really sorry and wants to fix things."

Clara knew her friend was right, but she wasn't ready to talk to him yet.

"Are you still going to his house for Christmas?" Sophie asked.

"I don't know. I was definitely going to, but now I think it might be too awkward and I don't want his family celebration to be filled with tension," Clara explained.

"I think if you don't resolve this and go, Clay will be miserable, which will make it a sad and horrible Christmas for his family too."

Clara heard a click on the phone and Sophie said, "Hey, it's Clay. I'm going to take it. What do you want me to tell him?"

"Tell him I made it home safely last night and thank him for the coffee. I'll call him later. Right now, I need space."

"Okay. Keep your chin up. Put on a Christmas movie and relax. Tonight's your last party, right?"

"Yes," Clara answered.

They said goodbye and promised to talk later.

The rest of the day was quiet. Clara tidied up her condo and did some chores she had put off for the last few weeks because she had been spending so much time with Clay. She took a leisurely walk around her neighborhood, read for a while before taking a nap, and ate the last of the Christmas cookies she made with Clay before getting ready for the party.

She wasn't as excited about this party as she had been in years past. She knew she would see Sam and Maria, and hoped of course that Santa would make another appearance. *At least he always seemed happy to see her.*

After a steamy shower, she put her hair in a wavy ponytail that fell over her shoulder. She put on mascara and a bit of lip gloss. Her face was puffy and red from all the crying, so she didn't add any blush. Pulling on her favorite jeans and boots, she needed to decide on a sweater. Swiping the hangers to the right to get a better look at her options, she saw the ugly Christmas sweater she wore on her day-long date with Clay. Fresh emotion swept over her, and she pushed it aside. She needed something that made her feel festive for tonight. Settling on a green sweater with a red and green plaid flannel underneath, she gave herself one last look before heading into the party.

Walking in the mall after closing was always strange. Most people only experience it with all the hustle and bustle of the crowds and open stores. It was different when stores were closed, with gates down and locked.

Clara found the crowd around the Santa display. The restaurants in the food court handled the food every year. Tables were full of the most-ordered menu items from each establishment. Because no one was technically working tonight, everyone was free to serve themselves. There were desserts from the food court as well on the other side. Everything looked delicious. It was too bad that Clara was too upset to eat.

Clara found Sam and Maria, and they caught her up about their plans. The boys would be in the next day for Christmas Eve. They planned to go to church and have a family dinner after. Maria invited Clara, but she explained her plans were still up in the air.

"Sam tells me you have a young man." Maria's eyes twinkled.

"I am not sure about that now," Clara said.

"Why, what happened?" Maria looked concerned.

Clara told them about the party. She explained she didn't know what to do.

"Look, why do you love Christmas movies so much?" Sam asked.

"Because they're magical. Everything always works out in the end," Clara replied.

"Well, things in the actual world have a way of working out too, you know," he teased.

"I don't know. I'm not feeling good about the whole thing. It bothers me he's so upset and I could make it better, but I just can't get that scene out of my head."

"Well, try. He's perfect for you. Don't wait too long to fix this," Sam said.

The party continued, with games and food and visiting. Everyone sat with Santa for a picture and told him what they wanted for Christmas. After the gift exchange, Clara was at the dessert table when Santa walked up next to her.

"Clara, isn't it?" Santa asked.

"Yes, and you are?" she asked.

"Santa Claus." He smiled.

"Well, it's so nice to meet you, Santa Claus."

"I've seen you at several parties this season," Santa said, filling his plate.

"Yes, I noticed you too. This must be a very busy season for you. You look like the real thing." She turned, loading up her plate full of cookies.

"That's because I am the real thing, as you say."

Clara studied him, wondering whether he was getting paid tonight to stay in character. There had never been a Santa at previous mall parties.

"Tonight, everyone came and sat with me for a picture and a request. Well, everyone except you. So, what would you like for Christmas this year?" Santa looked deep into her eyes and smiled.

"You know what," Clara said, exasperated. "I want my life to be like a Christmas movie."

"That is a big request, but I'll see what I can do. Merry Christmas, Clara." He patted her on the back.

"Merry Christmas, Santa." She turned to walk back to her seat.

She thought about everything that happened as she got ready for bed. She checked her phone and as he said, there were no new messages from Clay. Just messages from Sophie, her mom, and sister. She decided she would call them the next day. She chose *Miracle on 34th Street* to watch until she fell asleep. Hopefully, tomorrow would be a better day. It had to be.

Chapter 15

L ight streamed into her bedroom, over the Christmas tree lot decor, and onto her bed. Clara opened her eyes. Stretching, she felt light, almost happy throwing off the covers and beginning her morning. She stepped out of her room and stopped. Something was different. There were more decorations than she remembered. Some she had never seen before.

Slowly moving to the kitchen, she wondered whether Clay had come in and done this. Dismissing the thought, she remembered they weren't speaking. Or rather, she wasn't speaking to him. Opening the cabinet, she noticed her regular coffee wasn't there. Instead, Clara found Christmas-flavored coffee, spiced cider, and homemade hot cocoa mix. She couldn't remember buying any of these things. She chose candy cane-flavored coffee and started her morning coffee ritual.

Coffee steaming in hand, Clara sat in her usual spot on the sofa, to wait for the caffeine to do its trick. The TV came to life and played a Christmas movie. *That's nice.*

Settled under a thick, cozy blanket, she jumped when her phone played "Holly Jolly Christmas" and vibrated in her pajama pocket. She forgot it was there. Clara answered after the third ring, surprised to hear her mother's voice on the other end of the phone.

"Clara, I'm so glad I caught you. Have you left your house yet?"

"No." Clara hesitated. "Why?"

"Don't tell me you scheduled yourself to work today. We told you a month ago to keep today clear." Something clearly irritated her mother.

"Um, I'm sorry, I don't have my calendar right here with me on the couch. Can you refresh my memory?"

"We're going to the Christmas tree farm today. Last year we saw the most beautiful Fraser fir. It was only six feet and not quite ready, but it should be perfect this year. We're leaving here at one o'clock. Don't be late."

"Okay. Um..." Confused, Clara asked, "Are you back in town?"

"Why wouldn't we be in town? Honestly, are you okay? You don't sound like yourself," Clara's mother said, concerned.

"I thought you and Dad left for your trip already. In fact, where will you put the tree? You already sold the house."

"Did you fall and hit your head? Why would we sell the house or be on a trip during Christmas?"

"It must've been a really weird dream. I'll get it sorted out. I need another cup of coffee." She didn't want her mother worried. She just needed to figure out what was going on.

Assuring her mother she would be there on time, Clara hung up and looked out the window. Snow blanketed the backyard. It hadn't snowed in this town in over fifty years. It was much too far south. She flipped through the channels to find a weather report and couldn't find any news. There was nothing but Christmas movies or Santa documentaries on every channel.

Excited about the prospect of playing in snow, she threw on jeans, a jacket, scarf, gloves, and boots and ran outside.

Confused, she stopped. This wasn't her street. Looking from left to right, she noticed independent houses, not condos. She stepped out into the front yard and turned to look at her condo. Only it wasn't a condo; it was a cute Victorian-style home decorated for Christmas, like something just out of a Christmas movie. She heard laughter and looked around for the source. The kids from next door were having a snowball fight with the kids across the street. She had never noticed children next door. Just as she was trying to sort this out in her mind, a rogue snowball hit her in the chest.

"Hey, Clara, come play with us," shouted a little boy with a navy-blue puffy jacket and a red scarf.

"I'm sorry, do I know you?" she asked the boy.

"Are you okay? You look a little weird," he answered.

Another snowball hit her on the shoulder. She turned and this time a girl, about twelve years old, shouted, "Come on, Clara. Be on our side!"

Clara looked at the children. She did not know who these people were and was thinking she had lost her mind when the third snowball was a direct hit to her face.

"Oops! I'm sorry, Clara. I didn't mean to hit you in the face. I know your rule—'the face is off-limits.'"

Clara bent down to gather a handful of snow and packed it tight. Laughing, she lobbed it across the driveway and right in to the chest of the first kid. The snowball fight began.

A mom appeared from a house decorated in a candy cane theme with a platter of hot cocoa and freshly baked cookies. They called a cease-fire immediately. Running toward the woman, the kids called out, "Hey, Clara, come get some."

"Yes, Clara, there's plenty and you look like you might need to warm up too," the woman called out to Clara.

How do these people know my name? She didn't want to be rude, but she was confused. Nothing seemed right. Not the changes in her house, the call with her mother, or this.

She accepted hot cocoa and a cookie from the neighbor's mom, and it was perfect. The cocoa was rich and no matter how long she sipped, it never got cold. These were the best chocolate chip cookies she had ever tasted. There was a chocolate chip in every bite. Her face must have given her away because she heard the mom say,

"My goodness, Clara, you act like you've never had a chocolate chip cookie before."

"I've had them before, but not like these. They are amazing!"

"Yes, you have." The woman laughed. "Just yesterday you had some while you were getting the decorations ready for the block party."

Clara didn't know what this woman was talking about. She racked her brain, trying to remember yesterday. All she could remember was being hurt and sad about Clay, getting ready, and going to the Christmas party at the mall.

"I am sorry, what about yesterday?" Clara inquired, sounding very confused.

"Yesterday, we were all outside decorating our yards for the big Christmas block party."

"Um, when is the party? I seem to have misplaced my calendar and without it, I don't know what I'm supposed to be doing." Clara hoped this explanation would cover for her obvious confusion.

"Every year, we have a big block party. You know that. My goodness, you were the one who started the tradition, Christmas Girl!"

"I am sorry, what did you call me?"

"Christmas Girl. You know, because of your shop."

"My what?"

"Your Christmas shop. Are you okay? You look like you might be ill, and frankly, you seem off today. Is everything all right? Maybe you should sit down. You look a little pale." The mom stepped toward her with her hand out as if to feel Clara's forehead.

Clara dodged the outstretched hand and responded, "Yes, I'm fine. I, um, didn't sleep well last night and had some weird dreams. I'll be fine. Thank you for asking."

With that, Clara excused herself.

"Why are you leaving so soon?" the kids said as they begged her to stay.

"Kids, leave her alone. She has to go to work. I am sure today's a busy day," the mom said. "You can play without her."

"But she makes the best snowballs and is the only grown-up who will play with us," the kids whined.

"You'll just have to make do without her," the mom scolded. Then, to Clara, she said, "I hope you aren't coming down with something," and reached out and felt Clara's forehead.

This time she caught Clara off guard and she didn't have time to move out of the way.

"You don't feel like you have a fever. Take care of yourself. No one should be sick at Christmas."

Clara thanked the woman for her concern and accepted one last cookie. She turned and walked through the crowd of children, toward her own front door. She needed to figure out what was happening and why everyone thought she owned a Christmas store. Although that sounded like a fun business and perhaps one she should consider.

Showered, she went to her closet to get dressed and ready for the day. Standing in her bathrobe, Clara opened the door to her closet and noticed everything was Christmas themed. All her sweaters were green, red, or some other Christmas color or design. Dresses were all green or red. She knew she had many Christmas sweaters, but this seemed excessive, even for her.

Getting dressed, Clara decided she would go to Cool Beans for coffee. Something familiar might do her good this morning. She had to admit it had been a pleasant morning. She got to play. Overnight snow transformed the neighborhood into a winter wonderland, and everything seemed perfect. *This must be some kind of really strange dream*, she thought as she drove to Cool Beans.

The radio came to life as she started her car. A soundtrack of Christmas music played as she pulled away from her house. The drive seemed shorter than usual, and someone decorated every business and light pole along her route. She hadn't noticed that yesterday. *Did the entire city suddenly get into Christmas overnight?* Maybe she had been too busy spending time with Clay to notice things around her. Sadness washed over her as she remembered the situation with Clay. She still wasn't sure what to do, but she was tired of being sad about it.

Her mood lifted as she pulled into the parking lot of Cool Beans. She continued to notice her good fortune when she found a parking place right next to the door. Walking in, all the baristas called out, "Merry Christmas, Clara. Your coffee is ready at the bar."

"How did you know what I was going to order?" she asked. Then, before they could respond: "And, how did you know I was coming just at this moment?"

"Because this is exactly when you come every day, and we always have your coffee ready for you," they answered, looking at each other, a bit confused.

"Are you all right? You seem a little off this morning," the head barista asked.

"Yes, I'm fine. I didn't sleep well last night. I'm fine, really. Thank you for having my coffee ready. I'm sure it is perfect," she said as she walked to the bar to retrieve it. "How much do I owe you?" She reached for her wallet.

"There's no charge. Your coffee is always on the house."

"Oh, well, here...put this in the tip jar then." She handed the young man a few bills.

"Thanks, and Merry Christmas," he called out as he folded the money and put it in the cookie jar marked Tips.

"Merry Christmas," she said as she walked through the shop and into the mall.

She wasn't sure why she was going into the mall. It just seemed like the thing to do. The mall was familiar. Clara recognized the decorations because she was the one who put them there. She was sure of this and walked leisurely, watching everyone as she sipped on her coffee. It was spectacular this morning. She would need to compliment the baristas the next time she was there and made a mental note to do so. As she tried to figure out her morning, she passed by the Santa display. There he was! The Santa from last night. As he transferred one child from his lap to the floor before the next one climbed onto his lap, Santa looked at her and smiled. She smiled back and gave a quick wave. Remembering her wish last night at the party, she thought this must be a dream. Some kind of sugar- and misery-induced dream about Christmas. *Well, it is better than a nightmare, so I might as well enjoy it*, Clara decided. Only, it wasn't a dream.

Clara walked with purpose and confidence as "Holly Jolly Christmas" played over the mall PA system. Clara, determined to have a holly jolly Christmas experience until she woke up, began saying hello to everyone she met along the way, being sure to point out mistletoe throughout the mall so that couples would stop and steal a kiss as they went about their Christmas shopping and people watching. She even noticed her never-ending cup of cheer wasn't cooling off. In fact, it was the perfect temperature all this time and no matter how much she drank, there was still coffee in her cup.

Clara giggled to herself as she continued down the concourse, listening to the music overhead. She didn't even think about where she was going until she stopped right in front of the Christmas Shoppe. Looking up at the sign and into the entrance, she thought, *This is where I work? This is amazing*!

She wasn't sure what to do next, when she heard a voice from behind: "Merry Christmas! Today is the big day!"

Clara turned and found a young woman on the bench behind her.

"Good morning," she said as she tried to figure out who this person was.

"Not Merry Christmas? Are you feeling all right?"

"Yes, I am fine. People have been asking me that all morning."

Rolling up the security gate, Clara and the woman let themselves in. This was unbelievable. There were at least a hundred trees, all decorated with different themes or in a different color. Tables with Christmas place settings, outside decor, options for mantels and banisters, and decor specific to kitchens and bathrooms held prominent places. Christmas music and movies played throughout, and there was a hot cocoa and spiced apple cider machine and a single-serve coffeemaker on a long counter that had a platter for fresh cookies on it. Next to them were disposable Santa cups and napkins for customers to use. It even smelled like Christmas. Cinnamon and spice smells mingled with pine and fir.

Clara smiled and she took it all in, wanting to remember every detail. This might be a new business venture for her.

She made herself another cup of coffee while the other woman busied herself with opening the store. Then Clara took the woman cocoa and two cookies. Setting them down on the counter, she snuck a look at the woman's name tag.

"Maggie, how was your night last night?"

"It was great," Maggie said, telling Clara all about it, in great detail.

Clara listened as Maggie told her about her family going to a Christmas benefit concert after they served dinner to the homeless and then looked at lights as they drove home. It sounded like a wonderful, but busy evening to Clara.

"What did you do last night?"

Clara struggled to remember. "Um, well, I went to the party and then home to watch a movie and go to sleep. Were you at the party last night?"

"What party?"

"The mall Christmas party."

Maggie gave her friend a sideways glance. "The mall Christmas party isn't until next week. Maybe you should have a seat. Are you okay?" Maggie was very concerned and watched Clara closely as she continued getting the cash register ready for the day.

"I feel wonderful. I guess maybe I dreamed I went to a party. What a weird night. I fell asleep watching a Christmas movie, so that must be it," Clara explained. Now she wasn't sure which was the dream and which was reality.

"By the way," Clara continued, "I have to leave early today. I have plans with my parents this afternoon."

"I know. You put it on the calendar in the office. And your mom called to make sure I'd remind you so you wouldn't hang around here longer than you needed to."

"Oh," Clara said, "That was thoughtful and intrusive." *And unusual.* Her parents were not the plan-for-Christmas type. That's what *she* did. All of this seemed strange.

The register ready for the day, Clara began tidying up and dusting the store. She rearranged displays, fluffed pillows in the seating areas, and made sure the refreshment bar was fully stocked.

Customers streamed in and her morning flew by as she helped people find last-minute gifts or decor to add to their homes before the big day. At one point, she glanced at a receipt and noticed that it wasn't Christmas Eve as she thought; it was December 15. *Had she really lost nine days?* This must be a dream or some kind of Christmas stress-induced breakdown.

At noon, she heard, "Coffee?" from behind her. Turning so fast she almost knocked the coffee from his hand, she faced Clay.

Laughing, he said, "Whoa, I didn't mean to startle you." He stretched out the hand with the coffee, offering it to her.

She took it suspiciously. "What're you doing here?"

Taken aback, he answered slowly, "You and your parents invited me to go with you to the Christmas tree farm. Remember? Last night I said I'd pick you up and we could go together? Are you okay?"

Clara wasn't sure how to respond to this. No, she was not okay. This was confusing, and she was still hurt about the party.

"No, I'm not okay. I'm still upset. Why are you acting like nothing happened the other night?" she demanded.

"What are you talking about?"

"At the party, Alexis and mistletoe? Are you really going to tell me nothing happened? That it was all in my imagination?"

Clay calmly walked toward her. "Clara, I really don't know what you're talking about. I don't even know anyone named Alexis. Are you okay? You don't seem like yourself."

Clara allowed him to lead her to a couch, where she told him all about the party. Now she wasn't sure herself about anything. She was having difficulty discerning reality from whatever was happening.

"That must've been an awful dream. In the last few months, neither of us has kissed anyone else. At least, I don't think you have," he teased. "I think maybe you are a little stressed out. Let's have a fun day with your parents. I know they have been looking forward to today."

Clara gathered her things and told Maggie she probably wouldn't be back until evening to close. Maggie shushed her and said that she could make sure the store was closed properly.

Clay and Clara walked through the mall and it felt nice, like it had before the awful party, and she wondered whether she had been too hard on him before. They settled back into their familiar routine, talking about work and the holiday. They even watched people as they walked. Nearing Santa, Clara wondered whether he would acknowledge her again. She slowed as they walked by the display and all the children lined up to see him and take pictures. Nothing. He didn't turn and look at her, wink, wave, or nod.

"Huh," Clara said as Clay talked.

"What?"

"Did you see Santa? For weeks, he has been winking and waving to me here at the mall and at the Christmas parties I have attended. And just now, nothing. Isn't that weird?"

Clay blew it off. "He looks busy. And since you aren't a paying customer, there's no reason for him to pay attention to you."

"Ouch," Clara teased.

"No, I mean, it's getting close to Christmas, and he looks really busy. Come on, we need to get going to make it to your parents' house on time."

The drive across town was like old times with Clay. He opened and closed her door for her, warmed her seat, and they talked as they listened to Christmas music over the radio. Happiness bubbled up inside her. Things were just like they had been, and she allowed herself to soften toward him. He really was a good guy, and she was thinking she was crazy for getting so upset at the party.

Arriving at her parents' house, they went to the door together. As they waited, Clay pointed to the mistletoe hanging on the light fixture and raised his eyebrows. Clara leaned over and gave him a quick peck on the cheek.

"What was that?" he asked. "Are you kissing your grandparents?"

She stepped toward him and kissed him properly just as the door opened and her parents stood there.

"Come on in. So far you two are the only ones who noticed the mistletoe. We don't have time for that now. Let's get everyone together."

"Kayla," her mom called up the stairs. "Your sister and Clay are here. We need to go!"

"Coming," answered Kayla as she bounded down the stairs. She was all smiles as she welcomed Clara and Clay.

"Ready to get the perfect tree?" Clara's dad asked, not really expecting an answer.

"Let's go," Clara and Kayla said in unison, and laughed.

Her dad locked the house and announced, "Everybody get in and buckle up," as he did every time they had left the house since Clara could remember. Parents sat in the front and Clara, Clay, and Kayla shared the backseat. Clara was in the middle. It was a tight squeeze, but she enjoyed spending time with everyone.

Finally, she thought, *I am not the one in charge of planning a Christmas activity.*

Her dad turned on the Christmas station, and they all sang along as they drove the hour toward the Christmas tree farm. Clay reached over and held Clara's hand. It was nice, she thought. Every once in a while, someone made a mistake in the lyrics and everyone laughed.

As they turned onto the long, winding dirt road that led from the highway to the Christmas tree farm, *Last Christmas* played on the radio and Kayla shouted, "Turn it up!" Clara and Kayla sang their hearts out as they commiserated with the singer about an unrequited love. Clay rolled his eyes and laughed. Their dad let the song play to the end before turning off the ignition and saying, "Everybody out!"

There was a fine dusting of snow on the ground and trees as they walked from the parking area toward the farm. She looked around, unfamiliar with this place. As far as she could remember, they always went to a local lot or used a huge artificial tree that was pre-lit. There was a festive energy in the air, and Christmas music came faintly from the speakers. Families milled about the food trucks and picnic areas, or dragged trees from the farm to their cars. Smaller children rode the Christmas train as they waited their turn to talk to Santa. This Santa wasn't sitting on a red chair, waiting for pictures. He was standing with a swinging red kettle and ringing a bell. As children came, he would bend down, hands on knees, and visit with them face-to-face. She heard his jolly laughter as he talked with children and wished them a Merry Christmas. The atmosphere was perfect, magical even, and she felt Clay squeeze her hand.

Her dad led the way through the rows and rows of trees. The smaller trees were in the front and they became progressively taller and fuller as they made their way to the back of the field. Areas blocked off in red were not for purchase; they were too small. The trees in the green area were ready to be cut down.

"How about this one?" Clara stopped in front of a large Douglas fir.

"No, not tall enough," Kayla said. "What about that one over there?" Kayla pointed to a taller tree. This one, a Fraser fir, was fuller and six inches taller.

"No, that one is lopsided," her dad said, inspecting the base. "Keep walking."

They separated into two groups, each in search of the perfect tree. Her parents walked in one direction and Clara, Clay, and Kayla in another. Each group could hear the other as they debated whether the tree was the right one for the living room. After half an hour of searching, they all arrived at the tree at the same time. They were drawn to it, as a beam of light came down directly on the tree. The sunlight glistened as it fell on the snow still on the branches. This was their perfect tree.

As they waited, her dad went to get a saw and came back with an employee. The young man took the tag from the tree and wrote the family's name on it. Shoving it in his back pocket, he got to work cutting down their perfect tree. When it was down, Clay, her dad, and the young man wrapped and dragged it to the area where it would go through a machine to have the loose needles shaken out, netted, and purchased. There was a long line in front of them, so the young man put the tag with their name on the tree and told them to walk around and enjoy themselves, explaining it looked like an hour's wait before their tree would be ready to go.

There was plenty to do at the tree farm. There were hayrides, a maze built out of hedges and trees, more food trucks, a shed turned into a Christmas shop, and premium people watching.

Clara and Clay walked toward the maze and waited their turn to find their way through. The teenage girl, named Holly, offered them a map. "Just in case you get lost," she explained.

"How hard can it be?" Clay asked.

"We have many people who get turned around and we have to go in and help them find the exit. If you don't want the map, then at least take a bell to ring if you need help."

Reluctantly, they accepted the bell and walked through the entrance. The hedges were high and punctuated with holly bushes planted in raised beds, or large displays of very full red and white poinsettias. They anchored each corner with an eight-foot tree decorated with lights and glass balls of all shapes and colors. There were clear bulbs strewn above the path and with the daylight fading, the effect was beautiful. Clara and Clay walked together, sipping on cider and turning left, then right at each intersection until they came to a dead end and had to backtrack and try again in another direction.

The sound of laughter and Christmas music floated all around them as they joined in. *This is fun*, Clara thought as she relaxed and enjoyed the scene. She was here with Clay, her parents seemed to enjoy themselves, and even her sister wasn't complaining. *This is how Christmas should be.* After some time, they still weren't out of the maze.

"How long have we been walking?" Clara asked Clay.

Glancing at his watch, he answered, "Looks like thirty minutes."

"I didn't think this would be difficult. It really seemed like Holly was exaggerating when she offered us the map and bell."

"Yeah." Clay chuckled. "Maybe we should have taken her up on it."

Just then, a group of children came running by.

"Are you stuck?" they asked as they came to a sudden halt.

"Well, kind of," said Clara. "We aren't sure which way to go."

"Follow us," the leader of the little group said. "We have been rescuing people all afternoon."

"Oh, I think rescue is a bit of a strong word," Clay said as the kid stood in front of him.

"Really? Well, I see you both have large cups of cider in your hands. How much do you have left in your cup?"

Obediently, they removed the lids and peered in. Showing each other their cups, they realized they only had a few swallows left in the bottom of each paper cup.

"Just a little left, right? How long have you been in here?" the kid asked.

"Thirty minutes," Clay answered.

"In that time, have you seen one bathroom, or port-a-potty?" the kid demanded.

"Well, no, we haven't," Clara said timidly, a little afraid of this kid.

"Then, in a few minutes, you will need a rescue because you won't be able to hold all of that liquid. Just follow us." And with that, the leader waved to his group to come out in front with him and they walked, turning left at the first intersection they came to.

"See, this is where you went wrong. You turned right at the first turn," the leader explained as they rounded a corner. With each turn, the kid showed them their error.

From behind, Clay and Clara looked at each other, rolling their eyes. Neither appreciated being instructed by children. They followed anyway and found out the kids had been doing this maze year after year. Evidently, they were all cousins and came every year as a family. While their parents drank cider and cocoa, the kids wandered the maze. One of them explained they knew it so well, they'd tried it blindfolded, just to make it more challenging.

"How did that turn out?" Clay asked.

"That was a struggle. We finally had to choose someone to remove theirs and lead us through. We kept bumping into each other and the hedges. But it was fun!"

"Sounds like it," Clara said as they walked.

"Just one more turn and you'll be at the exit," the leader said.

When the opening came into view, they thanked the group and Clay handed the leader a ten-dollar bill.

"Thank you for rescuing us. Take this and get yourselves a snack. You deserve it for all of your efforts today."

The kids beamed and ran off toward the food trucks with their newfound wealth.

Clara and Clay watched them as they ran off. "That was nice of you," Clara said.

"It was the least I could do. They rescued us from the agony of having to finish that maze while we needed to find a restroom. And, now, I really need to find one. That kid was right."

They walked across the field that held the other attractions and found a restroom. Clay was waiting when Clara came out.

"Are you hungry?"

"Starving. Let's get a funnel cake and people watch," she answered.

Clay took her hand, and they walked to the nearest food truck. They ordered the extra-large funnel cake and two coffees and found a picnic table with prime people watching placement. Sitting with the plate between them, they watched as they ate, licking the extra powdered sugar from their fingers.

"Look at that family." Clay nodded in the general direction and she turned to see what he was pointing out. "They are not having a fun time."

She watched as the family melted down. Two young children both cried, seemingly for different reasons, as their parents tried to comfort them and no doubt salvage what they thought would be a fun time. One child had stumbled and fallen. The other was crashing from all the sugar in the hot cocoa and funnel cakes. Both kids had dirty and sticky hands and faces. Clara wondered how much longer the family had to wait for their tree.

Clara noticed another couple sitting a few tables away and nodded toward them. "What do you think is going on over there?"

"Hmm, it looks like they might be on a date, kind of early in their relationship."

"What makes you think that?" Clara asked.

"Well, for one, look how they are sitting. Close, but not too close. They like being with each other, but haven't spent enough time together to feel comfortable. Plus, there's a hardly eaten funnel cake between them, probably getting cold because they realized how messy it is to eat a funnel cake in front of someone."

They laughed as they looked down at their paper plate dotted with grease spots and clumps of powdered sugar.

"Not the case for us." Clara picked up a bit of powdered sugar and kicked it right off her finger.

"Nope," Clay agreed, smiling. Clay stood. "Let's see if your tree is getting close. I don't see your parents anywhere and your dad might need some help to get it tied onto the car."

Clara stood and stretched. "Okay. I'll catch up with you in a minute. I am going to put some money in the red kettle."

"Okay. See you in a few minutes," Clay said as he cleared their trash and headed for the checkout station.

She approached the bell ringer. Something seemed familiar about the man dressed as Santa. She knew him from somewhere. Shaking it off, she watched as others approached him—little kids sure he was the real thing telling him what they wanted for Christmas and adults making small talk as they dropped bills and change into the red kettle.

When it was her turn to approach, he looked right at her and continued to ring his bell. "I wondered when you would come over," he said without skipping a beat.

"What do you mean?" she asked. "Were you watching me?"

"You don't recognize me, do you?"

"Should I?"

"Think back to all the parties this season. Remember the last one, the one where you made a wish? You wanted your life to be a Christmas movie?"

In a flash, she knew this was Santa. The Santa she had seen all season at all the parties and the mall. Her eyes grew wide with excitement as she made the connection.

"Yes, I remember you! Every time I'd see you, you'd wink and wave. Sometimes you were the only person who acknowledged me. What are you doing here? And why didn't you wave at me this morning at the mall?"

"I was busy this morning at the mall. You know, the rush leading up to Christmas. Anyway, is this what you expected?"

"My day has been a little strange, but great! Why do you ask?"

"Well, I wanted to know if this is what you thought living in a Christmas movie would be like."

"What do you mean, 'living in a Christmas movie'?" she asked.

"Last night, you were so sad. It was quite pathetic. I believe heartbroken is not too strong a description. Anyway, I felt sorry for you, so I asked what you wanted for Christmas. You said you wished your life was like a Christmas movie, so here we are." He gestured to the surrounding space. "It's what you wanted, right? For everything to be Christmas and beautiful all the time?"

"Are you serious? No one can live like a Christmas movie."

"Well, you have been for about twelve hours now. Think about it. The snow that isn't freezing, the perfect drink every time. Your family is perfect, things are perfect with Clay, you have the perfect job, constant Christmas music, a ray of light beaming on the right tree at the right moment. Now you tell me, doesn't this feel like a Christmas movie to you?"

Clara thought about this for a moment and a gigantic smile plastered her face. "Yes! This is perfect. Exactly how I wish my life would be. Thank you."

"Now, wait. Before you get too excited, there are some things you should know." Santa's expression was serious. "It seems like fun now, but you really don't want to stay here. This is fantasy. In fact, it's someone else's fantasy of Christmas. That's what a Christmas movie is—someone else's story to keep you entertained."

Clara interrupted, "It seems good to me!" She couldn't believe her good fortune, excited for all the experiences to come.

"Listen, I'm serious. This isn't just a wish granted. You must take this time to reflect on your life. You live in a perpetual state of trying to make everything perfect around you, and it's causing you a lot of stress. In fact, trying to live up to your expectations of Christmas is what's making the magic of Christmas slip away from you, and you know it. That prompted the wish. Isn't it? Lots of unmet expectations." Santa looked at her with a very serious expression.

"Think about every Christmas movie you love. Pay attention to the story you are in and you'll learn an important lesson. I'll check in with you periodically to monitor your progress. Do you understand?"

"I understand everything is perfect and I never want to go back," Clara exclaimed.

"Consider that carefully before you wish this permanent. See you later. And remember what I said. There's something you must figure out or there will be consequences."

And with that, Santa disappeared. Santa, the red kettle, bell and all. Poof.

Clara looked around, confused, and noticed Clay waving her over. Walking toward Clay, she watched the people milling about for signs they had seen Santa vanish, but no one seemed to think anything was amiss.

Santa made my wish come true. "And I am going to make the best of it," she whispered to herself as she walked across the square to join Clay in her perfect Christmas movie life.

Chapter 16

C lara and Clay joined everyone in setting up and decorating the tree. Boxes of ornaments and lights lined the walls and entryway, almost floor to ceiling. Clara had never seen so many boxes of Christmas tree decorations in her parents' house before and wondered where they came from. There were smells of gingerbread and cocoa mingling with the fir. And she could swear that there was a faint Christmas refrain in the background as they opened and sorted through the boxes. The tree steady in the stand, they worked to hang what seemed like hundreds of strands of twinkling lights beginning near the tree's trunk and working each strand farther and farther out to the ends. The effect was breathtaking.

The conversation was lively, and Clara found it difficult to break in and say anything. *Since when do they suddenly have opinions about Christmas?*

The group laughed and swapped stories and memories about each ornament that was placed on the tree. Clara noticed Clay watching her as she joined in with her family, reminiscing about Christmases past or the significance of each ornament. Her face lit up when she saw ornaments from her childhood.

"Decorating the tree is like going from memory to memory for you, isn't it?" Clay asked, nudging her. "It is amazing that you never tire of it, even though you surround yourself with Christmas every day of the year."

"Well, not every day of the year. I take a vacation now and then," she said.

"Yes, but you are always thinking about it, planning for it, shopping for it," Clay answered. "I think it is great that you love it so much," he continued.

"Thank you," she said. "Not everyone appreciates what I do."

Hours passed since Clara and Clay arrived at her parents' house that day to begin the tree extravaganza. She was tired and content when her mom put the topper on the tree. Kayla turned the overhead lights off and they stood in wonder, looking at the perfect tree.

"Who's hungry?" Her mother broke the silence. "We never ate dinner. I can throw something together if everyone wants to eat."

Clay glanced at his watch and announced, "It's getting late. I really need to go, but thank you for the offer."

Clara went to collect their coats, saying, "Thanks, Mom, but I rode with Clay so I'm going to head out too."

With hugs all around and promises to talk the next day, Clara and Clay left.

"Are you hungry? We can grab some takeout," Clay asked as they pulled out of the neighborhood into traffic.

"No. Actually, I am not hungry at all." Leaning back in her seat, she felt great. Tired but reflecting on this perfect day.

"Tired?"

"Yes. It's been quite a day," she answered over the Christmas music playing on the radio.

"Well, get plenty of rest. Tomorrow's a big day."

"Oh, really? What is going on tomorrow?"

"You don't remember? Your mom has been going on and on about it for weeks."

"I don't. I didn't sleep well last night and my calendar is at home. What is tomorrow?" she asked.

"Bell ringer day. Your mom signed you up. I'm pretty sure there are matching ugly sweaters involved, so get ready," Clay warned.

"That sounds like fun! Finally, someone else is scheduling things during this season."

Clay looked at her. "What do you mean? Since I've known you, your mom plans out December."

The way Clara remembered it, she did all the planning and cajoling. This was a welcome change. "I'm excited and can't wait to volunteer tomorrow."

"That's the answer I expected." Clay smiled.

Pulling into the mall parking lot, they parked next to her car.

"I'll follow you home to make sure you get there okay."

Clara thought that was so thoughtful of him and knew better than to argue. She opened the door and let herself out and got into her own car. Clay followed her back across town to her house. Parking behind her, it surprised her as he walked her to the door.

"You didn't have to get out of your car. You could have just watched to make sure I got in safely."

"No way! I couldn't do this from the car." He kissed her. "Good night, Clara. See you tomorrow."

He turned and walked back to the car as she watched, thinking things were perfect. Everything in her life was the way it should be, just like in a Christmas movie.

Inside her cozy home, she showered and dressed for bed. She fed Mistletoe and felt content as the cat snuggled up next to her, purring softly. *Even Mistletoe is perfect*, Clara thought.

Snuggling under her covers, she replayed the day's events in her mind. Santa was right; she'd seen enough Christmas movies to know that, although magical things always happened, they were usually in a dream sequence. Sighing, she figured this was what this had been—a crazy dream—and tomorrow she would wake up and experience the emptiness of a Christmas without Clay, her family, or Sophie.

She settled on *It's a Wonderful Life* for tonight. *Well, that's appropriate*, she thought as she turned up the volume. Before drifting off to sleep, she watched Clarence helped George Bailey understand his life was perfect just the way it was.

Chapter 17

S he woke the next morning, certain the day before was a weird and wonderful dream. After a deep stretch and yawn, Clara decided it was time to face the day. Mistletoe purred, reminding Clara she was there, as she threw the covers to the other side of the bed. She reached over to uncover the cat, apologizing, and gave her a quick belly rub.

Going out into the living room, she noticed everything was as it was the day before. It was still her home, but better. She made coffee and settled onto the sofa before turning on the television. Again, Christmas movies on every channel. *This is perfect.*

Her phone buzzed next to her, and she noticed several messages from her parents. *Already? They are up early this morning.*

She listened to the messages. "Just wanted to make sure you were up already."

Next message: "Be sure to wear the red turtleneck. It's hanging in your closet next to your jeans."

Next message: "Wear comfortable shoes."

Next message: "Let me know you got these messages. I haven't heard from you since last night."

Clara punched in her mother's number. She answered before it rang.

"Well, good morning, sleepyhead! Did you get my messages? We'll meet at Cool Beans and get our assignments. Did you get coverage for the store? Remember, it was on the family Christmas calendar? We reviewed it on Thanksgiving to make sure everyone was clear on the schedule for this month."

Clara's mom went on and on, and Clara wondered whether this was what she sounded like to them every year.

"Yes, Mom, I'm sure there is someone to open the store for me. Remind me, what time are we supposed to meet at Cool Beans?"

"Eight thirty. And don't be late. They expect us to be in position before the mall opens for any employees who want to donate."

"Okay. Eight thirty it is. I will be there with bells on."

Clara heard her clock chime on the hour as it played "Jingle Bell Rock." She looked up and noticed it was eight o'clock. She leaped from her seat and dressed quickly. There wasn't much time. Fortunately, her clothes were exactly where her mom said. She put her hair in a ponytail that swung to the side and tumbled down her shoulder. No time for very much makeup, so she swiped sparkly gloss on her lips and one coat of mascara. She made a quick check of her reflection. "This will do," she said to herself as she bent to put on her most comfortable boots. Grabbing a scarf and gloves, she pulled on her jacket. On the way out the front door, she checked Mistletoe's food and water and left her a little extra. Today was going to be a long, but fun day.

As she approached the counter at Cool Beans, her mother called out, "Come sit down. We already ordered for you."

Clara walked to the table, draped her coat over the back of her chair, and sat. Waiting for her was a still steaming Americano, just the way she liked it.

"Thank you," she said, bringing her cup back to her lips for another sip. "How did you know what to order?"

"The guy at the counter said this is what you always order. Plus, we didn't want to wait for your order to go over our plan for the day."

Clara sipped on her coffee as her mom then explained the policies and procedures for bell ringing. *She is really into this.* It was nice she could relax and wasn't having to plan every activity for the

Christmas season. *This is how it should be. I shouldn't have to do everything.*

"Clara, did you hear what I just said?"

"Um, sorry, no."

"At the end of your shift, another bell ringer will relieve you. Leave everything with them. They will turn everything in at the end of the night. And, it should go without saying that you cannot, under any circumstance, leave your kettle unattended."

"Oh, what if you have to use the restroom?"

"Honestly, Clara. Haven't you been listening? You can't leave, so make sure you go before your shift begins. Once you accept that kettle, stay next to it."

"Okay, okay. I understand. Pee before I go, don't drink coffee while I stand there. Don't worry, it'll be fine," Clara said.

Her dad glanced at his watch, and his eyes narrowed. He forgot his reading glasses and stretched his wrist as far away as he could before announcing, "I think it says nine fifteen. What time do we meet the representative?"

"Nine twenty. We need to get going. Everyone, use the restroom and meet me at the main mall entrance. Here are your sweaters."

Clara accepted the sweater from her mom and was the first to unfold hers, revealing the festive design.

Laughing, she heard her sister say, "Where did you find these, Mom? I swear they get uglier every year."

They were spectacularly ugly this year. A red and green argyle pattern with blinking lights at each point. Across the front was a Christmas tree with presents along the bottom band. The top of the tree ended at the neck so that the wearer's head served as the tree topper. Clara turned the sweater to see what was on the back. A winking Santa face took up most of the space. Each year they wore matching sweaters for a family picture, but these sweaters were the tackiest yet.

"See why I told you which turtleneck to wear underneath? That way everything coordinates."

"Yes, very helpful," Clara agreed. "Let's get our kettles."

They arrived at the appointed spot and had a quick orientation that was pretty much everything her mother had explained over coffee earlier. Signing liability forms, they each accepted possession of their kettles and a schedule, including who would relieve them and what that procedure entailed. Before they separated, Clara's parents reminded the girls to meet at the end of their shift at the Santa display in the middle of the mall. They would take their annual family ugly sweater picture there.

Clara took her kettle and positioned herself at the mall entrance nearest the Christmas Shoppe. This way she thought she could give Maggie any last-minute instructions about the day and at least let them know where she would be should they need anything.

She didn't have her first contact until a little after nine thirty. Mall employees were showing up for their morning shifts, and many were excited to see her ringing the bell. It was fun to wish everyone a Merry Christmas and open doors for them as they made their way into the hustle and bustle of retail during the holidays.

There was a steady stream of people and as they walked by, almost all of them dropped money into the kettle. She knew it was better for the organization to get bills folded and shoved down the cross cut in the lid, but it was more satisfying to hear change clang to the bottom. She gave everyone a hearty "Merry Christmas!" and a candy cane. Almost everyone also responded with a "Merry Christmas" and a comment about her sweater.

Around nine forty-five, Maggie came by.

"Well, don't you look festive? Stopping by the Christmas Shoppe today?"

"I'm not sure. We signed up for a long shift and afterward I'm meeting my family for our annual ugly sweater Christmas picture. I'll try to stop by after that."

"Don't worry, I have it covered. Have a great day!"

"Thank you. You too. Oh, and Merry Christmas," Clara said, opening the door for Maggie as she stepped into the mall to begin her day.

That was the rhythm of the day: "Merry Christmas!", clang of change, open the door. Over and over, it went. People were cheerful as they walked by and laughed at her sweater, giving generously to charity. She wondered how the rest of her family were faring when she saw him.

Trevor walked toward her, squinting, like he wasn't sure whether he saw someone he recognized or not. As he got closer, he broke into a huge grin.

"Clara!"

"What are you doing in town?" she asked, shocked to see him.

"I came to spend Christmas with my parents. It's been a long time since I was home. It was time to give them a break from traveling and I needed a change of scenery, so here I am."

"That sounds nice, and very unlike you. I'm sure they're thrilled to spend time with you here."

"I see you are still mad. That was a really long time ago. Can't you just let it go?"

Trevor moved toward her when she started ringing the bell again.

A family dressed in matching sweaters commented on her sweater as they walked by. "Merry Christmas!" she called out as they dropped cash and coins into the slot on the lid of the red kettle.

Clara ignored Trevor's comment. She was still angry at how things ended between them years ago. He had a point; it had been a long time ago, and now she had Clay. Maybe he was right. She should let it go. Besides, she hadn't given him another thought in a really long time.

They grew up next door to each other and dated in high school. Like most teenagers, they thought they would be together forever. And, if she had gone off to school with him as they had planned, maybe they would have. The plan was to go to college together. He was going to major in business and she was going to study art and interior design. Things looked like they were going to work out until he changed the plan at the last minute and took a year off.

He and some friends were going to work for someone's uncle in the Keys as scuba instructors. They said a gap year would boost their résumés. Mostly, they wanted the opportunity to hang out at the beach.

What bothered Clara most was he didn't invite her on this new adventure. She wouldn't have agreed to go. Clara was much too sensible for that, but it hurt her he agreed to go without asking her.

Clara went off to college alone. Communication with Trevor was sporadic and though there was no official breakup, she moved on and so did he. The last time she saw him was the Christmas of her sophomore year when he brought a girl home to meet his parents. Unfortunately, she wasn't dating anyone at the time and it was terribly awkward when the couple walked into her parents' annual Christmas party.

Trevor stayed in Florida. He moved on from scuba instructor and after earning a business degree, he became a yacht broker. This allowed him to stay near the beach, and beautiful wealthy women. According to his mother, he had a string of relationships, but he never could commit to anyone. Clara and her mother would laugh as Trevor's mom would recount the latest news about him, and his mom would sigh and wonder whether he and Clara would ever find their way back to each other.

"Not hardly," Clara said under her breath, thinking about the most recent conversation her mother related to her.

"I'm sorry, what did you say?" Trevor asked.

"Nothing, just thinking out loud. So how long are you staying?"

"Not sure. There's been a slump in the yacht business. I let my lease go, my things are in storage, and I thought this might be a good time to think about my next move. Who knows, maybe I'll stick around for a while."

"Sounds like you have a lot to think about," Clara said absently, punctuating their conversation with "Merry Christmas" and "thank you," as people walked by and dropped money in the kettle.

"What time do you finish here? Maybe we could go to dinner? It would be nice to catch up. I hear you have a little Christmas business."

Clara's eyes flashed with anger. "Um, I'm sorry, but I already have plans."

"Doing what?"

"Well, if you must know, after this, I have to go check on my little Christmas business, and I already have plans for dinner."

"Oh, okay. Well, I'll be in town for a while. I am sure we can find some time to catch up." Trevor would not let this go.

"I don't know. It's busy this time of year, so I probably won't have time, but tell your parents hello for me."

"Will do. It was good to see you, Clara." He took a few steps past her toward the mall entrance doors and turned back. Smiling, he said, "You're still as pretty as you were in high school." And before she could respond, he was in the mall, merging into the crowd of holiday shoppers.

His last comment infuriated her. *What an amazingly shallow thing to say.*

At the end of her shift, she dutifully met her parents at the Santa display. Her mother paid for a portrait package. This was the tradition. They would stand in line with other families with little kids until it was their turn. Clara's mom had a display of these pictures starting from early in their parents' marriage before they had children, the years with just Clara, and then all four of them once Kayla was born. It was the thing that Clara loved the most every year. She and Kayla always had fun going through the frames, trying to figure out how old they were in each photo. This would be the newest picture for the wall.

Waiting in the line, Clara mentioned she saw Trevor.

"I didn't know he was back in town. Did you?" she asked her parents.

"His mother said that he was coming back for Christmas. Isn't that nice? She seems to think that he might be here for a while," her mother said.

"He mentioned that," Clara said.

"When did you see him?" Clara's mother asked.

"Today. He came through the entrance I was covering. He seemed as surprised to see me as I was to see him."

Kayla jumped in the conversation. "Is he still cute?"

"He looks the same as he always did. A little older, but yes, still cute," Clara answered, irritated.

They shuffled up the line a few places and Clara's mother said, "Wouldn't it be nice if you spent some time together before he left? You used to be inseparable."

Clara looked at her mother as if she had lost her mind. "Are you serious? I'm not interested in spending one minute with him."

"Clara, really, you were teenagers. It's time to let it go."

They moved a few more steps closer to the entrance. It would soon be their turn with Santa.

"Besides," her father interjected, "he'll be at our Christmas party with his parents. Can you at least be civil to him?"

"When have I been uncivil to anyone?" Clara asked, her tone giving away her annoyance. "I won't be rude, but I'm not interested in spending any time with him, reminiscing. I basically told him that, so I don't think he is expecting me to."

"Clara, you weren't rude, were you?" Her mother gasped.

"No, he asked me to go to dinner to catch up, and I told him I was busy. Just so you know, if he continues to invite me, I will continue to be busy. Besides, any extra time I have right now I want to spend with Clay."

The line moved again. They would be the next family to see Santa.

"My life is perfect right now just the way it is and I don't want anything, or anyone, messing it up."

"Come this way," the elf directing the photo shoot told Clara and her family. Their conversation ended for now as the elf placed the family members around Santa. Clara's mom and dad stood behind Santa on each side of his overstuffed red chair. Kayla knelt in front and Clara sat gingerly on his knee, careful not to put her full weight on him.

As they were getting settled, Santa whispered, "I heard you say your life is perfect now. Are you sure?"

Clara smiled and nodded.

Santa continued, "I'm glad you have everything you wished for."

The elf commanded everyone's attention and counted down to the smile. "One, two, three, Merry Christmas!"

"Merry Christmas!" they shouted, smiling, before the flash.

Thanking Santa, they stepped aside to wait for their print.

As she stepped away from his knee, Santa looked up at Clara and winked. "Merry Christmas," he said.

"Merry Christmas," she replied.

Before they went their separate ways, they confirmed plans for the next day. They were going to meet to plan for the party. Every year they divided up the duties. Now that Clara and Kayla were adults, it was much easier for their mother to delegate. Tomorrow night they would get their assignments. Clara was looking forward to the party, and she wondered how this would be different.

After their goodbyes, Clara walked through the mall toward her store. She loved the atmosphere of the mall at Christmas. She was happy as she made her way through the crowds. Satisfied that Maggie had things managed at the store, she walked into the parking lot.

At home, she fed Mistletoe and filled the water bowl. Making a sandwich in the kitchen, she carried her plate to the sofa to eat. Switching on the television, she watched Ralphie as he imagined how different his life would be if he had a Red Ryder BB gun. She laughed as she thought about how nice it was to get her wish. Her life now certainly seemed to be like a Christmas movie, where everything was perfect.

Clara noticed she had messages and checked them. There was one from Sophie asking when they could meet for coffee. Clay called to ask about her plans the next day and asked her to call him when she was home for the night. The last message was from her mother, reminding her about meeting the next day. She explained that she would have dinner at the house so Clara could come straight from work.

Getting ready for bed, Clara slipped on fluffy pajamas and slipped under the covers. She felt Mistletoe jump up on the bed and snuggle near her feet. Clara considered sitting up to pet her cat, but decided she was too comfortable where she was.

Instead, she picked up her phone and dialed Clay's number. She hadn't talked to him all day and missed him. It was nice that things were back to normal between them. She hated what had happened at his Christmas party, and had to remind herself that it had happened in actual life, not in her Christmas movie life.

Clay answered after only one ring. "Hello."

"Hey, how was your day?" Clara asked.

"Busy. Trying to get everything cleared off my calendar before vacation. How was your day? Tell me about being a bell ringer."

"It was fun. I think people like to see bell ringers. It sets the mood for them before they enter the mall. Everyone was really generous."

"That's great. Did you see lots of people you know?"

"Yes, lots of mall employees and customers who have been in the store in the last few months. Most of them recognized me, but you can't really have conversations beyond 'Merry Christmas' and 'Thank you.' Everyone is eager to get past you and on with their day."

She felt a pang of guilt not mentioning Trevor, but dismissed it. Clay didn't know him anyway, and she really didn't want to explain ancient history. That was over, and Clay probably wouldn't meet him.

"So, what's on the calendar for tomorrow?" Clay interrupted her thoughts.

"I am opening the store. After work, I'll go to my parents'. We have a party planning meeting during dinner."

"Sounds like a busy day. How about I come by after dinner? We could watch a movie and just hang out."

"Okay. I'll call you when I am on my way home."

"See you tomorrow."

"See you tomorrow." Clara hung up and snuggled down into her comfy bed.

Chapter 18

The next morning, light streamed into her bedroom, waking her before her alarm. She felt light, energized, and ready for the day. Over coffee, she consulted her calendar and made a few notes. There was a reminder to check inventory for the store and billing statements for her display business. She had a few outstanding accounts and wanted to have that wrapped up before the new year started.

Showered and dressed, she drove to the mall. Stopping at Cool Beans, she found her Americano waiting for her in a cup labeled Christmas Girl. Smiling, she put a few dollars in the tip jar and called out, "Merry Christmas!" She opened the door and walked out to the parking lot as the barista responded, "Merry Christmas!"

This is more like it, Clara thought. *Everyone is cheery, just like in the song.*

Relishing her newfound perfect life, she entered the mall, dropping coins into the red kettle, as she opened the heavy glass doors. The sounds and smells of Christmas. Crowds, music, and gingerbread. Smiling, she joined the crowds of people and walked directly to her store. It was already open. Maggie came in earlier to help with inventory.

Going to the counter, she called out, "Maggie, I'm here. Where are you?"

"Coming," was the muffled reply.

Clara put her things behind the counter in the center of the store. It was like several movie sets in one room and she loved it. It reminded her of the scene in *Elf*, when Buddy makes Gimbels toy section into the North Pole and it was beautiful.

Maggie came into the store, loaded down with new Christmas tree skirts and stockings. "We never put these out. Where do you want to display them?"

Clara looked around the store, slowly turning so she could see it from every angle. "Let's change out the existing skirts on the trees and put the skirts that have already been on display on the shelves and put the stockings on the various mantels and hangers."

They divided the work, Maggie taking the skirts and Clara the stockings. Maggie caught Clara up on what she had done so far on the store inventory. Clara took over so Maggie could assist the customers in the shoppe. Grabbing another cup of coffee, Clara took it to the office space in the back of the store to finish inventory and billing.

Several hours later, the women called in an order for lunch and took turns eating. They had an excellent system and worked well together.

The day progressed and Maggie continued to wait on customers, helping them find the perfect Christmas decorations while Clara worked steadily on her projects in the back office. Finally, later in the afternoon, Maggie's shift ended and her part-time holiday help arrived to relieve her. Clara had hired a college student home for Christmas to help with the holiday rush. Usually, she and Maggie ran the store, but she always needed extra help at Christmas. Beth was a trusted employee who had been working with Clara and Maggie since she was in high school. She loved being there and looked forward to coming home all of fall semester.

Maggie gave Beth a list of things to do in between customers. Beth made herself a cup of hot cocoa and began her shift. Clara worked through her entire list of things to be finished that day and was tired but content as she gave a few last directions to Beth before leaving for the day.

As she was walking through the mall back to her car, her phone vibrated in her purse, alerting her to a call. Finding her phone, she answered it. "Hello?"

"Hey, Clara. Are you heading to your parents' house now?" Clay asked.

"Yes, I just finished at the shop and I think I am going to grab a coffee and drive over there now. How was your day?"

"Pretty good so far. Are you still going to let me know when you are on your way home tonight?"

"Yes, I shouldn't be too long. We are meeting over dinner. I had a productive day, but it has been long and I am tired."

"Oh, do you still want to hang out tonight? We can meet up tomorrow if you are tired." Clay sounded disappointed.

"No, I want to see you. A coffee will perk me right up. I will call you as I am leaving my parents'."

"Okay. See you later."

The call ended as Clara walked into Cool Beans, where another Americano was magically waiting for her on the counter. Smiling, she picked it up and called out a thank-you and Merry Christmas as she opened the door to the parking lot.

Walking toward her car, she passed a Santa at the kettle and heard her name. She turned and there he was. She walked toward Santa as he asked, "So how are things going for you?"

"Are you kidding? Everything is perfect!"

"Everything?" Santa's eyes narrowed and his brow rumpled.

"Well, yes. I mean, things are better than ever with Clay, the store is great, and my family is excited about Christmas for once. This is how I imagined my perfect Christmas movie life would be. Thank you for making all of this happen."

"You're welcome. I'm glad it is everything you think you want. Remember what I said in the beginning. A Christmas movie is someone's fantasy, and not usually yours."

"I know what you said," Clara interrupted, "but this is exactly what I want and I'm going to enjoy every minute."

"Okay," Santa conceded, "it sounds like you have it under control. Just a warning—enjoy it while it lasts."

Before Clara could agree, argue, or ask questions, Santa and the kettle vanished. Just like at the Christmas tree farm, they disappeared, leaving Clara bewildered in the parking lot.

Clara found her car and drove to her parents' house, ready for a night of planning for the party. She hoped it wouldn't take too long. She really wanted to see Clay.

Elvis was crooning "Blue Christmas" through her radio as she pulled into the driveway at her parents' house.

Not me, she thought as he went on about memories of someone special who wasn't there this Christmas. *My Christmas is perfect.*

Smugly, she turned off the ignition and grabbed her purse and bag. Getting out of the car, she heard a door close and looked toward the next-door neighbor's house. Trevor bounded across the lawn, making his way toward her.

"Hey, Clara," he panted.

"Hello, Trevor," she answered.

"I wondered when I would see you again. I hoped you would come by soon."

"Well, it is Christmas, and this is my parents' house. Is there something you wanted?"

"Yes. It's boring around here. Everyone from high school has either moved away or gotten married, and there isn't anyone to do anything with. I'm desperate to get out of my parents' house. Do you want to grab dinner? Maybe go to a movie?"

"That's what happens when people grow up, Trevor. And, no, I can't. I'm having dinner with my family and then I have plans later."

"Come on. It'll be fun and we don't have to stay out late. Besides, how early do you have to wake up? You work at the mall."

Incensed, Clara slammed her door, a little harder than necessary. "Trevor, not that I have to explain myself to you, but I don't just work at the mall. I have a business I run that is in the mall. Now, if you will excuse me, I'm going inside."

She turned abruptly to walk away from him and toward the door.

From behind she heard, "So, that's a no, for tonight? That's okay. I'll be here a few weeks. We can get together another time."

"Bye, Trevor," Clara called out, as she opened the door and walked into her parents' house, closing it behind her before she could hear anything else he had to say.

"Who were you talking to?" her mother asked, coming to the door to greet Clara.

"Trevor. He seems to think we're friends. He asked me to go to dinner. Said none of his high school friends have time for him. Imagine that."

"His mother said that he was pretty much just hanging around their house. Would it be so bad if you spent a little time with him?"

"Are you serious? Yes, yes, it would be so bad. And, I don't think Clay would appreciate me spending time with my high school boyfriend. So, no, I will not go to dinner, or a movie, or anything else with him."

"Okay, okay. Just thought I'd ask. Come on, let's eat. Dinner is ready and we have a lot to discuss."

Clara followed her mother into the kitchen. Dinner smelled delicious and her stomach growled. It had been several hours since she had lunch, and she was so busy she only ate a few bites of that.

The mood at the table was festive. Everyone was telling about their day as they ate plates of lasagna, salad, and breadsticks. When dinner was over, her mother brought out coffee and dessert. Everyone got out their calendars to make lists of what they needed to do for the party.

"We still have to decide on the menu and any games or entertainment we want to have."

They tossed around different menu options and decided on appetizers and desserts.

Kayla, usually uninterested, offered a brilliant idea. "What about a fire in the backyard to make s'mores? We could rent a hot chocolate cart and a projector to play Christmas movies on the back fence."

"That's a great idea," Clara's father chimed in. "We could put chairs in a few rows like at a theater and have outdoor heaters set around if it's cold."

"Okay, so we have options for outside. Do we need to do anything inside?" Clara's mother asked.

"We could play Christmas trivia games for door prizes," Clara offered. "I could donate a few items from the store."

"Can you find a game?" Kayla asked.

"I think I have something that'll work," Clara said.

"Okay, anything else?" Clara's mother asked.

No one could think of anything else except the guest list.

"Well, I think we will just invite the usual people. What about Clay? Are you inviting him?"

"Yes, of course."

Kayla also wanted to invite a few of her friends. After reviewing the list, they counted twenty-five people. Clara's mother already had most of the invitations addressed and stamped. Clara and Kayla took the remaining invitations from her with the list and began addressing them and getting them stamped for the mail the next day.

Once they each had their assignments, Clara collected her things and promised to mail the invitations the next morning on her way to work.

Arriving home, she checked on Mistletoe and consulted her calendar about the next day. It was going to be another long one.

She was working again, from open to close, and had plans with her parents again.

Sighing, she fixed a cup of cinnamon tea and went to her room to get ready for bed. Clara knew she would need plenty of sleep to get ready for the next few days. In her Christmas pajamas, with her face washed, she and Mistletoe settled into her bed. She switched on the television and found *Christmas Vacation*. She just settled in to watch the movie until she fell asleep when her phone rang. Picking it up, she noticed it was Clay.

"Hello?"

"Hey, there. What are you doing?"

"Just settling in for the night. What about you?"

"I just wanted to call and see how the big party planning meeting went." Clay said. "I thought we were going to get together after, but you didn't call."

"Oh, I am so sorry. I've had such a long day, and I'm exhausted. All I could think about was getting home and going to sleep. It went pretty well. We all have our assignments. I have to mail the invitations tomorrow and take care of the trivia game and prizes."

"I understand, just disappointed. So, am I invited?"

"Of course. It wouldn't be a party without you," she teased.

"Looking forward to it, especially since I helped choose and decorate the tree. Hey, why don't you save the stamp and you can bring it to me tomorrow."

"Aren't you working tomorrow?"

"Yes, but I thought we could meet for lunch or after work for dinner. What does your day look like?"

"I am working all day at the store and then after, my mom has us going on her annual caroling at the nursing home. Or it might be at the children's hospital, I'm not sure."

"I'll call you in the morning and we can either meet for lunch or dinner at the mall, or I can pick something up and bring it to you at the store."

"That sounds great. See you tomorrow."

"Good night, Clara."

They hung up and Clara could not imagine a more perfect life as she watched Clark Griswold try to create the perfect Christmas for his family. *This is how Christmas should be*, she thought. *Family, friends, Santa, decorations, wonderful food—just everything perfect.* Content, she fell asleep.

Chapter 19

The next morning was what she expected. Sunlight streaming into her face, she woke before her alarm chimed, well rested and ready for the day. Walking into the kitchen, she fed and watered Mistletoe as she waited for her coffee to brew. Taking her coffee to the sofa, she turned on the television and surprise, surprise another Christmas movie. Smiling, she settled in to make notes in her calendar as the movie played in the background. This was becoming her usual morning routine, and she loved it. She noted any changes that needed to be made and was excited to begin her day. In the course of the next few days, she had caroling with her parents, and a day of baking to prepare for the party. There would be a day of shopping and wrapping, and of course the party. It was the perfect way to spend the time until Christmas.

In her closet, she chose jeans and a green Christmas sweater with red and gold trim. The emerald green brought out the color in her eyes, and she wanted to look especially nice when she met Clay.

Humming "Jingle Bells" to herself, she walked to her car and made the drive across town to the mall. As usual, she stopped in at Cool Beans for a steaming Americano that was waiting for her with her name on it on the bar. She put the tip in the jar and called out, "Thank you and Merry Christmas," and the barista replied with the same.

She walked back into the brisk air, through the parking lot and into the mall. Other than employees and mall walkers, the mall was empty. The crowds would file in later, increasing throughout the day as they hurried to complete their shopping before the big day. Her shop was all Christmas all the time, but it was nice to see the rest of the mall decorated and filled with the special energy Christmas brought.

She stopped to admire the tree in the intersection of two concourses of the mall. It was huge, almost reaching the ceiling, and beautifully decorated. She had helped in the tree's design and chose the theme for the decorations.

"It really is stunning, isn't it?" she heard a voice say next to her.

"Yes, it is." Turning, Clara was happy to see her friend Sam next to her. "How are you?"

"Great, thank you. And you? I haven't seen you lately."

"I know. I have been working in the shop and then pretty much with my parents when I am not at work. How is Maria? Will the boys be here for Christmas?" Clara asked.

"Yes, they're planning to come home. Maria is so excited to have them for a few days at Christmas. I believe they're staying through New Year's Eve, so we'll have a nice long visit with them. What about you?"

"My schedule is pretty packed. I have work, and then my mom has taken over all the festivities and has planned all kinds of Christmas activities. It is great because I haven't had to plan anything. I'm finding I don't have as much free time to spend with Clay. He helped us find and decorate the tree, but other than that, our schedules haven't allowed us much time together."

"Oh, I thought you loved all the festivities at Christmastime."

"I do. It is just a lot this year. I am enjoying everything. I just wish it was longer." She laughed.

"I understand. Well, I need to get going on my rounds. I may pop in later for some coffee and a cookie, if you don't mind."

"Of course! I'd love you to come by the store. The coffee bar is always open."

She gave Sam a quick hug and reminded him to give Maria her love, and they separated to get on with their day.

Maggie was already at the shop when Clara arrived. Making her way to the back, she noticed Maggie already set out coffee and pastries. She checked to make sure there were plenty of cups and napkins on the counter and then went to the back office to drop off her things. Maggie was there, sipping on a cup of cocoa and nibbling a cinnamon roll while she responded to emails from different vendors.

"Good morning," Clara said as she made her way past Maggie to the coatrack to hang her bag and purse.

"Good morning." Maggie swiveled around in the office chair to face Clara. "It looks like we only have one more large order coming in before Christmas. I'm not sure if you want to hold or approve it."

"Approve the shipment. If we don't have space available on the floor, we can always put it in storage until we are ready for a reset after Christmas."

"Okay." Maggie turned her body and attention to the computer once again. She typed a quick message, approving the shipment and charges, and stood after hitting Send. She caught Clara up on the progress of the inventory and then excused herself to finish getting the store ready to open for the day.

Clara thanked her for the update and busied herself with trying to finish inventory and made a note that she needed to choose some prizes to donate to her mother's Christmas party.

The morning went quickly and before Clara knew it, it was almost noon. Her stomach growling, she checked her watch. She hadn't heard from Clay and wondered whether they were still going to meet for lunch. It wasn't like him not to call to confirm plans. She thought he must have been busy at the office and called him before running to get lunch on her own.

He picked up on the second ring. "Hello?"

"Hey, it's me. I was just checking to see if we were still on for lunch or if you need to push it to dinner."

"Can we do dinner? A client meeting ran late this morning and I'm just now getting back to my desk."

"Sure. Call me when you are on your way and we can make a plan."

"Thank you for understanding. I'll see you later."

"Okay, see you later."

Grabbing her bag, Clara announced to Maggie that she was going to get lunch.

Walking through the mall at midday had a different feel than in the early morning or after closing. It was prime people watching time and Clara loved it. She ordered a salad and breadsticks from the pizza place. Finding a table, she set her food down her food.

As she was taking a bite, eyes focused on the salad in front of her, she saw a hand pull the chair away from the other side of the table. Her mouth full, she looked up and saw Trevor.

"You don't mind if I join you for lunch, do you?" he asked as he sat and scooted himself up to the table.

Choking down her salad, she answered, "Do you have something to eat?"

"Yes. What kind of weirdo sits down to a meal with no food?" He set his bag of takeout on the table.

"I'm sorry," she said, confused. "Why are you here?"

"Because I was in the mall and I got hungry. Isn't that why you're here?"

"Well, yes. But, I mean, what are you doing at the mall? Don't you have other things to do?"

"We've gone over this already. It's so boring at my parents' house. I keep asking you to hang out and you're always too busy. The only thing I can do is go to the movies and the mall. I've already seen every movie showing, so that leaves the mall. After I ordered, I noticed you were sitting alone and thought we could finally catch up." With that,

Trevor picked up his burger and took a bite, chasing it with a long swallow of his drink.

Clara, irritated at his boldness, felt a little sorry for him. She watched him as he took another bite and drink, unsure what to say. "What's really going on with you and your job? Why are you thinking of staying around here? You couldn't wait to get away from this place."

"Well," he swallowed the bite he had just taken, "business is very slow right now. There are plenty of sellers, but not enough buyers. I'm not sure what to do next, but I can't make a living in that market. Mom and Dad invited me to come home and consider my options. I have plenty of savings to carry me for a while. Real estate has been something I considered before, so I'm looking into it."

"Sounds like you have things all worked out." Clara took another bite.

"What about you? Mom told me you created a Christmas empire around here."

"I wouldn't call it that. I have two businesses. There is the shop, and I also do Christmas displays for various businesses and throughout the mall."

"That makes sense. You've always been over the top about Christmas."

"Not over the top. Very enthusiastic."

Trevor swallowed the last of his French fries and wiped his fingers on a napkin. "So, which displays did you design in the mall this year?"

She listed the store windows and told him about the Santa display in the center of the mall.

"Wow, the Santa one is impressive. How long did that take?"

"A couple of weeks to get the design worked out in my mind, another month to find everything, and then a few days to put it all together."

"When do you plan these designs?"

Clara explained the process to him as he nodded, looking interested in her work and what it entailed. Finishing her salad, she looked down at her watch. "Well, speaking of work, I really need to get back to it."

She stood and began clearing her side of the table. She collected her bag as Trevor did the same. Standing, they walked toward the large trash bins in the center of the food court.

"I hope things work out for you, Trevor."

"Thanks. Me, too," he said. "Hey, you want to go see a movie when you get off work? *Gremlins* is showing tonight. They have a Christmas movie every night until Christmas, some kind of countdown to the big day."

"You know that is not a Christmas movie." She laughed. They had had this argument since middle school. Trevor insisted that it was, and Clara held to her opinion that just because a movie took place at Christmas, it was not a Christmas movie.

"Anyway, I can't. I already have plans with my parents."

"Okay, how about tomorrow night? It's *Die Hard.*"

"Hard pass. Definitely not a Christmas movie. You enjoy it."

Laughing, Trevor said, "Okay. But you don't know what you are missing."

"I do, and I really need to get back to work. See you around, Trevor."

"See you around, Clara."

The rest of the day was a blur of helping customers, resetting and stocking displays throughout the store, and finishing end of the year inventory. She loved this job. It was exciting to feel the magic of Christmas in this space. All the lights twinkled, the glass balls glistened, and the place smelled of the best of Christmas. Children and adults of all ages enjoyed just being in the store, and she found they lingered in the sections with sofas and stuffed chairs, most likely wishing they decorated their homes like this. Because she did sometimes have little visitors shopping with adults, she created a space that was very child friendly. There were no glass ornaments in that area to break. Clara had smaller furniture and character themed trees. She also had Christmas activity sheets to occupy little hands and minds while their parents shopped. She loved to watch them walk by the Santa that would sing and dance when they tripped the sensor. Their eyes would go wide, mesmerized. A train went around the top of the store that they could watch as they played or just sat quietly, taking it all in. This was the area that had to have special attention each night, especially on the weekends when there were more families shopping together.

Toward the end of the day, as things were winding down, Clay called about dinner. "I am finally free and will leave the office in about ten minutes. What would you like for dinner? We can meet somewhere after work, or I can pick it up and bring it to you."

Clara thought for a minute. She planned to go to her parents' for a night of caroling with the friends they had caroled with since she was a teenager.

"I can leave here in about an hour. My parents are expecting me for caroling tonight after work. How about we meet at the food court in an hour? I think that is the quickest option."

"Okay. How late will you be caroling?"

"I am not sure. Usually a couple of hours. Why don't you come with us?"

"No, I don't want to mess up the tradition. Everyone already knows all the words and harmonies. If dinner is all I get, then that will have to do."

They agreed he would come to the store when he arrived at the mall.

Hand in hand, they strolled down the concourse toward the food court. He listened attentively as she recounted her day, telling him about the customers she helped and some of the new inventory she set out. He smiled as she spoke. It was obvious in her face that she loved her job, and even on long days like this one, she wouldn't trade it for any other.

Arriving at the food court, they stopped to consider their options.

"What are you hungry for?" Clay asked.

"Um, I'm not sure. I had a salad for lunch from the pizza place. What sounds good to you?"

"Stir-fry?"

"Stir-fry it is," she agreed, and they headed in that direction.

They carried their plates to the nearest table and sat. It was quiet at first. Clara didn't realize just how hungry she was until there was a plate of steaming chicken and vegetables in front of her. They were starving and hardly spoke as they ate their first few bites.

"So, tell me about the caroling tonight."

"We meet at my parents' house and caravan over to a nursing home and sing during their activity time. There is an enormous room where they meet to play games and have other activities. We've been going to the nursing home for years. It's always fun to see the residents year after year, and sad to notice who's missing from years past."

Clay swallowed his food. "It sounds like fun. And not as cold as I imagined it would be."

"Come with us. We aren't professionals, you know." Clara scooped up a forkful of stir-fry.

"It sounds fun, and I really do hate to only see you for a few minutes at dinner."

They finished eating, continuing to catch each other up on their day and laughing as they watched other people in the food court.

After clearing the trash from their table, Clay escorted her to her car. Her house was on the way, so they dropped her car off at her house and she rode with Clay to her parents'. Clara was happy. She was thankful Clay came with them. She felt torn between spending time with Clay and meeting her parents' expectations.

He turned down the Christmas music, and they talked and laughed as they made the short drive to her parents' house.

Clara knocked on the front door and Clay leaned in for a quick kiss under the mistletoe as they waited for someone to come to the door. It opened before they had time to pull apart and there was Trevor.

"Well, well, look who the cat dragged in," he said.

"What are you doing here?" Clara asked, shocked to see him standing in her parents' doorway.

"You don't have to sound so surprised. Don't our parents do this every year?"

"I guess so. It just didn't occur to me that this would be something you'd want to do."

Looking at Clay, Trevor answered, "Well, I had no choice when I found out you would be here. I had to see how this was possibly more interesting than going to a movie with me."

Clay reached out his hand. "Hi. I don't believe we've met. I'm Clay," he said as he put his other hand around Clara's waist and stepped closer to her.

"Hi. I'm Trevor. My parents live next door," he answered.

Clara explained, "Trevor is home for the holidays. I believe this is the first time in years he has been kind enough to come home instead of making his parents take a long trip to see him."

"Yes, but I think I may stay in town awhile this time. I am considering making a change, and coming back to something familiar may be exactly what I need," he said, smiling like a toothpaste advertisement.

"Let's go inside. I want to say hello to my parents and, Trevor, I'm sure you have other people to catch up with," Clara said, annoyed.

Trevor stepped aside and invited them in to Clara's parents' house. "No, I really just came to see you."

Clara shot him an angry look and took Clay's hand as they walked into the living room. Her mother had set out trays of cookies, finger sandwiches, and other appetizers. She also had hot apple cider and coffee available.

As they made their way across the room, Kayla rushed up beside her and quietly said, "By the way, Trevor is here."

Clara looked at her sister and under her breath said, "I know. That's who answered the door."

Kayla's eyes grew wide as she looked at Clay. "Awkward."

Her mother saw her and announced, "Clara, I am so glad you made it. We weren't expecting you for a while. And, I see you brought Clay. Wonderful! Everyone, you obviously remember Clara, and this is her young man, Clay. Clay, we are so glad you joined us."

The party welcomed Clay warmly, except for Trevor, who stayed at the back of the room near the snack tables. It was obvious he was unaware that Clara was seeing someone. Clara noticed him staring at her, and she redirected her attention to Clay and led him to the table for some cider or coffee.

"Coffee or cider?" she asked.

"Coffee, please," he answered and Clara busied herself with pouring two cups of coffee. "Is it like this every year?"

"Sometimes the crowd is a little different, depending on who is in town, but this is the usual group. My parents have been doing this for years."

"I can see why. It seems like everyone is excited. Well, except Trevor."

Clay gave a slight nod in his direction and she looked over to see him scowling, looking miserable. He quickly averted his gaze when their eyes met. She felt a little sorry for him. He was obviously uncomfortable here.

"Yes, this isn't his thing. I guess you must have picked up that we have a history."

"Yeah, I figured there was something there the way he was looking at you."

"We grew up together and dated throughout high school. He was my first boyfriend, and I was his first girlfriend. We had plans after high school and he bailed on them, leaving me alone at college. It wasn't an ugly scene; he just dropped the relationship. The few times he came home after that, he had a different woman with him on each visit. I have talked to him more in the last two days than in the last ten years."

"I think he has some unresolved issues around the breakup," Clay suggested.

"Maybe. He always only thinks about himself. Anyway, I feel sorry for him. He seems lonely and sad."

Clay squeezed her hand. "You're too nice. I don't know if I would feel the same way if I was in your place."

Clara's mother announced everyone should move to their vehicles before Clara could respond. Clay led Clara toward his car when Trevor appeared.

"Hey, can I ride with you? I can't stand another minute with my parents and their incessant questions."

Before Clara could object, Clay agreed. As he got Clara settled into the front seat, she mouthed, "What are you doing?" to him.

He leaned in to give her a quick kiss and said, "It'll be fine," but she wasn't so sure.

Trevor let himself in the backseat, and they pulled away from the house. At first it was quiet, except for the cheery Christmas music coming from the radio. Clara felt awkward with an old boyfriend and a current boyfriend in the same car. She didn't have to wait long until Trevor broke the silence.

"Look at that house! They always had the best lights. Clara, remember when we used to drive by here every night during Christmas break? It seemed like they were putting something new in the yard or on the house every day until Christmas."

Clara craned her neck to see as they drove passed. "It was the best Christmas house in the neighborhood, for sure."

Trevor began talking about old times. Clara continually tried to involve Clay, but he didn't have the history they did.

As they pulled up to the nursing home, Trevor said, "So you couldn't go to a movie tonight because of this? Do we even know anyone here?"

Clara felt Clay looking at her from the seat next to her, and heat rose to her face. "Trevor, seriously. Can't you just do something nice for people?"

"Whatever," Trevor said as he unfolded himself out of the backseat.

Clay came around to open Clara's door, and as she got out, she heard Trevor make a comment about chivalry as he rolled his eyes. Just to spite him, Clara gave Clay a kiss full on the mouth.

Trevor looked away as Clay asked, "What was that for?"

"Just my way of thanking you for being chivalrous."

Trevor walked off ahead to join the group, giving Clara a chance to explain.

"I wasn't going to a movie with him. He was in the food court when I went there today for lunch and invited himself to sit at my table. Anyway, he's lonely and asked if I would go with him to dinner or the movies. I feel kind of bad for him. He is just so out of place."

Clay listened and nodded. "So, at lunch, did you mention me?"

"I just said no, and I didn't think I needed to offer an explanation. Why?"

"But you did, something about having plans with your parents."

Clara panicked, stammering, "No, it wasn't like that. I am not going anywhere with him. It was an awkward moment that caught me off guard. I just wasn't expecting to see him, that's all."

"It's okay. I'm just surprised you didn't mention it to me. How much has he been around since he has been back in town?"

Clara counted silently. "I ran into him when we were bell ringing, then in the driveway when I came to help my parents plan the party, and then today."

"Clara, I don't want to sound like a jealous boyfriend, but you need to be careful. He has regrets and still has a thing for you."

"I don't think so. He's just arrogant. We dated a very long time ago."

"Maybe, but coming home, back to familiar people and places, might make him think you can pick up right where you left off. Especially since there wasn't an actual breakup. Just think about it. In the meantime, let's have fun messing with him."

Holding hands, they walked across the parking lot and joined the rest of the group.

The director led them into the activity room, which was sparsely decorated. There was a tree with multicolored lights and cheap green and red balls. A lopsided angel dressed in white satin with gold trim sat atop the tree. There were empty packages under the tree, their paper faded and ripped on some corners from being tossed in storage. There was a construction paper mantel someone created and attached to the wall next to the tree. Hanging from it were actual stockings with the names of residents and staff on the white cuff on the top. Clara walked over to read the names and noticed they were all embellished differently.

"A group of our ladies made stockings for everyone during their activity time. Aren't they pretty?" the director asked.

"Yes, they are. You know, I own the Christmas Shoppe in the mall. If you'd like, I'd be happy to donate some decorations for this space or even your lobby."

"Really? Our budget is tight, so we have used these same decorations for years. They are getting worn."

"Sure. Let me put some things together, and I can drop them by tomorrow after work."

"Thank you, so much. The residents will love it." The director gave Clara a quick hug.

Clara found Clay in the group, and he stepped closer to her, putting his arm around her waist. The director got the residents' attention and introduced their carolers for the evening. Turning everything over to Clara's mother, they were to begin.

Singing Christmas carols was always fun. Clara thought no matter what was going on, Christmas carols made things better. After several songs, the director invited everyone to stay for cookies and punch so they could visit with the residents.

Clara and Clay made a plate and found a table to sit together with an older gentleman. He was white headed and wore glasses he had to look over when he talked to them, dipping his head down almost as if his face were parallel to the floor.

"Can we join you?" asked Clay.

"Sure," the man answered.

Clay pulled out Clara's chair for her and then sat next to her.

"You don't see that anymore," the man said. "In my day, a man wouldn't think to sit down before pulling out a chair for a woman, even if it wasn't his wife or girlfriend. Now you see men just ignoring everything around them. Like that one over there." The man nodded toward another table.

Clara winced as she noticed Trevor in a chair next to his mother as she tried to balance a plate and cup while she slid the chair out with her foot.

"No manners. What is the world coming to?" the man grunted.

Clay reached out his hand and introduced them.

"It is nice to meet you. My name's Frank. Thank you for coming tonight. Yours was the best group we have had all season. It's pretty dreary around here, you know."

"Thank you for saying that, Frank. I am sure this is not the Christmas you grew up with," Clara said.

"No, that's for sure." Frank chuckled. "When we were kids, Christmas was a big deal. We had little money, but Christmas was huge. There were all the foods we didn't get any other time of the year. We spent every minute with our cousins, getting into all kinds of trouble. One year..." Frank continued telling them about all the trouble he and his cousins got into while together. His eyes lit up, and he laughed from his belly, remembering the good times he had as a child and young man. Clara and Clay sat back and listened as his memories poured out, stories of people they would never meet.

Eventually, the director announced it was time for the residents to begin their night routine and thanked the carolers again for such a special treat.

Clara and Clay stood and shook Frank's hand and thanked him for a wonderful evening. He looked shocked as he thanked them, wondering why they were thanking him.

"Your stories were wonderful, some of the best I have heard. Thank you for taking the time to share them with us," Clara said.

"Thank you for listening to an old man reminiscing about things from a hundred years ago." He smiled. "It was the most fun I've had in a while. Now, don't be a stranger. Come back and visit."

"Thank you, we will!" They made plans to return later and visit Frank since he was alone.

Walking out to the car, Trevor asked whether they could give him a ride home.

"We aren't going back to the house. We rode together, so I am taking Clara home," Clay explained.

Trevor's face hardened for a minute. "Oh, okay. I will just catch up with her tomorrow then." He waited for Clay to respond when Clara approached the car, interrupting the conversation.

She could feel the tension, but didn't know what happened.

Clay opened the door, and as he shut it, she heard Trevor say, "See you tomorrow, Clara."

Clay came around and got in the driver's seat. "Wow, that guy has some nerve."

Clara, clicking her seat belt, asked, "What do you mean?"

"He wanted us to take him home. He got a little weird when I mentioned we weren't going back to your parents' house, that I was taking you home since we rode together."

"What do you mean?"

"I don't really know how to explain it, except it seems like he thinks we are in some kind of competition and you are the prize."

"Surely not." Clara laughed. "He is competitive, for sure, and selfish, and lots of other things, but I am not interested in him in the least bit. There is some history, but that is long over."

To prove she meant what she said, she leaned over to give Clay a kiss. "See, I'm where I want to be."

Clay smiled, and Clara leaned back into her seat. Then, reaching to the floorboard, she panicked. She leaned over the center console, twisting to look into the back floorboard. "Clay, have you seen my bag?"

Looking everywhere she had already looked, Clay said, "No. Maybe you left it inside? Do you want to go check?"

"Yes, I will be right back."

"Do you want me to go with you?"

"No, keep the car running so it will be warm."

She jogged across the parking lot and entered the lobby. Clara went straight to the activity room. The cleaning staff were the only ones in the room, sweeping, mopping, and wiping off tables.

"I think I left my bag in here earlier. Have you seen it?" she asked, worried.

"No, but check the front desk. The director keeps things like that behind the desk."

"Okay, thank you." Clara rushed down the hall to the information desk. "I think I may have left my bag here earlier," Clara explained to the nurse on duty.

"What does it look like?"

Clara described her bag and some contents.

Satisfied that this was her bag, the woman unlocked a cabinet directly behind her and retrieved it. "Frank noticed it after you left. He thought you might be frantic without it and brought it here himself. He enjoyed the visit with you and your gentleman, you know."

"Thank you, and please tell Frank thank you for me. I'll come by for a visit as soon as I can." Clara took the bag and slung the straps over her shoulder as she turned to walk back to the car.

As she passed through the lobby doors, she heard a familiar sound: bell ringing. Thinking this was a little late in the evening and a strange place for a bell ringer, she looked around to find the source of the sound. There by the benches at the entrance was Santa.

"Merry Christmas, Clara," she heard him call out.

"Merry Christmas, Santa," she answered, stepping closer and looking around to see whether anyone else was around.

"How were things today?" Santa asked.

Not wanting to admit that things were becoming a little tense, she responded, "Great."

"You know I can see you when you are sleeping and when you're awake. You can't fool me. Now, do you want to try that again? How are things going?"

Clara let out a heavy sigh. "Okay. Things were perfect, just like a Christmas movie, and it was amazing. Now things are hectic. My mom has every minute filled, and I don't have any time to myself or to spend with Clay."

Santa nodded, and she continued, "And now this thing with Trevor. I was so happy that things are as they should be with Clay, and then Trevor has to show up and now things are getting weird and Trevor won't go away, and Clay is acting strange, and I am in the middle."

Santa looked amused. "I thought you liked a packed schedule during the holidays. You know, baking, parties, decorating, shopping and wrapping, caroling—just all of it."

"I do, but this is overwhelming because I am not the one making the schedule."

"Maybe this is how your family has felt for years?"

"No, they just don't like Christmas as much as I do. That's what has been so nice. Finally, they are interested, but they are taking it too far."

"Okay. Well then, what is the problem with Clay and Trevor? Isn't it nice to have options?"

"No, it isn't. I am afraid that Trevor is going to ruin everything."

"That's a possibility. Remember, a Christmas movie is a fantasy and maybe this one isn't yours. I tried to warn you."

"Wait, what do you mean?" Clara asked, but it was no use. Santa disappeared, and she was standing there talking to a bench.

Frustrated, she slid into the warm car next to Clay.

"Great, they found your bag," he said, oblivious to what just happened.

"Yes," she answered curtly.

"Are you okay?"

"I'm fine. Hey, did you notice a bell ringer outside the entrance?"

"No. This doesn't seem like a place they would set up. Why?"

"No reason. I just thought I heard a bell ringer."

"Okay, where to?" Clay asked. "We can stop for something to eat or just go straight to your house."

"We can just go to my house. I have plenty of snacks and hot chocolate."

Clay agreed and reached over, taking her hand.

She relaxed again, thinking that maybe she could still manage a perfect Christmas.

Chapter 20

T he next few days were a blur. Clara went to work each day and spent the evening on fun and festive activities with her parents.

She felt something was off with Clay. Since the caroling incident with Trevor, he seemed different. She couldn't exactly say what it was. She didn't want to pry. Clara wished Trevor had never come home. He was constantly intercepting her at her parents' and taunting her about Clay. It was unnerving. She thought it better to keep it to herself rather than worry Clay unnecessarily.

When she saw Trevor, she heard Clay's warning to be careful. Clara thought Trevor was annoying but harmless. She assumed he was unhappy and messing with her because of that, not because he wanted her back. With Trevor, it was all about Trevor, and she could handle him without making things worse with Clay.

As Christmas approached, her excitement grew. Clay's family planned to celebrate with him, and she would spend Christmas Day with them. When her mother found out they would be in town, she invited them to their Christmas party. Clara was nervous about the party because Trevor and his parents would be there too, but dismissed it. Perhaps she shouldn't have.

The morning of the party, the sun woke Clara before her alarm. She rolled over and found Mistletoe curled up at her feet. She stretched and scratched her cat behind the ears. Mistletoe stretched, waking and ready for the day, and the two headed into the kitchen. Clara made coffee and thought about her recent conversations with Santa.

She had encountered him in the strangest places. He was at the grocery store, the coffee shop, and he even joined her for a cup of hot chocolate at her Christmas shop. Every time, he asked her if she was enjoying her experience and every time, she reported things were more difficult. The last conversation they had was worrisome. It ended with an ominous warning about time running out. Then he disappeared.

Clara had thought living a Christmas movie meant everything would be perfect, and things weren't perfect anymore. She was on eggshells every time she was around Clay, and she was resenting her parents and all the time they took from her plans. It was fun at first, but now it was overwhelming.

"And, what did Santa mean, 'before it is too late'?" she wondered out loud to Mistletoe, who was rubbing up against her ankle. Mistletoe purred in response.

Taking her coffee to the sofa, Clara sat down and looked into the backyard when her phone rang. It was Clay.

"Good morning."

"Good morning, yourself," he answered.

"Did your parents make it in last night?"

"Yes, and they are excited about meeting your parents tonight."

Clara's stomach fluttered with nerves. Trevor had been so obnoxious just meeting Clay, she wasn't sure what would happen in front of Clay's parents.

"What are you doing today?" she asked.

"Mostly just being together. My mom wants to go to the grocery store to stock up for Christmas Eve and Christmas Day. I thought we'd stop by your shop so they could see where you work. My mom will love it. I'll probably have to drag her out of there."

They made plans to meet before Clara opened the shop. She thought he seemed like his usual self, and she was excited to see him and his parents before the party.

She wore a cardigan that brought out her green eyes. With mascara and lip gloss on, she ran a brush through her hair and was ready to go. Clara pulled on her most comfortable boots, grabbed her coat and bag, and was ready to leave for the day. Checking to see that Mistletoe had food and water, she headed across town to meet Clay and his parents.

Maggie was opening the store, so she didn't have to be there right when it opened. Clara was glad she had this flexibility in her schedule. She wanted to have a leisurely coffee with Clay and his parents.

She arrived first and as usual her coffee was ready at the bar. This time in a glass mug. Clara dropped some bills in the tip jar and took her coffee to claim a table and wait. She watched the customers come and go, when she heard Clay call her name. Clara turned to see Clay and his parents walk toward her. She rose and gave him a hug, and he kissed her cheek. It relieved her he seemed relaxed. Things were back to normal. She hugged his parents and welcomed them to town, explaining that she was happy they could come and her parents looked forward to meeting them.

"Oh, we wouldn't have missed this for the world," his mom said, smiling.

Clara noticed Clay shot his mother a look, but she dismissed it.

"What should we order? It smells wonderful in here."

"Everything is delicious. They roast and grind their beans so the coffee is amazing, and we order pastries from here for the shop," Clara explained.

Clay and his family dropped their coats at the table, folding them over the back of their chairs. Clara sat at the table, waiting as they ordered coffee and muffins. Their conversation and laughing continued as they waited at the bar for their order. Clara smiled. *Maybe he was anxious about his parents' visit.* Now that they are here, he could just enjoy them.

She smiled up at him as he approached the table with his parents in tow. They settled into their seats, arranging their coffee and plates before them.

Clay's father asked, "Clara, how does your business do in the months after Christmas?"

"There is a lull January through June. That's when I reset the store and do a very intense cleaning. I use that time to see what trends are coming for the next Christmas and ordering inventory. By February, I have a lot of my contracts for window or lobby scenes completed, at least for my repeat accounts. March is full of design meetings and sketching out their vision and getting approval. Then the rest of the time until October is ordering or finding what I need from what I have in store or in storage and setting a schedule to get them all set up. In October, I hire a team to help me get everything put into place. As you might have noticed, companies are doing their Christmas decorations earlier and earlier each year, so that means I need to have things in place and ready to go by mid-October. Once things are up, I can concentrate on the store until Christmas, and then I start over."

She took a swallow of her coffee.

"That sounds like a lot of planning and prep for a quick season."

"Dad, wait until you see what she has done with the displays in the mall. They are amazing." Clay smiled at Clara.

Turning toward Clay's dad, Clara said, "It is, but I love it. I've always loved Christmas. Since I was a little girl, I couldn't wait for December. There is something magical about Christmas. It's the time of the year when everything is perfect. Anything can happen at Christmas," she said, beaming.

Clay and his parents exchanged a glance, and his mother said, "Yes, wonderful things happen at Christmas."

They continued to visit comfortably as they emptied their cups and plates, and Clara checked her watch.

"This has been wonderful, but I really need to get to the store. Clay mentioned that you might pop in to see it, and I hope you do."

She stood and put on her coat and collected her bag from under the table. As Clara picked up her cup to take to the counter, Clay stood and gave her a hug and a quick kiss. "We'll come by later." He smiled at her, and her anxiety about him and the party melted away.

Maybe things will be fine after all, she thought, entering the mall.

There weren't many shoppers in her store this close to Christmas, but she had a lot of mall employees and others who popped in for cocoa and a break. The energy in the rest of the mall was at a fever pitch as people rushed about to get last-minute gifts. The line for Santa was the longest of all season. As she passed by, he smiled and winked at her. This put even more pep in her step as she continued to make her way to the store.

Clay and his parents dropped by that afternoon. They were impressed and enjoyed browsing the decor options. They told Clay and Clara stories from their childhood Christmases. She watched Clay as his parents explored the store. He was proud of her and the business she built and wanted to share that with his parents.

She left the store in Maggie and Beth's capable hands, later in the day, to get ready for the party. She took items she was donating for the prizes from the office in the back of the store and headed back through the mall to her car.

Making her way across town to her house, she smiled as she thought about the party. Things were finally coming together. She thought about Santa's warning and dismissed it. Everything was perfect. Her business was booming, her relationship was back on track, and she was excited about her parents' party.

She hummed along with the radio as she pulled into her driveway. Letting herself in, she checked on Mistletoe as she set down her coat and bag. She checked her messages and found several from her mother about the party: a reminder to get there early, another to bring the trivia game and prizes, and a third confirming that Clay had contacted her to let her know his parents would be there.

Clara smiled to herself and sent a message that everything would be fine: she would be there early, she already had the game and prizes in the car, and she knew that Clay and his parents would be there because she had seen them earlier that day.

Walking into her room, she noticed someone laid her clothes out for her. It was the dress she had worn to all the Christmas parties, the black one. It was all there, just like the night of Clay's office party. The jewelry, purse, stockings, and shoes were next to it on the bed. Beside her purse, she found a note handwritten on white and red candy striped paper. It read, "Dear Clara, Tonight is a do-over, a chance to make things right. Merry Christmas, Santa Claus."

Humming Christmas carols, Clara spent the next hour getting ready. She was excited about the party. Clay was going to pick her up and take her to the party early to help her parents with any last-minute preparations before the rest of the guests arrived. Clay's parents were coming later on their own.

When she was almost dressed and ready, Clara's phone rang. She quickly answered as she slipped on her black heels.

"Hello."

"Hey Clara, just letting you know I am leaving in about ten minutes. Is there anything I need to pick up before the party?" Clay asked.

"I don't think so. I have the game and prizes in my car. We can transfer them when you get here."

"Okay. By the way, I have a surprise for you."

"It isn't Christmas yet."

"Well, this one's a little early. I'll see you in a few minutes."

Putting on the finishing touches of her makeup, she was about to shut off her bedroom light when her mother called.

"Clara, I know you are in a rush to get ready, but I wanted to remind you about the prizes."

"Mom, I already told you they are in the car."

"Yes, but isn't Clay driving you over here?"

"Yes, and we are going to move them from my car to his."

"Okay. Well, don't get dirty doing that. You are going to want to look your best tonight."

Clara rolled her eyes. "Okay. I have to go. Clay will be here any minute. See you soon."

Hanging up, she looked around her house at all the decorations. She felt butterflies in her stomach in anticipation of the big night. First Santa leaving a cryptic message, and now Clay and her mother. She wasn't sure what was afoot.

Clay arrived and knocked on the door, interrupting her thoughts. When she opened the door, he stood under the mistletoe with a cup from Cool Beans.

"Wow, you look great." He stepped toward her. "I thought you'd like coffee more than flowers." He smiled.

"Thank you, and yes, coffee is always a better choice." She gave him a quick kiss.

Walking toward the cars, Clay explained, "Your mother called and asked me to make sure that I transferred the prizes. She insisted. Something about not wanting you to get dirty."

"I know. She called me too. She's never worried so much about my appearance."

"Tonight is a big night. She probably doesn't want you to be self-conscious about pictures."

"Yeah, but there are always pictures from her party. And may I remind you it was at her insistence that we had to take a picture with Santa wearing those crazy sweaters?"

"Whatever. Let's just get the prizes and get over there before she gets worried that you might make mud pies in that beautiful dress."

Clay was quieter than usual, and Clara was anxious. Usually, he had no trouble carrying on a conversation. Clara wondered whether he was concerned about running into Trevor at the party. Surely his parents would be there, and that would mean he would be there too.

"Why are you so quiet?" she asked.

"Just thinking about the party and wondering who will be there."

"There should be enough people there to avoid Trevor, if that is what you are concerned about."

She saw Clay's jaw tense at the mention of Trevor's name.

"Are you worried about avoiding Trevor?" she asked.

"It is just that he seems to insert himself whenever we're together, but even he can't ruin tonight." Clay squeezed Clara's hand.

She settled back into her seat, ready for what the evening would bring.

The house was buzzing with activity when they arrived. Taking the prizes from her store into the house, she asked her mother where to display them.

"Over there, on the table next to the desserts," her mother directed.

As she stepped toward the table, her mother said, "Tonight is going to be a very special night." Smiling, her mother continued, "You look happy and beautiful."

Thinking that it was a strange thing to say, she responded, "Well, luckily I didn't ruin my dress leaning into the trunk to get all of your stuff." She smiled at her mother and continued, "Mom, everything looks perfect."

Her mother beamed, hearing this compliment from Clara. Everyone knew what Clara did for a living, and it was hard to compete with her creative decorations and displays.

Everyone had a role to make sure the party ran smoothly. Kayla and Clara took turns meeting everyone at the door to take their coats and welcome them into the party.

Clara knew this party was mostly for her parents and their friends, so it surprised her when some of her friends arrived.

As she was walking down the hall from a coat run, she heard Sam's and Maria's voices. She didn't remember seeing them on the guest list but was excited to see them.

"There she is," Sam said as she walked toward them. Stepping toward her, he and Maria both gave her big hugs.

"I'm so glad you are here." Clara looked from them to her sister. "I didn't know you were coming tonight."

"I made sure they were on the guest list, and I think Clay delivered the invitation," Kayla explained. "I knew you'd want them here."

"Well, I am so glad you did." She turned to Sam and Maria. "Through there you will find lots of food and drinks. In the backyard, we are going to have a s'mores station set up shortly. Help yourself. Clay should be in there somewhere. I'm not sure where Mom put him to work."

They walked through the entryway and into the living room as directed.

More guests arrived, and Clara and Kayla continued their system. Clara was the one to open the door when Trevor's parents rang the doorbell.

As with everyone else, she welcomed them in, taking their coats and his mother's purse. "It's so good to see you." She stepped aside to make room for them in the entryway.

"Well, don't you look lovely," Trevor's mother said.

"Thank you. You look lovely yourself," Clara answered. And she was right. Trevor's mother was stunning.

"We're sorry Trevor won't be joining us tonight. He had other plans," his mother said. "He has a date tonight."

"That's nice. I know he's had a difficult time adjusting to being at home."

"You know, we always hoped that the two of you would work things out. You were so perfect for each other," his mother said as her husband tried to shush her.

"We may have been perfect for each other in high school, but we're different people now," Clara said, as Clay came over to stand by her.

"I know. And you found a wonderful young man, for now." She smiled at Clara as they walked into the party.

"What was that all about?" Clay asked.

"She was being nostalgic. They're Trevor's parents, and evidently she always wanted us to end up together." Reaching down, she took Clay's hand. "But then we found each other and I'm not interested in working anything out with anyone."

"Is Trevor coming tonight then?"

"I don't think so. His mom said he had a date."

"Good. I guess I was wrong to judge him before."

"Let's stop talking about Trevor and enjoy the party," Clara said as they walked toward the food tables set up in the dining room.

A moment later, she heard a familiar voice above the din of the crowd and Christmas music. Sophie had just arrived. Clara turned and saw Sophie come in with a date. His back was to her as he handed Kayla his coat. Clara thought he looked familiar. *Sophie was on vacation. What was she doing home so early, and why hadn't she mentioned she was dating someone?*

They made eye contact and Sophie waved. Clara smiled and waved back just as the mystery man turned around. It was Trevor. She had little time to recover before they made it to Clara.

"Clara, why do you look so surprised?" Sophie asked.

"I didn't see you on the guest list. I thought you were on vacation."

"A turn of the weather meant I needed to leave early rather than get stuck. I have to get back to work the day after Christmas. I couldn't risk it."

Clara nodded.

Sophie continued, "Hey, did you know Trevor's back in town? I ran into him last night at the coffee shop on my way home from the airport. We had a great visit, and he invited me to come to the party tonight. It's like old times, the three of us hanging out together. You don't mind, do you?" Sophie's face fell.

"No, absolutely not. I am so glad to see you. Yes, I knew he was in town. He keeps showing up. It's been awkward with Clay and all."

"What has been awkward with Clay?" she heard from behind her.

"Oh, I was just explaining to Sophie that Trevor keeps showing up places, and it has been awkward. I kind of feel sorry for the guy."

"Sophie, it's so good to see you," Clay said as he gave her a hug. "And, why are we talking about Trevor?"

"I came with him," Sophie explained. Looking around, she said, "We walked in together, but I'm not sure where he went. He was just standing next to me."

"Maybe to find his parents," Clara offered.

"I better find him then." Sophie walked toward the other guests and the food.

"I thought he wasn't coming tonight," Clay said under his breath.

"That's what I was told, that he had a date. I guess he brought a date. It's weird that he brought Sophie. He knows she is my best friend. I am not sure that she knows she is on a date, or maybe she does, but it still seems out of character."

"You wanted him to move on and leave you alone, so this is perfect. Don't you think? Now everyone is happy."

"I guess. You just never know with Trevor."

"Come on. Let's get some food and find a place to sit."

Clara followed him through the crowd, aware that people were watching them. It was unsettling, as if everyone knew something she didn't.

The party went as parties do. There was plenty of eating, drinking, and merrymaking. Clara and Clay made the rounds, spending time with each guest. Clara didn't enjoy Christmas parties, but this one was fun and she had known all these people for a long time. It was wonderful to catch up during the holidays.

Throughout the party, she sensed someone watching her and would catch Trevor staring at her. He quickly averted his gaze when she caught him. She wondered again why Sophie was here with him. *Was he interested in dating her, or maybe she was interested in dating him?* Clara decided to just let it go. *It really isn't any of my business, anyway.*

Clara and Clay went into the brisk backyard for s'mores and to check out the movie setup. There were a few couples in the backyard enjoying the fire and the movie. She and Clay were roasting marshmallows when she realized she needed to replenish the napkins. They were going fast because of the melted marshmallows.

"Here, hold this. I'll be right back," she said to Clay.

"Where are you going?"

"To the kitchen. I need to get more napkins and wet wipes for everyone's hands. They have to be a sticky mess and a regular napkin won't work." She tried to wipe her hands and part of the paper napkin stuck to her fingers and ripped off from the rest of the napkin.

Inside, she made her way through the house to the kitchen. The counters were full of plates, napkins, cups, cutlery, and platters of food to be brought out. The only illumination came from the windows and the light above the sink.

Clara made her way to the napkins and looked around for some wet wipes. She knew they bought some, expecting the marshmallow mess. As she sorted through piles and opened and closed cabinets, she heard a noise behind her. Startled, she whipped around.

"For goodness' sake. It's just me," Trevor said.

"Why didn't you say something when I came in? You scared me to death."

"That's an exaggeration. I can see that you are still alive."

"Whatever. Why are you in here, anyway? Where's Sophie?"

"Oh, you know Sophie. It's just like when we were in high school. She hasn't changed a bit. She walks into the room and captivates everyone."

"Well, if you don't like her, why did you invite her to come with you?"

Ignoring her question, Trevor got up from the table and walked toward her to help in her search. "What are you looking for, anyway?"

"Wet wipes for the marshmallow mess. And you didn't answer my question."

Continuing to help her look, he answered, "I know I hide it well, but things haven't been going well for me lately. I lost my business, I had to move home to stay with my parents while I figure things out, I have nothing to do and no friends to spend time with. And really, who wants to date a thirty-year-old guy still living in his parents' basement?"

Clara stopped looking for the wet wipes and turned to listen to him. She hadn't realized that he was so miserable and felt guilty.

"Anyway, you were busy and obviously moved on with Mr. Perfect. When I ran into Sophie, I thought it might be nice. You know, just see what happens."

Clara was about to answer when the overhead light flipped on.

"Oh, there you are. Why are you looking in the dark?" Clay asked and then stopped, staring at the scene in front of him. "I brought your s'more," he said, holding it out.

Looking directly at Trevor, he added, "I didn't know you needed help to look for napkins."

"Thank you," she said, taking the s'more from him. "I don't. I didn't know anyone was in here when I came in. In fact, funny story, I was looking around these piles and heard Trevor behind me. I nearly jumped right out of my skin."

"Yeah, I was in here getting a break from the holiday cheer," Trevor answered. "If you'll excuse me, I better find Sophie. She is probably wondering where I am."

"Yes," Clay agreed, "you should go find your date."

Trevor stepped out, and Clara sighed. "It wasn't what you think. He was in here all sad and depressed, and I was just about to leave when you came in."

"Really? Because it looked like he was making you feel bad for him because he's lonely and you have a history."

Clara wondered how Clay could tell she felt sorry for Trevor. Then she was angry that Trevor kept putting her in this position.

"Well, if so, he was unsuccessful." She stood on her tiptoes and kissed Clay. "For the rest of the night, I will stay with you. Is that better?"

"Not really. You should be able to enjoy your parents' party without having to worry about me or anyone else. I will get over it," he said, smiling mischievously. "Besides, I have a surprise for you later that even Trevor can't mess up."

"Really? What is it?"

"You will find out. Come on, let's get back to the party."

They walked out in time for the first game. Her parents set up a huge whiteboard on an easel with a box of multicolored dry erase markers.

"This should be fun," Clara said to Clay. She loved games at Christmastime.

Clay seemed nervous and pulled his hand from hers, wiping it on his pants.

"Are you all right?" she asked.

"Yeah, why?"

"I don't know. You seem off, really nervous."

"I'm fine. Come on, let's find out who our partners are."

Clara noticed her mom giving a look that appeared to be some kind of signal to Clay, and he nodded. They took their places in the living room and waited for their names to be drawn. The guests laughed as they reminisced about how competitive previous years had been.

Kayla stood by the board to give rules. "There will be two groups, the left side of the room and the right side of the room."

Clara looked around to see who would be on her team. *Oh no*, she thought, irritated. Trevor would be part of their team.

Kayla went on, "Each of you has a slip of paper and each group has a jar. Write your name on the slip and put them in the jar. Each team will pull two names out of the jar. These players will come to the board. One will draw and the other will guess. Each team has one minute. The team with the most correct guesses wins."

"What do we draw?" someone from the other team asked.

"I forgot. I'll give the person who is drawing a Christmas movie or item they will have to draw. Those are right here in this box," Kayla explained, shaking a box wrapped like a present. "If there are no other questions, let's get started."

The other team went first. Their clue was *Rudolph the Red-Nosed Reindeer*, and the one guessing got it when the artist drew a red circle. The crowd exploded with cheers and complaints that that was too easy.

"Settle down. Some are easier than others," Kayla admitted.

Clara's team was next. Kayla drew two more names, and they got their first point when the player correctly guessed *Elf on the Shelf*, after seeing a stick figure sitting on a brown line.

It went like this, back and forth for a few rounds, with some more difficult than others, and some drawings were hilarious and way off course. Each team accrued a few points, and the competition was heating.

Kayla reached into their team's jar to draw two players for the next round and called out, "Trevor." Reaching in again, she swirled around the slips, building the anticipation. Pulling one out, she opened it and gave a slight frown in Clara's direction as she said, "Clara," mouthing "I'm sorry" to her sister. She stepped away from the board to make room for the two.

Clara glanced over at Clay.

He smiled and squeezed her hand. "Good luck."

She breathed a sigh of relief as she walked to the board, glancing back at him one more time for reassurance. He smiled and nodded, calming her nerves as she took her place.

They agreed Trevor would draw, and she would guess. Trevor reached into the box with the clues and his face broke out into a huge grin. Kayla counted them down as she set the timer and when she yelled, "Go!" he grabbed a gray marker and started drawing a large rectangle.

In high school, they had been very good at this game and had developed a system. As soon as one started drawing, the other began guessing. They immediately slipped back into that strategy and Clara began yelling out, "Present, package, *Miracle on 34th Street*, Empire State Building, *Home Alone 2*."

Trevor continued drawing, adding details and tapping his watch, showing she was running out of time. Kayla gave them the thirty-second warning. Clara kept guessing as Trevor was drawing a stick figure Santa, yelling out "*The Santa Claus, Scrooged*." Trevor shook his head as Kayla began counting down from five, four, three. Trevor grabbed the orange and red markers and, holding them together, drew a big colored circle with lines coming off right on the rectangle building. Just as Kayla said, "One," Clara jumped up and yelled, "*Die Hard*!"

"And this team gets another point," Kayla said, adding to the tally.

The partygoers were still cheering when Trevor enveloped Clara in a bear hug, lifting her off the floor.

"I knew you would get it. As soon as I thought about the explosion. We always were an excellent team," Trevor said, looking at Clay over Clara's head.

Suddenly, Clara was aware of what was happening and tried to remove herself from the hug. That was when Trevor leaned in and kissed her.

Clara shoved him away, but the damage was already done. "Trevor, what are you doing!"

"We won! Just like old times."

"This is not old times, you idiot! What is wrong with you?" She looked around for Clay, turning from him and trying to get away as fast as she could.

Trevor grabbed her hand. "Wait, where are you going?"

"I have to find Clay. You are ruining everything. My life was perfect until you came back. I wish I had never met you."

The rest of the partygoers didn't know how to react to this outburst and were silently watching the uncomfortable scene unfold.

In tears, Clara ran from the room, bumping into Sophie in the entryway.

"Move out of my way," she said to Sophie as she tried to get to the door.

"Clara, I tried to go after him. I explained Trevor is a jerk and tried to get him to stay and talk to you, but he wouldn't listen. When he got to his car, he just said, 'I tried to warn her. I guess she chose a history with him over a future with me.'"

Pushing her friend aside, she ran through the door to the driveway just as Clay's taillights turned out of the neighborhood. Standing there, out of breath from running and calling out to Clay, she heard angry voices behind her.

She turned and looked up from the street to see Sophie trying to hold Trevor back.

"Stay away from her," Sophie said.

"Let me explain. I didn't even think about it. It was a reflex."

"No one believes that, Trevor. I saw you look at Clay as you kissed her."

Clara's blood boiled as she stormed up the lawn toward the two of them. "Is that true?"

"No! Why would I do that? I just got carried away. But I'm not sorry. If that is all it took for Clay to leave you here humiliated and alone, then he doesn't deserve to be with you."

Clara heard all she could stand. "Clay was right about you. You are a terrible person. All you care about is yourself. Clay was patient, trying to give you the benefit of the doubt at first. I even felt sorry for you, all miserable and alone. You were the one who humiliated me."

As the party moved outside, Trevor took a step toward Clara. "Come on. You don't mean all of that. You're upset. Let me drive you home. I can help you sort this out with Clay. It really isn't a big deal."

Clara's eyes narrowed as she stepped back. "Trevor, get away from me. I hate you and never want to see you again." Shooting her parents a look, she emphasized this by saying, "Ever!"

She turned toward her friend. "Sophie, please take me home. I have to find Clay and fix this."

"Um, I rode with Trevor. I don't have a ride home either," Sophie said.

Clara tried to understand what was happening and tried to figure out how to get home, when she heard a voice from the house. "I'm coming. I'll take both of you home."

Kayla ran out of the house with her keys jangling. Shaking them in the air, she said, "What are you waiting for? Hurry."

Clara and Sophie followed Kayla to the car. She had grabbed both of their bags and tossed them in the backseat. The women barely had enough time to buckle their seat belts before Kayla peeled off toward Clara's house.

"Don't worry," Sophie said.

"We'll help you explain everything," Kayla agreed, looking over at her sister in the passenger seat.

Clara rummaged around in her bag to find her cell phone. She dialed Clay and waited while the phone rang and rang.

"He isn't answering," she said, crying.

"Leave a message and then call back," Sophie said from the backseat.

Clara suddenly put her hand up to shush the other women. "Clay, please call me back. I need to explain what happened."

They continued to drive to Clara's house. A few minutes later, she called again.

"Clay, please call me. I know what Trevor did. Sophie and Kayla explained everything. We need to talk about this."

After a few minutes of no call from Clay, she made another attempt.

"Clay, please, please call me back. I am really sorry about what happened, and I am worried. Can we please talk about this?"

The three women continued to drive. Kayla and Sophie took turns trying to comfort Clara.

"Look, I'll go talk to him, explain everything and tell him about the big argument in the middle of the yard after he left. He is a very understanding person," Sophie explained.

"Everything's ruined," Clara wailed as her sister tried to find a tissue in the center console.

Kayla handed a distraught Clara a wadded-up napkin she found. "Here, use this," she said, and Clara blotted her eyes and blew her nose.

Sophie tried again to console her friend. "Try to calm down. We'll help get this worked out."

Kayla looked in the rearview mirror at Sophie, and they exchanged a look.

Clara saw it and immediately said, "Kayla, what was that for?"

"What was what for?"

"That look you just gave Sophie. What was that for?"

Kayla let out an enormous sigh. "Tonight...was supposed to end differently." She looked over at her sister before going on. "At the end of the game, the last time it was your team's turn, I was going to make sure that you and Clay were picked for the last round. He was going to draw a ring on the board."

A fresh round of tears flooded out of Clara. "I can't believe this happened. He warned me about Trevor. Trevor ruined everything."

Kayla reached over and patted her sister's leg. "He really loves you. He had this whole thing worked out. Why do you think we made sure Sam and Maria and all of Mom and Dad's friends were here? Even his parents came."

"Oh no, his parents. They must have seen the whole thing and think I am a horrible person." She sobbed.

"At least they have a ride home," Sophie tried to joke from the backseat to lighten the mood. It didn't work.

Clara continued to cry. She was beyond consolation and the two other women sat in silence as they pulled into Clara's driveway. They got out of the car and went inside with her as Clara settled in for the night.

"Come on, let's wash your face and get you in some cozy pajamas," they said, guiding her to her bedroom. She laid down on her bed as Sophie dug through drawers to find the softest, comfiest pajamas she could find.

"Here, go into the bathroom and wash your face and change into these," Sophie said.

Kayla stayed in the kitchen while Sophie helped her friend. She got Clay's number from Clara's phone and dialed it from her own. There was no answer, so she left a message.

"Clay, it is Kayla. I'm calling from my phone. Listen, none of this is what you think. Clara is really upset. After you left, there was a huge argument on the lawn. You can ask your parents about it. Everyone saw what happened. I know Trevor is a jerk, and Clara is beside herself. Please call her back so you can sort this out. Please, Clay. It's Christmas, for goodness' sake."

While Clara was changing, Sophie went to talk to Kayla.

"Why did you tell her about the proposal? I think that made everything worse."

"I thought it would explain his reaction. He thought he was going to propose and there she was, kissing someone else," Kayla answered. "I wanted her to know why he reacted that way. That it wasn't something petty."

"I can't believe Trevor." Sophie shook her head. "I mean, I know he's arrogant and entitled, but that was cruel and so public. What was he thinking?"

"He thought he could get rid of Clay and swoop in and comfort Clara, winning her back."

Clara finished changing and could hear the conversation from the other room. She began crying again when she thought about how it must have looked to Clay, and rage toward Trevor coursed through her body. She walked out, interrupting the conversation, and the women fell silent.

"Sit down on the sofa and I'll bring you some cocoa." Kayla took the ingredients and mugs out of the cabinet and made three cups.

Sophie led her to the sofa and unfolded blankets to wrap her friend in a cozy cocoon. Once Clara was comfortable, she went to the bathroom and found a box of tissues and set them next to Clara.

"Now, listen. Clay will come around. If he was planning to propose tonight, he'll want to work this out. Think about it from his perspective. What if you saw someone kissing him? How would you feel at that moment? Wouldn't you be willing to listen to his explanation once your emotions settled down?"

Clara felt a shock move through her body as she realized that this was exactly what happened. In her regular life, this was what prompted the wish she made when Santa asked what she wanted for Christmas. Now she felt terrible. She never considered what Clay was feeling when she refused to listen to him after Alexis kissed him at the party.

Jumping up, she almost knocked the hot chocolate from Kayla's hand. "I have to go find Santa," she said, in a rush to find her shoes.

Sophie and Kayla exchanged glances.

"What do you mean, you need to go find Santa? I'm not sure that will help," Sophie said.

"I need to find Santa and ask him to fix this. He can make everything work out. He'll know what to do."

The girls tried to persuade her to stay. Besides, they explained, the mall was already closed and Santa was only around during the hours of businesses.

"You don't understand. Santa is everywhere. He was the one who put all of this in place, and he is the one who can give me a chance to make it all right again."

"Okay, look. That might be true, but you look a mess. You are much too upset to drive, and I...well, we"—Kayla nervously looked at Sophie and then back at Clara—"think it's better if you stay here and get some sleep. Then first thing in the morning, we'll help you find Santa. You're not thinking clearly. Besides, as you said, if Santa is everywhere, then surely he knows what happened and can help you tomorrow. Maybe he is already working out a solution."

Clara looked at her sister and her best friend and knew they thought she was crazy. Maybe she was. For goodness' sake, she was an adult who wished her life was a Christmas movie. Santa warned her, and she went ahead, not paying attention to what he said; Clay warned her, and she didn't take that seriously either. Maybe she was losing her mind.

She joined Kayla and Sophie on the sofa and let them cover her and dry her tears. They drank their hot cocoa in silence while *It's a Wonderful Life* played in the background. When they thought she had cried all the tears her body could make, the women suggested Clara go to bed and get some sleep. Things would look different in the morning.

They decided to spend the night with her and found pajamas they could borrow for the night. After they tucked her in bed, they found blankets and pillows and made themselves comfortable on the floor next to her bed.

Before turning the lights out, Clara checked her phone for any calls she may have missed. There was one. Excited, she listened, then fresh anger flashed across her face. The message was from Trevor.

"Hey, Clara. Listen, I'm sorry about what happened. I hope you don't hate me, that you are just furious with me. But do you want to be with someone who leaves you at a party like that? You didn't deserve that. I know you're upset and don't want to talk to me tonight, but maybe tomorrow we could grab coffee and talk about all this. Everyone was so mad at me after you left. Please call."

Clara couldn't believe what she was hearing. She replayed the message for Sophie and Kayla, and they were just as incensed.

"It is all about him. Of course people are mad at him. He is an arrogant, entitled idiot! What did he expect?" Sophie asked.

"You won't call him, will you?" asked Kayla.

"What do you think? He ruined everything. No, I will not call him tomorrow or ever."

She picked up her phone and tried Clay's number again.

"Clara, it is really late. Don't you think you should wait until tomorrow?"

"Just one more call and then I will go to sleep. I promise," she said as she heard the recording: "This is Clay. I can't answer the phone right now. Please leave a message and I'll return your call as soon as possible."

"Clay, please call me. You were right about everything. I am so sorry. If I were in your shoes, I would be mad and hurt too. Please call me tomorrow so we can talk about this."

Hanging up, she let out a ragged sigh. There were no more tears, and she wondered whether a person could become dehydrated from crying. Her eyes and head hurt, and she thought she might never be happy again. With only a couple of days left until Christmas, she had to have Santa fix this. She made a plan to find him tomorrow and ask him to put everything back to normal.

Chapter 21

The next morning, Kayla and Sophie woke up before Clara. This time Sophie called Clay. After the third ring, he answered.

"Hello."

"Clay, don't hang up," she said.

Clay sighed on the other end. "How is she?"

"Still asleep, which is why I'm calling. She doesn't know I'm talking to you. Look, we all know what happened. Trevor is a horrible person. She feels terrible and cried herself to sleep last night. Kayla and I stayed with her so she wouldn't be alone. She's devastated."

"What do you want me to do?"

"I want you to talk to her, let her know you care about her and that you want to fix this."

"I care about her, but I don't know if we can fix it. She didn't listen when I tried to warn her about Trevor. I am upset too."

"I know, and everyone except Trevor feels horrible about what happened. Please talk to her."

"I know it upset her, but I need time to think. I don't know what to do and as long as Trevor is in town, finding himself, it will be a problem."

"Will you at least listen to her messages? I know she left you several."

"I have, and they are painful. Tell her I'll call her when I'm ready to talk."

Sophie heard Clara stirring in the next room. "She's awake. I have to go. Please call her soon. Don't wait too long. You know you care about her and can fix all of this."

Clara walked into the kitchen as Sophie ended the call.

"How did you sleep?" she asked Clara.

"Terrible. My head hurts and my eyes are so puffy I can barely see out of them."

"Come here and have some coffee. You'll feel better."

Kayla poured her sister a cup and handed it to her.

"Who were you talking to a minute ago? It is pretty early for a phone call." Clara took a long sip from her cup.

"Clay."

Putting her cup down, Clara leaned closer to her friend. "What did he say? Did he call you?"

"No, I called him."

Clara's face fell.

"But he answered, so that's progress. He's understandably upset. He promised to call you when he's ready, but right now he wants to think about things."

Clara's tears came all at once. They expressed all the feelings that were overwhelming her. She was angry, sad, humiliated, exhausted, and hopeless. She wasn't sure what to do next, so she reached for her phone.

"Don't," Sophie said. "He's listened to your messages and knows how you feel. Give him some time. He'll reach out. He said he would, and he's dependable. If he said he'd call, he'll call."

Clara set the phone on the table and picked up her cup. "What am I supposed to do today?"

"Mom and Dad are expecting us to spend the day with them, putting the house back together after the party last night."

"I am not doing that. I can't risk seeing Trevor, and you know he'll try to talk to me when he sees my car pull into the driveway."

"I'm sure Mom and Dad will understand. I'm going to get dressed and go home. Can you give Sophie a ride home later?"

"Yes."

"Sophie, can you stay with Clara for a while today? I will go deal with Mom and Dad. Try not to worry, Clara. Things have a way of working out. Christmas is a magical time."

Kayla changed back into her clothes from the night before and poured another cup of coffee for Clara and Sophie, and fed and watered Mistletoe before she left.

Alone, Sophie and Clara sat, quietly drinking their coffee.

"What do you want to do today?" Sophie said.

"I don't know. Don't you have things to do?"

"No. I'm supposed to be on vacation, remember? I have a completely clear schedule."

"I'm not sure I'll be good company today. I'm so miserable I can hardly stand to be around myself."

"Why don't you get a shower and get dressed. We can go to Cool Beans and maybe a movie. I'll check to see what is playing while you're in the shower."

Obediently, Clara rose from her nest of blankets and walked toward her bedroom.

They made it to Cool Beans after the morning rush. Clara was grateful she was less likely to run into anyone she saw regularly. She knew the store was in excellent hands and called in to tell Maggie she might not be in. Maggie said she understood and not to worry. Maggie reminded her that the mall Christmas party was that night.

"Oh no, I forgot all about that," Clara said.

"You're coming, aren't you? You know they are judging all the window scenes and you will most likely win."

"Yes, I'll be there."

"Are you bringing Clay?"

A new round of tears flowed. "I don't think so. We had a little situation last night and I'm not sure he wants to see me right now."

"I'm so sorry. Surely, you'll work it out."

"Everyone keeps saying that. I'll see you tonight." Clara was eager to get off the phone. She didn't want to hear anyone else's assurances that things would be fine.

She checked her phone to see whether there were any messages. Her parents called to find out when she and Kayla were coming home. No message from Clay. She slipped her phone back into her bag.

"No message?"

"No message."

"Come on. Let's go walk around the mall."

Clara let her friend lead her through the parking lot and into the mall. They passed by a bell ringer and she dropped some money into the kettle. "Merry Christmas," the bell ringer sang out. "Merry Christmas," she said in return as she walked through the doors.

Frantic last-minute shoppers were trying to get the gifts on their list. There was a line of families waiting to see Santa. She thought about getting in line herself, but thought even Santa couldn't fix this. They stopped and looked at the scenes she created in different shops and eavesdropped on shoppers' conversations. Everyone was happy, everyone except Clara, and she could barely stand it.

"There she is," a man's voice bellowed behind her. She turned.

Sam walked toward her. "How are you?" he asked, concerned. "Last night was a doozy."

"I know. He won't return my calls. I don't know what to do."

"Trevor humiliated him, but he cares about you. He'll come around." Sam gave her a hug. "Are you coming to the party tonight?"

"I guess so."

"Yes, she will be there," Sophie confirmed. "I will make sure of it."

"Then I'll see you tonight. Keep your chin up, kid. Things have a way of working out." He gave her another quick hug and went about his rounds.

They walked toward the food court and movie theater in silence. Sophie was quiet, allowing her friend to talk when she needed to.

Sophie purchased two tickets for *Miracle on 34th Street* and Clara stopped at the counter for drinks, popcorn, and candy.

"You must feel terrible to get all this," Sophie joked.

Clara offered a feeble smile. "Well, I don't have to share, so I'm getting all the things I like—Junior Mints, M&M's, and Red Vines. I can wallow in my misery and get a sugar rush at the same time."

They handed their tickets to the teenager manning the booth, and he directed them to a theater down the hall on the right. Clara remembered the last time she was in this theater was with Clay. It seemed like a lifetime ago.

Most likely everyone in the audience had already seen the movie. It was the remake of the classic. She looked around. It looked like a lot of them were taking a break from shopping based on the bags on the floor in front of them and in the seats beside them. Others were maybe escaping family and just needed a couple of hours of peace. Silence fell over the theater as the lights dimmed and the movie began.

Clara had hoped that the movie would distract her from her misery. She occasionally pulled out her phone and checked for messages. The third time, Sophie took her phone, promising to give it back after the movie.

Clara forced herself to watch as Bryan Bedford tried desperately to win the heart of Dorey Walker as he tries to defend Santa, proving he is real. She thought about her encounter with Santa. *How did everything go so wrong? She wished for her life to be a Christmas movie. Christmas movies were happy, magical, filled with merriment and joy. She was living a nightmare.* She expected things to be perfect, not have all this drama.

The movie continued, and she felt empathy for the characters. Little Susan wanted to believe in Santa and his magic. Dorey wanted to protect herself and her daughter from getting hurt, and all Bryan wanted was the chance to be a family. She watched the story unfold and by the end she knew, she had to find Santa. He could fix this mess. But first she had to get rid of Sophie. Sophie would never go along with her plan.

The movie ended. Of course, everything worked out perfectly, as a Christmas movie should. Leaving the theater, Clara said, "I think I am going to take you home. I really need to take a nap before the party."

"Are you sure you want to be alone the rest of the day? I can grab a change of clothes and stay with you."

"No, really. You and Kayla were very helpful. I just need some sleep."

"You aren't going to his house, are you?"

"No, I'm going to respect his need for time and space. But I have to go to the party tonight, and I really need to rest and depuff my eyes. I can't wear sunglasses to a party at night." She laughed.

Sophie looked at her friend. Finally, she said, "Okay, but if you need to talk, you can call me and I'll be right over."

"I know. And thank you."

"Okay, let's go," she said as they headed toward the parking lot.

When they got to the car, Sophie handed over Clara's phone.

She checked for messages and felt a pang of sadness that there weren't any.

Clara dropped Sophie off at her house, promising to call her later to check in. Sophie hugged her friend and encouraged her to get some rest. Clara watched Sophie enter her house before taking off for her first stop on her search for Santa. She had to get this straightened out, and she intended to have him put everything right again.

Checking her watch, she drove quickly across town to the tree farm. She hoped they would still be open this close to Christmas. The parking area only had a few cars when she pulled in. Clara paid her entrance fee and went inside. She thought of the day she was here with her family and Clay and felt sad, but then determination kicked in and she retraced her steps. She walked through the field with a few trees dotted here and there. Then she went through the maze, this time following the map, so she made it through quickly. She was the only one in the maze, and it was a little strange. After the maze, she made her way to the food trucks. Ordering a coffee and funnel cake, she sat at the same table she sat with Clay. She choked down a few bites, looking around for any signs of Santa. Finishing the funnel cake and coffee, she rose in search of a trash bin. Dumping her plate and empty cup in the bin, she heard bells ringing in the distance. She turned quickly and looked in that direction. There was Santa, ringing the bell next to the red kettle. She made her way, walking as fast as she could without drawing attention to herself, determined to reach Santa when no one else was around. She was about to tell him all of her troubles and ask him to fix things when she noticed it wasn't him. This was just a guy dressed like Santa.

"Where is the other Santa? Is he coming today?" she asked.

The man looked at her, puzzled. "I'm the only Santa who works here."

It was confusing. "I was here a few days ago and there was a different Santa working. He looked like the real thing. Real beard, real belly, real jolly." She was getting upset. "I have to talk to him."

"Are you okay? Maybe you should sit down for a minute." The man dressed as Santa stepped toward her. "I can assure you I am the volunteer assigned to this post. I've been here all month."

She stepped back. "I must be mistaken. I'm sorry." Clara dropped some coins in the kettle and turned to hurry back to her car. "Merry Christmas," she heard the man say. "Merry Christmas," she called over her shoulder.

In her car, she thought about the last few days and tried to remember all the places she saw Santa. She realized where to go next.

She started the car and was off. Christmas music played from the radio, and hope grew in the pit of her stomach as she reached her next destination.

Getting out of the car, she jogged across the parking lot toward the nursing home entrance. She had seen Santa there the night they went caroling. He had to be there. As she entered the building, she almost ran into Frank, the man she and Clay visited with days before.

"I knew you would come back for a visit," Frank said.

"You did? How did you know?"

"I just knew. Your fella was here not too long ago. We had a nice long chat. I was sorry that you weren't with him. He explained you had had a falling-out."

"What else did he say?"

"Well, he was pretty broken up about it. I told him to talk it out. Things have a way of working themselves out when everyone is honest. You know, he really cares about you. I think he'll come around."

"I'm sorry. Why did he come here? I didn't think that you were friends."

"Oh, we aren't. He came to drop some gifts off that his business collected for the residents. I asked him to join me for coffee and he just started spilling his guts like a heartbroken teenager. If it makes a difference, I told him not to wait too long. Someone else will come along and then he won't have a second chance."

"Oh, I see."

"Would you like to join me for coffee too?"

"I don't really have time right now, but I will come back. Soon. Um, do you know where the bell ringer is who was right outside the entrance the other night? He looks like Santa. Real beard and everything."

"I don't think we have had a bell ringer here," Frank said.

Clara persisted. "Are you sure? I am positive there was one here the night we came to sing Christmas carols."

"I've never seen one. But you can ask at the desk."

"Okay, thank you. And, I will be back to have that cup of coffee. I just need to find someone right now."

"Well, you know where to find me. I'm not going anywhere." He laughed as he turned to walk down the hall.

At the desk, she asked about the bell ringer from a few nights before. The nurse looked at her, confused, and said that they didn't have bell ringers. Clara was getting frustrated; she knew she spoke with a bell ringer that night. Just to be sure, the nurse called the director on duty and confirmed that they had not had a bell ringer, but thought it was a good idea and something to pursue for next year.

Clara thanked them and walked back to her car, unsure of what to do next. Thinking that she couldn't just go home and accept defeat, she went back to the mall. She stopped in for an Americano to go at Cool Beans and then made her way around the mall to every entrance, looking for Santa. She saw him here as a bell ringer one day on her way to work and thought he would have to be here this close to Christmas. As she went from bell ringer to bell ringer, her confidence that this plan would work waned. At the last stop, she put in the rest of her change and turned to walk away. "Merry Christmas," she heard the ringer say. "Merry Christmas," she replied and continued walking.

She checked her messages. There were none from Clay.

Clara had a few hours until the mall Christmas party and she was overwhelmed with exhaustion, so tired it was difficult to keep her eyes open. She took the last few swallows of her coffee, put the car in drive and made her way home. Inside, she collapsed in a heap on the sofa. Two hours passed before she stirred. She felt her phone buzz and grabbed at it in the dark.

"Hello."

"Hey, I was just checking on you," Kayla said.

"I'm okay. I was asleep. I'm glad you called. It's time to get ready for the mall Christmas party."

"Oh, you're going to that?"

"Yes, I kind of have to. It is a work thing. At least I won't be here waiting for the phone to ring."

"Okay. Look, I ran into Trevor today. I think he really feels bad about what happened."

"I don't care how he feels about anything."

"I just thought you should know. You can't stay away from Mom and Dad's house forever."

"I'm not. Just for right now."

"So, you aren't coming for Christmas Eve then?" Kayla asked.

"Nope, not this year. I need to get ready. I'll call you later," Clara said, eager to get off the phone.

Clara went to her closet. This was it, her last chance. Hopefully, Santa would be at this party like he was when she made her wish. The wish she now regretted because it had turned out to be anything but perfect.

Opening her closet, she chose the same outfit, down to the socks and shoes. She fixed her hair the same way and wore the same color lip gloss. She thought if she could recreate the exact conditions, maybe it would conjure up the magic she needed to go back to her regular life.

She hurried to get ready and to the party as soon as possible. Before she left, she checked on Mistletoe and turned off the lights.

She walked into the mall at the entrance nearest the Santa scene and saw the tables full of food. Everything was exactly like it was the night she made the wish. People were visiting and having a good time, and just like last time, she spent most of the evening with Sam and Maria. She kept looking for Santa, and finally Sam asked, "Who are you looking for?"

Feeling silly, she answered, "Santa. Isn't he going to be here?"

"I imagine he will be," Sam said. "Why, did you forget to send your letter this year?" he teased.

She laughed. "No, I just wondered if he was coming."

Just then the doors opened, and she heard the large man say, "Ho, Ho, Ho, Merry Christmas!" Relieved, she sat back in her seat.

"I told you he would probably be here."

Clara was desperate to see whether he was the one, the Santa who had granted her wish. After all the disappointment of the day, she wasn't sure she could take another one.

Santa settled into his seat and people gathered around to take pictures with him.

"Now is your chance," Sam said. "Go sit on his lap and tell him what you want for Christmas."

"I think I will," she said, smiling as she made her way to the line.

On the way, Maggie intercepted her.

"Clay came by the store today, looking for you. He seemed pretty upset."

Clara looked at the line. It was dwindling, and she really wanted to speak to Santa.

"Um, he came by the store? Did he say what he wanted?"

"No. He just asked if you were there. I told him you called in and said you would not be at work today and he seemed, I don't know, sad or something. He wanted to know if I knew where you were, and I said I didn't know. He just kind of wandered around awhile," Maggie continued.

Clara was trying not to be rude, but she really wanted to get to Santa. "Maggie, I need to do something really fast. Can we talk about this later? I'll tell you what happened, I promise, but right now I need to go talk to someone before they leave."

"Oh, of course. We can talk later."

Relieved, Clara continued to make her way to Santa. When she was just a few feet from the line to see him, the mall manager grabbed her.

"Where are you going so fast? I haven't had the chance to tell you how wonderful the Santa scene was this year. It looked like the real thing."

"Thank you. I was just heading over there to see Santa for a minute."

"Oh, there'll be time for that. It is time to announce the winner of this year's window display contest."

"Oh, okay. I will be right back, I promise. I just need to tell Santa something really important."

She looked over. No one was in line and a couple of employees were taking pictures with Santa. She had to get over there before he left.

"This will just take a minute." Then, louder, the manager shouted, "Everyone gather around. It is time to announce the winner of the Christmas window display contest."

The manager waited a minute, while Clara kept a close eye on Santa. The guests quieted down and drew closer to the prize table.

"As you know, each year customers vote for the display they like the best. There are several categories and we will start with the most creative." They announced the winner and they came forward to accept their prize. The manager went on and on, announcing one category after another. At a different time, this would have been exciting for Clara. Right now, she wanted to bolt as she saw Santa packing up his things to go.

Trying to get to him before he walked out the door, she heard her name called.

"Are you coming over to accept your prize?"

"I'm sorry, what did you say? I didn't hear you."

"I said, they chose you for the most whimsical scene for the gingerbread scene in the bakery window."

"Oh, um, thank you."

"Well, come and get your prize."

Clara stepped forward and anxiously looked in Santa's direction as she saw the back of his big red bag walk out of the door into the parking lot.

She grabbed her prize, said a quick "Thank you very much," and ran out of the party, toward Santa. Once outside, she yelled for him and, not hearing anything back, ran out into the parking lot. She looked around and didn't see him anywhere.

She let out a deep sigh and felt the tears again. This was a disaster. She wanted to go back to her old life. If she had the chance, she would accept Clay's apology and make things right again. She wouldn't be so hard on her parents now that she understood how exhausting it was to live up to someone else's Christmas fantasy. She wanted nothing more than to go back to her regular life and out of this Christmas movie nightmare.

Defeated, she walked back into the party and made her way to the dessert table. She thought she would make a plate and sit with Sam and Maria until she could excuse herself and go home to cry herself to sleep for a second night in a row.

"Hey, why didn't you come see me?" she heard from across the dessert buffet table.

Looking up, relief flooded her body. It was Santa. The same Santa who she had spent the day looking for. "I thought you left. I kept trying to get to you but every time I got close, someone would interrupt me."

"So, how was the party last night? I assume you got my note?"

"Yes, I got your note and last night was a disaster." She quickly recounted what had happened the night before at her parents' party.

"Oh, that's too bad. So, you really didn't see that coming?"

"Are you kidding? No! Everything was perfect, just like I wanted. You know, like in a Christmas movie. Then, out of nowhere, it all fell apart."

"Why are you confused by that? I believe I warned you. Didn't you take that seriously?"

"I guess not. Clay isn't even speaking to me, and my parents are mad that I don't want to do Christmas their way. I am exhausted and heartbroken. I just want my old life back."

"Really? That's interesting. I thought you didn't like your old life. Isn't that why you wished your life was a Christmas movie?"

"Well, yes," she stammered.

"As I recall, the night you made the wish, you were irritated with your family, you weren't speaking to Clay even though he was desperate to speak with you, and your job was ending."

"Yes, that's all true."

"So, what changed?"

"What do you mean, what changed? I want to exchange my wish, take it back, or whatever. This is worse than what was happening in my life before. Just change it back. You changed it before, why can't you change it back?"

She was getting hysterical.

Santa looked over his wire frames at her. "What makes you think it will satisfy you if you go back to it now?"

"Please, help me. I thought making everything perfect meant I would get to decide what was perfect. It would be what was perfect for me. I didn't consider that maybe my family didn't want to do all the things I wanted to do my way. I should have listened to Clay instead of being so insecure. By not giving him the chance to explain, I hurt him, and by making my family feel guilty about the holidays, I damaged my relationship with them. I can't create a perfect experience. What I think is perfect for me may not be perfect for everyone else around me."

Santa looked closely at her while she spoke, nodding in agreement. After a long pause, he said, "It sounds like you have done a lot of soul searching. But what happens if you go back to your life and tomorrow you forget all of this? Are we going to get in a cycle every year of you wishing for perfection and expecting others to deliver it for you?"

She thought a minute. "I hope not. I have to be content and accept people as they are and hope they do the same for me. But they're under no obligation to do so."

"Clara, I am going to ask you one more question."

She nodded, waiting for the question.

"What would you like for Christmas?"

She looked right at him and said, "Santa, I want the opportunity to make things right with Clay and my family."

"Well," he said, eyes twinkling, "let me see what I can do about that." And just like before, he disappeared.

Chapter 22

C lara woke with a start, her alarm blaring "Jingle Bell Rock." She looked around her room. It was exactly like she remembered, from before her Christmas wish.

She rolled over and, finding Mistletoe curled up in a ball, Clara gave the cat a quick pat. She hurried out of bed and into the kitchen. It was as it was before the two wishes.

Humming, she looked at her phone. Five messages. She listened to them as her coffee brewed. There were a few from her parents and sister wishing her a Merry Christmas and hoping they could talk later in the day. There was an automated message wishing her a Merry Christmas from one of her clients. The last message was from Clay.

"Clara, I'm sorry I've left so many messages. I don't know what else to do. I've tried to explain what happened and I know you don't want to talk. This is the last message I'm leaving. I'm sorry about what happened. I am sorrier we can't talk about it. Now, I've lost my friend and the girl I love. I hope you have a Merry Christmas. Goodbye."

Clara immediately called his number, desperate to make things right. Her family could wait. Now she knew how he felt, and she wanted to fix things.

His phone went straight to voice mail.

"Clay, I'm so sorry about how I acted. Please call me back. I really want to talk. I understand this was a huge misunderstanding. Please, if you get this, meet me at Cool Beans. I think they're open today. I'm headed there now."

She raced to her room and threw on the clothes she wore the night before. Clara glanced in the mirror and threw her hair in a bun on the top of her head and decided not to take the extra step of putting on mascara and lip gloss. If he didn't show, she would cry it off, anyway.

She decided her slippers would have to do, considering she couldn't find two of the same shoes.

Grabbing her keys and coat, she took a deep breath and opened the front door.

Clara was in such a hurry that she almost ran right into him. Clay stood at her front door, one hand up to knock and another with his phone to his ear. He was as startled as she was and quickly stepped back to avoid being knocked to the ground.

"I thought you might want coffee. It seems I was right." Clay motioned to the drink carrier and bag labeled Cool Beans. "I got your message as I was pulling up. You came running out before I knocked. After I left the message last night, I knew I had to make one more effort. I said I wouldn't call again, not that I wouldn't show up."

"Clay, I am so sorry. I was insecure and ruined everything. I know you had nothing to do with what happened. You were being you—a thoughtful and generous person—and Alexis took advantage of that. I should have listened to you."

She stepped aside from the open door. "Come in. Unless you have somewhere you need to be. It is Christmas."

Clay took a step forward as if to follow her and then stopped. Looking up, he pointed toward the mistletoe still hanging above her door. Shrugging, he said, "You know the rules. I don't make them, I just follow them."

She laughed as she stepped toward him and, standing on tiptoes, wrapped her arms around his neck and kissed him.

"Merry Christmas, Clay."

"Merry Christmas, Clara."

Epilogue

A year later, both Clara's and Clay's families were in town for Christmas Eve. They spent the day cooking, visiting, and playing games at Clara's condo. It was crowded, between the people and all the decorations and gifts. When they finished the meal and packaged the leftovers, they gathered in the living room to play a game.

Kayla divided the living room into two groups. One side was Clay's family and the other, Clara's. Kayla announced the rules of the game as she handed out little slips of paper. Everyone put their name on the slip, folded it and put it into the cup she provided. She pulled out a giant whiteboard and propped it up on the fireplace along with a box of dry erase markers. Each team would pull out two names to represent them at the board. The two would have one minute to choose a clue from the box and draw it on the board while the other guessed. At the end of the game, they would declare the family with the most points the winner.

The families did as they were told, Clara with her family and Clay with his. It was neck and neck until the very end. After all the clues, it was a tie. This was a competitive group, and no one would accept a tie. Kayla made a show of relenting and wrote a clue on a slip and handed it to Clay. She called up Clara and said this would be the tiebreaker. If she got the clue, the point went to her family. If she didn't guess correctly, the point would go to Clay's family.

Clay opened the clue and nodded.

She counted down: "Five, four, three, two, go!"

Clay drew a circle, and Clara shouted out guesses. At the top of the circle, he drew an upside-down triangle. "Ring, the bells ring on Christmas Day," Clara yelled. Clay kept pointing at the ring and shaking his head. She kept guessing. Inspired, he drew a church next to the circle and upside-down triangle over the circle.

"Church, Christmas Eve."

He added a plus sign in between the drawings. She jumped up off the sofa. "*The Bishop's Wife?*" Clay shook his head. "*The Preacher's Wife?*" she asked. Clay shook his head as the timer buzzed.

Clara looked at her sister. "That was not a minute," she said.

"Yes, it was." Kayla showed her the timer.

"Girls, stop arguing," their father interrupted. "I think Clay has something he wants to say."

Clara turned back to the board and saw Clay kneeling, with a small black velvet-covered box in his hand. As she stepped closer, he opened it, revealing a ring that looked a lot like the one on the board.

"Clara, I love you. Will you marry me?"

Anticipation filled the room as they waited for her answer.

"Yes, of course I will," she answered as he slid the ring on her finger.

He stood up and kissed her as the family congratulated them.

Admiring her ring and bursting with joy, she asked how he planned all of this.

"I was ring shopping in the mall, and the guy they hire every year to be Santa saw me. He said he recognized me from the parties we went to last year. Anyway, he assumed things were going well since I was buying a ring. In fact, I had narrowed it down to two, and he suggested this one. After I bought it, he asked how I planned to propose. I told him I wasn't sure. He gave me this idea. I guess he was right. It worked and we have Santa to thank."

Clay kissed her again as she agreed, "Yes, we have Santa to thank for a perfect Christmas."

Don't miss out!

Visit the website below and you can sign up to receive emails whenever Brooke Baxter publishes a new book. There's no charge and no obligation.

https://books2read.com/r/B-A-KMLQ-GYNSB

BOOKS 2 READ

Connecting independent readers to independent writers.

About the Author

Brooke Baxter is obsessed with Christmas and lives in South Texas with a family who isn't. She is an avid Christmas movie watcher, and when she isn't creating the perfect boyfriend for a wholesome holiday romance, she is trying new coffee shops in search of the perfect cup of coffee.